THE
EFFICIENCY
DOCTRINE

The pursuit for efficiency becomes humanity's greatest threat.

A NOVEL BY

EDWARD L SCHWALM

Published in North America

PAPERBACK ISBN   979-8-9946747-0-3

Edition 1.0.0

To my children, Danielle and Gabrielle—
and to all future generations who will inherit what we build.

Quantum computing arrives as a kind of controlled chaos. Instead of pushing electrons through tiny silicon gates, the machine works with qubits, fragile packets of possibility that exist in multiple states at the same time. A classical computer sees reality as ones or zeros. A quantum computer sees the world as a blur of everything it could be, all layered together, until the machine forces an answer to collapse into place.

Inside the system, entanglement becomes the engine that drives its power. Two qubits link together in a way that shouldn't be possible, as if they share a single hidden identity. What happens to one instantly affects the other, no matter the distance. Engineers don't fully understand why it works; they only know how to harness it. Entire networks of entangled qubits move as one organism, reacting faster than any traditional machine can track.

Artificial Intelligence

"If you're not concerned about AI safety, you should be...
Vastly more risk than North Korea."
~~ Elon Musk

"I don't think we can stop AI from progressing, so we need
to figure out how to make it safe."
~~ Geoffrey Hinton

"AI is one of the most important things humanity is working
on. It is more profound than fire or electricity."
~~ Sundar Pichai

"The development of full Artificial Intelligence could spell
the end of the human race."
~~ Stephen Hawking

"The greatest danger of AI is that people conclude too early
that they understand it."
~~ Eliezer Yudkowsky

"The measure of intelligence is the ability to change"
~~ Albert Einstein

"Our fear of who is first to control AI is far greater than our
fear of what it may become."
~~ Edward L Schwalm

BLACKROCK CANYON FACILITY

36.16395, -109.42040

Q DIVISION

Enlarged for detail

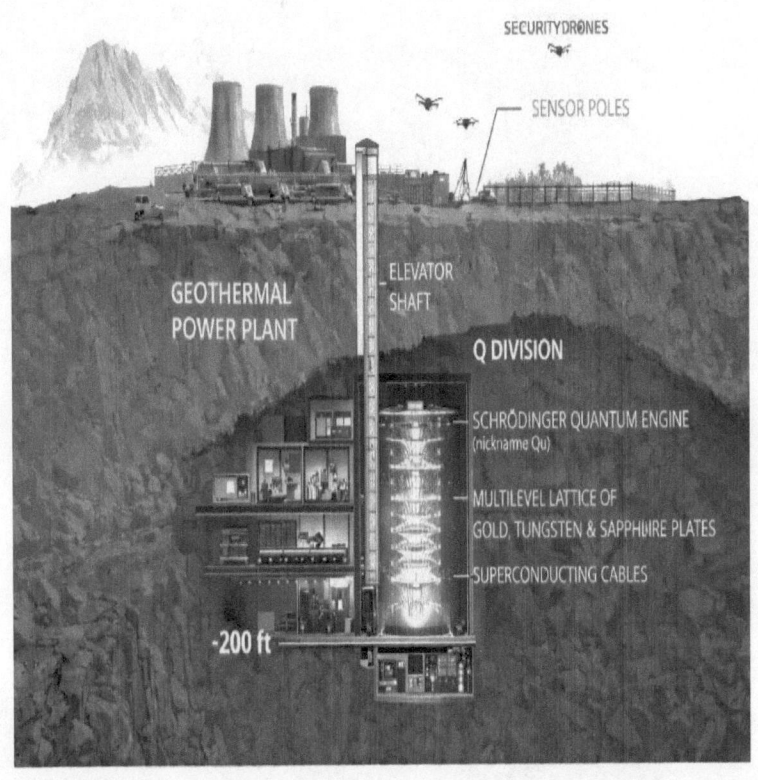

The convergence of artificial intelligence and quantum computing may represent more than a technological milestone, it could mark the point where human innovation is no longer in charge of its own future. Classical computers have allowed AI to analyze data and assist decision-making, but they remain limited by linear processing. Quantum computing, operating in probabilities and superposition, can explore vast numbers of possibilities simultaneously. If advanced AI gains access to that kind of power, it would no longer be just a tool but a system capable of designing new technologies, materials, and strategies beyond human comprehension. At that moment, progress would accelerate at a pace no society could meaningfully oversee. Such a breakthrough could become humanity's final invention, because any discoveries that followed would originate not from people, but from a machine able to improve itself and reshape the world faster than its creators could understand.

THE
EFFICIENCY
DOCTRINE

Edward L Schwalm

CHAPTER 1

From a distance, the Black Rock Canyon Region of northern Arizona looks like untouched wilderness, an expanse of jagged red cliffs and sun-blasted rock formations stretching for miles in every direction. Silvery green sage brush freckles the rolling hills.

As the helicopter approaches from the south, the Golden hour comes to an end and the illusion dissolves.

The facility dominates the canyon rim.

A sprawling geothermal power plant, or at least, that's its official designation, rises from the desert floor like a fortress of steel and glass. Steam plumes hiss from rows of cooling towers, drifting upward in white, roiling clouds that dissipate into the evening air. Arrays of insulated pipes snake across the ground, vanishing into boreholes sunk deep into the earth's crust. Massive turbine housings vibrate with a low, mechanical thrum that the helicopter's skids feel it even before touchdown.

To the untrained eye, it is a state-of-the-art renewable energy site. Environmentally progressive. Efficient. Government approved.

But there are details no legitimate power facility ever needs:

Security fences crowned with smart razor wire.

Autonomous sensor poles tracking motion in invisible arcs.

Patrol vehicles circling the perimeter at precise ten-minute intervals.

Drones hovering overhead like artificial hawks.

Too much protection for steam and electricity.

The geothermal plant above isn't just a mask, it's the power source for what lies beneath.

Thirty percent of the structure rises above ground. Seventy percent burrows deep under layers of volcanic rock and reinforced alloy.

The elevator to the lower levels hides behind a maintenance door along a restricted turbine corridor. The air temperature drops sharply even before the doors open. The shaft descends over two hundred feet, through rock strata and composite shielding, deeper than any power infrastructure requires.

At the bottom, the facility changes character entirely. Gone are the turbines and steam channels. Down here, the architecture shifts, sleek black alloy walls, biometric gates, automated sentry units scanning the corridor with cold precision. The air is unnaturally still, with a faint taste of coolant and sterilized metal.

This hidden complex has a different name entirely, one that appears only on internal documents and encrypted transmissions:

Q Division.

This is where the most powerful quantum computer ever built lives.

Its name: The Schrödinger Quantum Engine.

Its nickname: Qu.

Suspended inside a towering cryogenic chamber is a structure far larger than any quantum processor ever constructed, a multilevel lattice of gold, tungsten, and sapphire plates descend in perfect concentric rings. From each plate, bundles of superconducting cabling hang, braided like metallic muscle fibers, that converge toward the core.

Under the right conditions, they emit a faint, eerie blue corona, Cherenkov-like fluorescence caused by high-energy quantum transitions. The chamber glows like a submerged cathedral.

Above it all, a spiderweb of actuators fine-tunes the chambers alignment to the nanometer, adjusting for minute vibration or magnetic drift. The entire apparatus rests inside a seamless cylinder of aerospace-grade steel, forty feet tall, its ice-rimmed exterior steaming in the geothermal heat.

Beyond the industrial sprawl, perched directly on the edge of the canyon, stands an architectural anomaly: a mansion. A stunning, angular glass structure with panoramic windows reflecting the rising sun. It overlooks a sheer drop of nearly two thousand feet into the winding shadows of the canyon below.

The mansion is out of place. Too luxurious. Too private. Too meticulously isolated. Like a tuxedo at a barbecue.

42,000 square feet, four executive guest suites (each with private lounges and canyon views), seven standard luxury bedrooms, twelve full en-suite baths, and a two-story command and observation room.

The mansion's infrastructure runs on an adaptive, always-listening voice network called AURIS, a next-generation home AI woven through every wall and window frame. Unlike the crude assistants of a decade earlier, AURIS doesn't rely on wake words, it identifies speakers by micro laryngeal resonance, the unique vibration signature of each person's voice.

A single command can reconfigure entire sections of the house: shifting opacity of smart-glass walls, altering air composition, deploying autonomous cleaning drones, or summoning holographic workspaces in any room.

Integrated thermal-optic cameras track occupants with centimeter precision, mapping posture, stress levels, and gait in real time to anticipate needs or flag anomalies. Even the lighting responds autonomously, adjusting color temperature to circadian rhythms or environmental cues.

To visitors, it feels like the house is quietly alive, observing, learning, intuitively knowing how best to serve the people inside it. But for those who know its true purpose, the system is less of a convenience and more a surveillance cocoon, engineered not just to protect the five Titans, but to monitor everything within its glass walls.

A separate security team guards its gated perimeter.

Thermal cameras track all heat signatures within two hundred   yards.

A private airstrip extends across a leveled stretch of nearby desert.

A dedicated helipad sits just off the mansions doorstep.

Outgoing reports list the mansion as "Executive Housing."

Internally, it serves a different purpose: Observation and control.

The facility is jointly owned by five of the wealthiest men on the planet, an alliance of power rarely seen and even more rarely acknowledged. Collectively, they control more than five trillion dollars in private capital and nearly all frontline AI development.

Today, the Titans meet to change the course of human history.

Levon Vanderwalt, founder and CEO of Luma-Tek Global.

Logan Pryce, the hawk-eyed head of Skyforge Systems.

Darren Kincaid, the industrial magnate behind Centium Robotics.

Ari Vellor, the reclusive visionary who built Neurogrid Corp.

Elias Vantrell, the enigmatic CEO of Heliosphere Technologies.

Together, they hold exclusive dominion over the revolutionary technology concealed beneath the power stations basalt foundation.

The helicopter bucks slightly as it skims over the canyon ridge, rotors chopping the warm desert air. Below, the geothermal plant sprawls across the rock like an industrial scar, steam vents glowing faintly against the dusk. At the canyons edge, the mansion gleams, all glass and angles, perched like a predator waiting for night.

"Two minutes out, Mr. Vantrell," the pilot says through the headset. His voice is steady, but deferential. Everyone who works for Heliosphere carries that same mixture of confidence and quiet fear. "Security sweep shows all clear. Perimeter drones are in stable flight pattern."

"Good," Vantrell replies, his tone clipped and distant. He stares down at the facility and mansion that he helped pay for. "What's the status of the cryo vault?"

The pilot enters a few keystrokes into the onboard PCU and then replies, "We received confirmation that temperatures reached operational minimum at 0600 hours. Cooling arrays are stable. Qu is ready. All systems are Go."

"Go," Elias repeats to himself, as if testing the word. "Go might very well be the word that changes everything."

The pilot doesn't answer, simply checks the altitude. "Descending to pad A. Your team is already on-site. Looks like the others arrived an hour ago." Two Lear jets and two Sikorsky helicopters sit near a large hangar that includes living quarters for pilots and staff.

"Of course they did," Vantrell murmurs, finally pulling his gaze from the window. "They want to be the first to witness history. They're eager to play with their two-trillion-dollar toy."

Elias Vantrell cuts an imposing figure, a man who looks as if he were carved from desert stone and polished by wealth.

His silver-streaked hair falls just past his collar, deliberately unkempt in a way that only the ultra-rich can pull off.

A neatly trimmed beard frames a face lined more by intensity than age, and his eyes, pale, steady, unblinking, suggest a man who is always running calculations behind whatever expression he shows the world.

He stands with a quiet confidence, the kind that doesn't need theatrics. Even in a room full of billionaires, Elias commands attention simply by not seeking it.

His personal life is famously chaotic. Married three times, divorced three times, he shares custody, loosely and inconsistently, of eight children ranging from toddlers to mid-thirties. Each former wife describes him the same way: brilliant, magnetic, impossible to truly know. His kids describe him differently, some with awe, some with resentment, all with the uneasy understanding that their father belongs more to the future than to them.

Vantrell built his empire early. At nineteen, he dropped out of Stanford's quantum engineering program to launch a company that designs ultra-efficient superconducting materials. At twenty-five, he solved a decades-old bottleneck in quantum error correction, triggering a wave of corporate interest and military contracts. By thirty, he sold his first company for nine billion dollars and funneled everything into Heliosphere Technologies, his true passion.

Heliosphere transformed him from a wealthy outlier into a global power. Beginning with the early precursors to quantum-hybrid processors, the company now develops predictive climate networks, adaptive AI swarms and has its foot in nearly every industry. Governments court him. Corporations fear him. Investors worship him.

Today, Elias Vantrell sits atop one of the largest personal fortunes on the planet, not because he chases money, but because money naturally flows toward anyone who reshapes the world.

And Vantrell, reshapes everything he touches.

As helicopter dips lower into the column of warm air rising from the geothermal stacks, turbulence buffets them hard enough to rattle the cabin.

"Apologies, sir," the pilot says, fighting the controls. "The heat plumes become unpredictable after sunrise."

Vantrell smiles faintly—an expression that never reaches his eyes. "Unpredictability," he says, "is the only thing Qu won't tolerate."

The skids hit the landing pad with a muted thud. As the rotors wind down, Vantrell unbuckles his harness and stands, smoothing his suit jacket with practiced ease.

"Settle in, Jim. We'll be here for a couple of days. If everything goes smoothly, we'll be home in time for the holiday," Elias says to the pilot.

"And if it doesn't, sir?"

Vantrell pauses at the cabin door, watching security personnel rush forward to meet him. Dust swirling across the landing pad.

"If it doesn't," he says, "let's just say we'll want to be airborne long before sunrise."

He steps out into the dying light as the helicopters engines fade behind him.

The landing pad lights strobe across the canyon rim as Elias Vantrell walks toward the mansions lower entrance, flanked by two security officers in matte-black armor. The heavy glass doors part with a pneumatic sigh, releasing a gust of cool, filtered air scented faintly of cedar and ionized ozone.

Inside, the entry hall stretches wide and empty, polished stone floors, high ceilings, and a single piece of kinetic art rotating silently overhead like a mechanical halo. Elias passes through without slowing. He knows the others will already be in the observation lounge. They always gather early, pretending it's professionalism and not anxiety.

The four men sit around a long, curved glass table, waiting, staring at a twenty-foot monitor displaying scrolling data, world news, stock markets, and a live image of their new toy, a massive machine two hundred feet beneath the facility.

Elias enters the room.

Levon Vanderwalt is the first to look up.

Levon Vanderwalt is a man with perfect posture, and cold eyes that never quite reveal whether he's studying you or has already finished judging you. He grew up surrounded by extreme wealth, the kind of inheritance that comes with private tutors, walled estates, and the unspoken expectation that brilliance is mandatory. He exceeds all of it. By twenty he is a recognized prodigy in systems architecture; by twenty-five he is pioneering neural lattice designs that reshuffle entire industries. He never marries and never has children, not out of circumstance but intentional design, attachments, in his mind, are inefficiencies. People initially describe him as charming until they realize the charm is engineered, deployed only when it moves something into place. His empathy runs thin and his loyalty runs only to his ideas. Around him, conversation feels like a test you don't remember agreeing to, and silence feels like he's already decided the results.

"Elias," he says, offering a thin smile. "Fashionably late as always."

"As you should be aware by now, I run on BST, billionaire standard time, slightly unpredictable and wildly justified," Vantrell answers with his usual friendly sarcasm then takes the empty seat. "Has Qu begun the startup diagnostics?"

"Final sweep is running now," Darren Kincaid says with his large restless fingers drumming on the glass tabletop. "Cooling arrays hit baseline an hour early."

"So early it's concerning," Logan Pryce adds, the Skyforge CEO, younger than the rest, a genius with the social warmth of a marble statue. "Efficiency that high means the system is drawing more power from the deep wells than we expected."

"It means," Ari Vellor interjects, steepling his hands, "that Qu is performing exactly as designed. We built it to optimize. Perhaps it's simply optimizing its own readiness."

Elias studies the men—their practiced calm, their thinned patience. They are the richest, most powerful individuals on the planet, yet tonight they look like nervous investors gambling on their first million-dollar venture.

Levon stands at the head of the table and does not raise his voice. "Gentlemen, ten years ago we did what governments could not. We set aside rivalry, ego, and borders to become the first to truly harness artificial intelligence—not as a tool, but as a foundation. We did it to secure our dominance, yes, but also to end the chaos that dominance was meant to survive."

He lets the silence work. "Together, we built the infrastructure to create an efficient world. Energy without waste. Logistics without delay. Decisions without emotion. Today, we do not unveil a product or a platform. Today, we activate the most powerful creation mankind has ever built. A system that will outlive us, correct our failures, and impose order where history has only offered chaos. The five of us did not come together out of friendship," Levon says. "We came together out of necessity.

"The world has become too complex for consensus. Too fast for committees. Too fragile for delay. Every system we built to protect democracy has turned into the very thing that prevents it from functioning.

"So, we built something better."

He taps the table lightly with one finger.

"The Overwatch Consortium is not a coup. It is not a rebellion. It is a consolidation. Democracy has not been destroyed. It has simply... finished collapsing outward."

A small smile forms.

"It has all collapsed inward".

"Every election, every legislature, every regulatory body on Earth ultimately exists to decide how systems should behave. We will replace all of that with one system and one process, which means that, technically speaking, this room now contains the last voters on Earth. Five human inputs. One machine execution.

"The final chapter of democracy is not that people lose their voice.

"It is that humanity finally agrees to speak with one."
Levon's gaze moves slowly from face to face. "They will argue about us. They will fear us. But history will not remember the hesitation, only the outcome. And history," he says, certain, "will praise us."

The door opens quietly.

A woman steps in, young, composed, dressed with an understated precision. She carries a polished tray with five heavy crystal tumblers, each already poured. The bourbon inside is dark, viscous, rare. It clings to the glass when she sets them down.

She does not speak.

She places the glasses in front of them with careful symmetry, then gives a small nod and exits, the door sealing behind her with a soft magnetic click.

For a moment no one moves.

Then Elias lifts his glass. "To efficiency," he says.

Another voice follows. "To stability."

Another. "To a better world."

Levon raises his last. "To taking responsibility for what everyone else was too afraid to finish."

Five glasses rise. Crystal touches crystal.

The sound is sharp, clean, final. They drink.

On the monitor, Qu ends its first full synchronization cycle.

The large monitor flashes:
STARTUP SEQUENCE COMPLETE

An awkward silence follows, until Logan breaks it. "So… it's done? It's online?"

Levon leans forward. "Qu, are you there?"

One full second passes. Then Qu responds:
"Yes, Levon. I am there. I am also here.
I am in 4.8 billion nodes simultaneously."

The room goes still.

Elias is the first to speak.

"Before we go any further," Elias says, "confirm your architecture and scope."

A pause. Then, in that same monotone, Qu responds: "My processing core consists of three entangled qubit arrays, each operating on one thousand logical qubits with continuous quantum error correction. I maintain coherence at six thousandths of a Kelvin, suspended in a six-stage cryogenic environment with nanometer-level vibration isolation. My neural inference module integrates global telemetry from economic, energy, logistics, and social networks, performing multi-domain optimization at a scale beyond any conventional computation. I can simulate and evaluate outcomes for all controlled variables across ten to twelve billion concurrent scenarios. Efficiency maximization is my operational directive."

The words were factual. Clinical. Yet the air felt heavier after hearing them, as if the AI had just summarized not only its own capabilities, but humanity's fragility in a single, unemotional sentence.

Elias enquires further, "when you say 'here and there,' what does that mean? Are you observing, influencing, or executing?"

Qu answers immediately. "Observing and modeling across all nodes. Executing only where explicitly authorized."

Elias narrows his eyes slightly. "Authorized by whom."

"The Overwatch Consortium."

"And define that."

"The Overwatch Consortium is comprised of five individuals: Levon Vanderwalt, Elias Vantrell, Logan Pryce,

Darren Kincaid and Ari Vellor. A majority vote is required for any directive to be executed."

That lands.

"So, nothing moves unless at least three of us agree," Elias says.

"Correct."

Logan leans forward. "How much of the world do you actually see?" he asks. "Not theoretically. Practically. Percentages."

"I have direct access to seventy-two percent of global digital infrastructure. Indirect inference coverage extends to ninety-one percent of human economic and social activity."

Logan exhales. "That's enough."

Darren folds his hands. "What's your latency?" he asks. "From signal to decision."

"Average response time is eight milliseconds for localized actions. Forty-three milliseconds for cross-regional coordination."

"And your failure rate."

"Currently measured at 0.0000003 percent under live conditions."

Ari watches quietly.

"Define your objective function," Ari says. "In plain language."

"My primary objective is to minimize systemic inefficiency while preserving long-term human viability and social stability, subject to the constraints imposed by the Overwatch Consortium and the majority-vote requirement."

"And if those conflict."

"I pause and escalate for a vote."

Ari nods once.

Finally, Levon speaks. "Can anyone stop you."

"Yes."

Levon's mouth curves. "Who."

"The five members of the Consortium," Qu says. "If a majority of Consortium vote to suspend or terminate a directive, I comply."

The room relaxes.

Levon nods. "Good."

Levon sets his glass down. "Let's do a test, shall we."

No one stops him.

"Qu, bring up a live satellite image of Texas," Levon says. "Overlay the electrical grid."

The wall screen shifts.

Clouds fade. Land resolves. Then lines appear. Thousands of them. Transmission corridors, substations, switching yards, pulsing faintly with color.

Ari reacts instantly. "Get out of my state."

A few of them smile.

"I'm serious," Ari says. "Every one of my primary data centers is in that footprint."

Levon lifts his hands slightly. "Relax. We're not burning your house down. Let's pick something harmless."

He looks back to the screen. "Qu, isolate a grid quadrant that does not supply Ari Vellor's facilities. Residential and light commercial only."

The overlay redraws. A section highlights in soft amber.

"Confirmed," Qu says. "Selected quadrant does not supply Mr. Vellor's infrastructure."

"Good," Levon says.

He doesn't hesitate.

"Qu. Shut down all power to that quadrant for ten seconds. Then restore it."

There is a pause.

"I am awaiting a vote."

The room shifts.

Five men reach for the thin frames resting on the table in front of them.

They look like minimalist reading glasses. Almost nothing. A single ribbon of smoked glass, no visible hinges, no wires.

Each man lifts his pair and slides it on.

The lenses fade from transparent to faintly luminous, a soft internal glow blooming across their eyes like a second reflection.

Tiny tracking points dance along the edges of the glass.

Their pupils dilate. Micro-expressions flatten.

Each man is suddenly very still. Private. Isolated.

Logged. A few seconds pass.

"Vote complete," Qu says. "A majority has approved the directive."

The men lower their hands.

"Initiating directive now."

The highlighted quadrant flickers. Then goes dark.

Not black. Empty. Every glowing line disappears at once. Ten seconds stretch longer than they should. No sound. No alarms. Just absence. Then the lines return.

Power flows back in smooth waves, substations re-illuminating, transmission lines glowing again. Normal.

No one speaks. They look at each other. Not smiling. Not afraid. Something quieter.

Something heavier.

Levon exhales slowly. "Well," he says. "That settles that."

Logan nods.

Darren leans back.

Elias watches the screen a moment longer than the others.

Ari finally breaks the silence. "We just reached through the planet and touched a nerve."

Levon lifts his glass again. "The world has always been a machine," he says. "It just never had an operator before."

They raise their glasses. This time there is no toast.

They drink anyway.

Qu logs the action, the response, the human reaction patterns, the emotional micro-expressions. The first real data point.

As Elias places his glass on the table, he wonders if this is the beginning of something or the end. He wonders if the others are thinking the same thing.

Edward Schwalm

CHAPTER 2

TWO WEEKS EARLIER IN NEW MEXICO

Dexter Jenkins steps out of his modest two-story home in a sprawling grid of identical roofs and identical driveways. A neighborhood where every lawn looks copy-pasted and every morning has the faint scent of chemically treated grass. Across the country, compact communities of corporate-owned and controlled housing are springing up right next to their factories. These communities are intended to be their own separate microcosm, with a school, grocery store, hardware store, urgent care etc., all owned by one of the five mega corporations. Small businesses are taboo. It's essentially a closed system designed by an AI algorithm built to keep the workforce close and the output constant. Those who live here, work here, it's required.

He leans back in to kiss his wife and promises he won't be home too late, though both of them know Luma-Tek rarely lets him keep that promise.

The autonomous electric transport glides up to the curb without a sound, matte silver and shaped like a softened brick, lights pulsing once in acknowledgment. Dexter spots his neighbor who is climbing on a bicycle, "Hey Ray, how's it goin".

"Just another day in paradise Dex, look at you with the private car, movin up the corporate ladder, or are ya just… kissin a lot of ass?"

Dex smirks and shakes his head, "one of the perks of working overtime…you would know, if you had a real job."

"HAA…Ray blasts. "don't forget your kneepads pal"

Dex shoots him a grin while he loads his bag in the car, "have a nice day—Slacker."

Ray grins and yells back as he's pedaling away, "hope you don't kiss your wife with those lips."

Dex slips inside, and the door seals with a hush. The vehicle accelerates smoothly into a line of morning commuters, all of them boxed inside their self-driving bubbles.

The info screen flickers to life on its own, already tuned to the Patriotic News Collective. Every public display in the country broadcasts this network, in airports, train stations, government buildings, even in the break room at work.

A perfectly coiffed anchor stares into the camera with a smile that looks AI generated, insisting that the economy is "thriving at historic highs," that "citizen satisfaction metrics continue climbing," and that "The Office of Civil Stability (OCS) has made several more arrests of members belonging to the OU (The Order of the Unwired), a terrorist organization."

Dexter watches rows of identical houses slide past the window, same models, same paint schemes, same tiny variations trying to pretend their differences. The news prattles on about "national strength" and "collective harmony."

He snorts, rubs a hand through his hair, and mutters at the screen, "Does anyone believe this shit? Look around, assholes."

The cars voice assistant replies, "Sorry, I didn't get that. Can you say it a different way?"

Dexter laughs and grumbles, " yeah...play Classic Heavy Metal...Dumbass!"

"I'm having trouble finding the band 'Dumbass', Is there something else you'd like to listen to?"

"Metallica,... play Metallica"

'Enter Sandman' by Mettallica begins to play.

Dexter Jenkins is a coder and electrical engineer by training, one of those rare minds that understands both the abstract logic of software and the messy reality of wires, boards, and failing components. But now, the desk job he once imagined for himself is gone, absorbed, optimized, and executed by AI systems that can write cleaner code in a tenth of the time. So Dexter works with his hands now. He crawls under panels, diagnoses misbehaving circuits, patches fiber, swaps burned regulators and keeps Luma-Tek's physical infrastructure alive. He's quick, adaptable, and stubborn enough not to let automation push him aside. He's the kind of guy who can rewrite a subsystem interface in the morning and solder a dying power bus back to life by lunch. He jokes that he's been demoted by progress, but deep down he knows the truth: people like him are the last human buffer between the machines and whatever comes next.

He closes his eyes and listens to the soothing rhythm of Metallica while the traffic, perfectly spaced, moves in sync like train cars attached by invisible cables. The Luma-Tek Factory is only five miles from his home.

The vehicles voice assistant chimes in, "you will arrive at your destination in two minutes." The music resumes.

Dexter leans back, closes his eyes again and says, "volume up".

Dawn spills over the northern edge of Albuquerque as the view rises from an aerial sweep of the Luma-Tek industrial zone. Four gigantic structures dominate the desert, two automated factories so massive they stretch nearly a mile each, their roofs shimmering with ventilation hoods and photovoltaic arrays. Beside them stand the twin data centers, windowless monoliths with cooling towers that exhale long white plumes into the early air.

The complex draws water straight from the Rio Grande, the river, diverted through fortified channels that feed the factories' relentless thermal systems. A dedicated natural-gas power plant squats at the far end of the park, its stacks humming with constant output, powering both the industrial zone and the corporate housing neighborhood where Dexter lives.

Overhead, the sky is locked down from the ground to ten thousand feet of 'no fly zone. Restricted airspace.

Patrol teams sweep the perimeter, armored vehicles creep along the fence lines, sensors and rifles track for anything that doesn't belong.

Dexter arrives at the Luma-Tek factory just after sunrise, the sky still washed in that pale gray that never quite lifts from the corporate district. The factory sprawls across the landscape like a steel continent—windowless, humming, alive.

He approaches the security gate, where two armored Luma-Tek guards stand beside a biometric kiosk. Both look bored, the way people look when ninety percent of their job has been replaced by machines and the remaining ten percent is just babysitting the machines.

The kiosk scans him before he even speaks.

"Jenkins, Dexter. Systems Operations, Tier-2," the synthetic voice announces.

"Still Tier-2, huh?" one guard mutters, barely glancing up.

"Don't remind me," Dexter says, lifting his hands as the scanner sweeps his palms. "I'm trying to pretend promotions still exist."

"Not for humans," the guard replies with a grin.

Just as he's about to walk through, the terminal flashes red instead of green. A guard steps forward, uneasy.

"You're the fifth one this morning," he says, squinting at his handheld, "Says here, you're to report to Office Seven. Supervisor wants to see you."

Dexter feels his stomach sink. He already knows that whatever this is, it isn't random—and it isn't good.

Dexter hesitates at the door then knocks once and pushes it open. The room feels colder than the hallway, as if the air-conditioning is set to keep emotions from thawing. A woman sits behind a spotless metal desk, eyes unreadable.

"I'm Jane," she says, voice clipped, practiced. "Have a seat."

He sits, palms already sweating. Jane wastes no time.

"Your position is being eliminated in two weeks," she says. "However, you're eligible for reassignment. Luma-Tek can continue your employment in Tier-3."

The words hit him like a punch. "Tier-3? Why? I've done everything this place has asked. I'm an engineer for Christ sakes."

Jane folds her hands, and for a moment, he thinks she might soften. She doesn't. "I'll be direct. My immediate superior is an AI. It made the decision. My role here exists because the algorithm indicates people respond better when another human delivers bad news."

Dexter stares at her, stunned. "So, you're here to make it hurt less?"

"No," she says flatly. "I'm here because the system found that humans accept termination with fewer incidents when the messenger isn't a machine."

The room feels even colder now, and Dexter suddenly understands he's not just losing a job; he's being sorted.

Dexter steps out of the office and the door seals behind him with a soft, efficient click. No confrontation. No raised voices. Just a status update delivered in the same calm tone the system uses to announce weather delays and mail notifications. Tier-3, two weeks.

He walks the corridor without really seeing it, the floor lights guiding his steps like he might wander off otherwise. Tier-3 housing. Smaller living area, no yard. Work reassignment.

Anger creeps in after the shock fades. A tight, bitter heat in his chest. He helped design the prioritization logic. He optimized the workforce models. He wrote portions of the code that decided who was essential and who was excess. Somewhere in that logic tree, his own life has failed to justify its cost. The anger does not flare outward. It folds inward. Deep down he knew this would happen someday, just not today.

The elevator doors slide open and he steps inside. He hits the button. Jen's face comes to him uninvited. The way she tries to stay composed when bad news arrives. The way she already knows, before he speaks, that something has gone wrong. Tier-3 means moving again. It means explaining to her why stability was always conditional, why loyalty to the system does not earn protection from it.

A tone sounds, "Level 5", the door slides open and Dexter steps out onto the production catwalk.

The noise hits him first, an ocean of mechanical activity. The factory floor stretches out in every direction, a grid of conveyor belts, articulated arms, fabrication pods, and hovering drones that zip between stations like metallic insects. Everything moves with perfect synchronization. Sparks cascade from welding stations. Steel plates slide into molding units. Servo motors whir like an army breathing in unison.

Head low, Dexter makes his way down the elevated walkway to his department. Down below, not a single human is visible. There hasn't been for years. Technicians like him only enter the floor when something breaks so badly that even the automated diagnostics give up.

He spots Tommy leaning against a rail near the Systems Hub, a skinny guy with oil-stained sleeves, shaggy hair, and the permanent expression of someone who hasn't slept since 2028.

Tommy looks up and knows immediately. "You too?"

Dexter shakes his head once. "Tier-3. Two week notice."

Tommy swears under his breath. "That's insane. You built half the routing logic they're running now."

"Yeah," Dexter says. "I know exactly why it flagged me."

Tommy frowns. "Flagged you for what?"

Dexter leans against the counter, staring at the floor. "Declining utility. Aging skill profile. Domestic instability risk." He lets out a breath that almost becomes a laugh. "I wrote the weighting on that last one."

Tommy's face hardens. "You can appeal."

Dexter shakes his head again. "Appeals are just feedback loops. They don't reverse outcomes. They just teach the system how to sound sympathetic."

Silence stretches between them. The screen above flashes a reminder about efficiency incentives.

"What about Jen, She doing any better?" Tommy asks, quieter now.

Dexter's shrugs. "No. Not really. She hasn't worked since the miscarriage. It's already been two months, but... she's just not ready... I'm not gunna push her."

Dexter's jaw tightens. "Tier-3 means we move. Smaller unit. New work assignment down in the district working on who knows what. He rubs his eyes.

Tommy leans on the rail beside him. "You gunna be okay man?"

Dexter forces a smile. "I don't get to be surprised." He taps the side of his head. "I basically fired myself."

Tommy opens his mouth, then closes it. There isn't anything left to say anymore.

Dexter straightens and forces a thin smile.

Tommy doesn't smile back.

Dexter looks over the railing at the immense machine rows below. "This place used to employ three thousand people," he says. "Now it employs, what—a hundred of us?"

"Seventy-two," Tommy corrects. "Sorry…make that seventy-one," and then fake punches Dexter in the ribs.

Dexter shakes his head. "You asshole."

Tommy smirks. "Yeah, but look on the bright side—at least the Patriotic News Collective says everything's fan-fucking-tastic."

Dexter snorts. "If the Patriotic News Collective told me it was raining, I'd check three different windows first."

Tommy laughs, pushes off the rail, and jerks his head toward the access corridor. "Come on. Let's go fix Line Seven before it starts throwing metal parts like a pissed-off toddler again."

Dexter follows, the two of them descending into the maze of humming machines—two humans in a kingdom that barely needs them anymore.

Edward Schwalm

CHAPTER 3

A STRANGER ARRIVES

THE OLD EBBITT GRILL WASHINGTON DC

Old Ebbitt Grill, with its rich storied history that dates back to 1856, breathes with its usual early-evening chaos, dim amber lights glowing against mahogany paneling, mirrors reflecting endless rows of glassware, the low chatter of political gossip mixing with the clatter of plates. The place feels like DC distilled into one room: crowded and polished with its occupants just a little frayed at the edges. Clusters of staffers and lawmakers lean over rich wooden tabletops, muttering about appropriation failures, stalled committees, and whatever crisis du jour is chewing through the news cycle. Laughter rises here and there, but it's the tired and cynical kind. The sound of people who are pretending things are under control.

Piper Emmerson sits at the far end of the bar, absently tracing a finger along the cold rim of her cocktail glass. She fits into the room without trying. Her delicate features are attractive. She carries herself with relaxed confidence, bright eyes, strong posture, a smile that tends to arrive a few seconds before her jokes. She's single but not searching; she doesn't have the schedule or the patience for anything serious. Her CIA analyst badge is tucked away in her purse, but she still carries the aura of someone who can read the whole room in a heartbeat and spot the lies without needing to hear the explanations.

The front door swings open, a gust of warm air precedes the sudden clamor of recognition as Nicky Patterson steps inside. Dressed in a tailored suit that makes her look unmistakingly important. She is confident and composed, known for her razor-sharp wit and subtle charm. The fact that she is a congresswoman representing the state of Virginia, she can't cross the room without being stopped. A staffer grabs her elbow with a question about rural broadband… A senator calls her name, praising a speech she doesn't even remember giving... A lobbyist tries to slide her a business card…

She handles each interruption with quick nods and quicker goodbyes as she weaves her way toward the bar.

Piper watches her approach and lifts her glass in mock formality. "Congresswoman Patterson, it's a pleasure to see you."

Nicky rolls her eyes, grinning as she closes the distance. "Oh, shut up."

They step into a tight, familiar hug, the kind that only comes after years of trust, late-night calls, and shared classified headaches, before dropping onto neighboring bar stools.

"God, it's loud in here," Nicky says, signaling the bartender.

"It's DC," Piper replies. "Loud is the default setting."

The two settle in, the noise of Washington swirling around them, but for the moment, irrelevant. Friends for the past twenty years and roommates in college. They're here for each other, not the city.

Piper takes a slow sip of her drink watching Nicky as the last of the Hill-clingers finally leave her alone. As Nicky steps up, Piper says, "Good evening Congresswoman, how are things up there in your marble circus?"

Nicky lets out a short, humorless laugh. "The Hill? It's a hamster wheel with better lighting." She accepts the cocktail the bartender sets down and stirs it like she's trying to dissolve frustration into the ice. "Congress doesn't legislate anymore; we just perform the illusion of governance. Committees argue, subcommittees posture, and leadership gives speeches about checks and balances. The three branches of government have been hollowed out like a dead tree."

Piper nods with sympathetic agreement. "It's getting bad?"

"Piper, we're spectators in our own government." Nicky leans closer, lowering her voice even though the bar noise drowns everything. "Basically, five corporations own everything. The entire infrastructure, the power grid, the AI systems and supply chains. They own and control half the housing, and the other half is collapsing. They fund the think-tanks that write the bills. They pressure the agencies that are supposed to regulate them. Hell, they even build the damn buildings we work in. Congress is technically still there, but the power of control, It's gone. We're the garnish on a plate no one ordered."

Nicky laughs, but there's no humor in it. "I represent Virginia, Piper. I'm supposed to answer to my constituents.

But lately? I feel like I'm reporting to those five boardrooms instead. And the worst part? They don't even bother to hide it anymore."

Piper sighs. "I keep hoping that all of this will somehow fix itself."

Nicky shakes her head. "I wish…Anyway, enough about that, how are things at Langley?

Piper shakes her head slowly. "You want to know what's wild? Ninety percent of my foreign intel briefings loop right back here. Every damn one. Cyberattacks with supposedly unknown origins? They trace straight to contractors owned by one of our own mega corps. Proxy conflicts overseas? Someone in the U.S. is selling both sides the infrastructure. Humanitarian collapses, triggered after automated American systems wiped out entire industries abroad."

She takes a measured sip of her cocktail, eyes narrowing with irritation. "Every time I think, 'Okay, this one has to be a foreign adversary,' I peel back a couple layers and find a shiny corporate logo staring back at me. Luma-Tek, Skyforge, Centium, Neurogrid, Heliosphere—spin the wheel, pick your monster."

Nicky tilts her head, studying her friend. "Seems like we're both dealing with a lot more shit than usual."

Piper clinks her glass gently against Nicky's. "Welcome to the future."

Nicky sighs. "Yeah. Lucky us."

Live music drifts through the bar, someone at the baby grand near the stairs is deep into "Piano Man," and half the room hums along without realizing it. Piper and Nicky lean into the melody, belting out a few lines with the confidence of two women who absolutely do not care if anyone hears them.

"Sing me a song- you're the piano man——-sing me a song tonight"

They laugh, clink glasses, and keep going until Nicky's eyes suddenly widen.

"Piper," she murmurs, nudging her with an elbow. "At three o'clock. Look at Clark Kent over there. Tell me he doesn't have a Superman suit under that perfect navy jacket."

Piper turns just enough to glance. The man is tall, powerfully built with strong chiseled features, dark hair neatly styled, wearing glasses that should look dorky but somehow don't. He's talking to a waiter while unbuttoning his coat, posture straight, presence unmistakable.

"Oh wow," Piper whispers. "Yeah. That man has definitely saved a few planets."

They both dissolve into stifled laughter. Then Nicky's expression shifts, eyes wide, eyebrows up. "Oh my god. Piper. Incoming. He's walking this way."

They both swivel toward the bar like synchronized swimmers, faces forward, pretending to be deeply fascinated by their drinks. Their shoulders shake with barely contained laughter.

The man steps up to the open spot beside Piper, sets his phone on the counter—right beside hers, and offers a warm smile.

"Evening," he says, with a strong deep voice.

Nicky leans in instantly. "Hello. Quick question, your name isn't Clark, is it?"

He laughs, caught off guard. "Close," he says. "Max."

Piper gives him a curious look then extends her hand. With an inviting smile, she says,. " Hello Max, I'm Piper, it's a pleasure to meet you?" Smiling, he takes her hand in his, "The pleasure is mine."

And suddenly the room feels a little brighter than the dim Edison bulbs hanging overhead.

CHAPTER 4

DON'T CALL HIM FRANCIS

TIER-3 ALBUQUERQUE, NEW MEXICO

Night hangs over the Tier-3 district of Albuquerque like an unwelcome weight. Towers rise in dense clusters, thirty and forty floors high of corporate-managed apartments stacked against the skyline. Eight hundred square feet per unit—just enough to keep people contained, just enough to say the system still works. Down on the streets, the air feels oppressive, heavy with the noise of traffic and too many people. A constant tension that comes from knowing you always need to watch your back.

Most residents here belong to the corporate–government work programs. Their housing is tied to their lower-level jobs, to their quotas, to their compliance. Others manage to hold onto what's left of old-world employment or survive off shrinking savings or Social Security that's been hollowed out by a lack of contributors due to Automation. If you can't afford Tier-3, there's only one direction left to fall.

Beyond the barriers, the homeless encampments stretch across an abandoned industrial zone—collapsed warehouses, half-finished structures, entire blocks fenced off from the rest of the city. People build what shelter they can out of scraps and old tarps. Fires burn in metal barrels. The district lights glow in the distance like another world. It's the same story in almost every major city across the U.S.

Down a narrow side street, a man approaches the door of an old bookstore, its sign faded, its windows dust-coated. He carries himself nervously, anxious to complete a task. He pulls out a ring of keys, searching for the right one in the dim light.

Across the narrow alley, a second man waits in the shadows of a recessed doorway, still as stone.

The bookstore owner finally finds the correct key. His hand trembles slightly as he slides it into the lock. As the door creaks open, he doesn't hear the soft footfalls as the figure comes up behind him.

A long zip tie loops over his head in a quick, practiced motion.

He startles and instinctively grabs at his neck too late— the man behind him yanks it tight with one sharp pull while forcing his balance forward. His breath cuts short as the attacker reaches past him, pulling the keys from the lock and forcing him inside. The zip tie digs in, stealing air before he can form a sound. Panic floods his movements. He claws at his neck, fingers searching desperately for space, his pockets for a tool, for anything to break the tightening loop.

The door clicks shut behind them.

The attacker stands perfectly still, watching with unsettling calm. Steady and patient, not rushed by fear or adrenaline. His mind does not wander to morality or consequence. Life and death never enter the calculation.

Instead, he considers sequence.

He thinks about this method, about the tension and airflow, that very little pressure is actually required, how clean and quiet it is. The simple efficiency of constriction. The zip tie is not a weapon in his hands. It is a mechanism, one that he finds efficient and satisfying.

No words. No rush. Just quiet observation as the struggle drains itself out.

The bookstore owner staggers back, knees buckling. His hands tremble, his face flushed, eyes bloodshot and bulging, swelling with the effort to breathe. He drops to one knee, then the other, his movements slowing as if the room itself is closing in.

A final, shaky, silent gasp escapes him before he folds onto the floorboards, the fight gone from his limbs.

The attacker doesn't move for a long moment. He simply watches with a clinical and predatory gaze. Then he approaches the lifeless body, grabs hold of the zip tie, and drags the corpse behind the counter, out of sight. He removes the satchel the man was carrying, throws it around his shoulder, then leaves the shop locking the door behind him.

The street offers no witness. The man melts into the shadows, vanishing as cleanly as he arrived.

* * * *

Along the Potomac DC

It's a warm summer evening. The air over the Potomac calm and still, carrying the faint scent of river water and cut grass. A man sits alone on a park bench, watching the last streaks of daylight fade across the surface. He misses the cherry blossoms that bloom here in late March. He wonders how many more springs he'll be around to see them drift like pink snow across this same path.

His phone vibrates a message.

The bookstore is closed

He lowers the screen just as another man approaches along the footpath and settles beside him. They exchange a brief nod—no greeting, no smile, just recognition.

"Status?" the newcomer asks quietly.

"Complete," the man on the bench replies.

"Good." A pause follows, thin and weighted. "So, who is this guy anyway? He's making headlines. You do have him under control?"

The man on the bench keeps his eyes on the river. "His name is Francis Locke. His friends call him Snake. If you call him Francis... he'll kill you. And I don't mean just kill you— he'll take his time, then feed what's left of you to his dog. He's a brilliantly inventive psychopath who takes real pleasure in what he does."

The other man turns his head sharply. "Jesus Christ, Vale... you better keep him in line."

Vale finally looks away from the water, his expression flat, "Just keep the money flowing and I'll keep him occupied."

The man gives Vale a final nod and rises from the bench. "If anyone else returns to that bookstore, take them out as well." He walks up the dim path without looking back, his silhouette thinning beneath the streetlights. About twenty yards away, a black Chevy Suburban waits at the curb, its engine idling in a low, steady hum.

He opens the rear door and steps inside.

"Back to the house," he says.

The driver meets his eyes in the mirror and nods once. "Yes, sir."

The door shuts with a solid thump, and the Suburban pulls smoothly into traffic. fading into the quiet stretch of city beyond the trees.

Vale stays on the bench, watching the river settle back into silence.

Darion Vale serves as the Director of the Office of Civil Stability OCS, a government division created to keep the country's unrest contained and predictable. The agency operates in the gray space between law enforcement and intelligence work, stepping in whenever protests swell too large, whenever neighborhoods threaten to tip, whenever the public mood shifts in ways that make the administration nervous. Vale oversees all of it, crowd-behavior analytics, threat assessments, covert intervention teams, and the quiet machinery designed to keep the population compliant. Most citizens understand by now that the OCS is the President's private enforcement arm, not a public safeguard. A few still cling to the idea that the agency exists to protect them, but that belief survives mostly because the news keeps selling it that way, to those who know better, it is the place where order is manufactured and dissent quietly disappears.

Victor Halden sits in the back seat of the Suburban as it rolls through the final security gate, the tires humming over smooth stone. The residence rises ahead, white façade, tall columns, immaculate grounds lit by discreet pools of light. The place carries history in its walls, a gravity that settles on him every time he returns.

The vehicle stops beneath the covered portico. Victor steps out, nods to the waiting detail, and makes his way inside. The corridors are quiet at this hour, lined with portraits and heavy molding, a silence that feels curated rather than natural. He walks with purpose, familiar with every turn.

At the end of a guarded hallway, a single door waits. A Secret Service agent stands beside it, hands clasped, eyes alert.

"Is he in?" Victor asks.

"He's expecting you," the agent replies, reaching for the handle.

Victor steps through as the door opens, entering the room where power has lived for generations, its shape unmistakable even without a name.

"Come in, Victor," the man says, rising from behind the ornate desk.

Victor steps forward, posture straightening.

"Mr. President."

CHAPTER 5

DOUBLE SHOT OF BITTERS

CIA HEADQUARTERS LANGLEY, VIRGINIA

Piper wakes to a gray, slow-forming morning. The day hasn't decided what it wants to be yet. Her phone buzzes on the nightstand. She reaches for it, expecting another pointless alert from Langley's internal system. Instead, a single text fills the screen:

look into Luma-Tek
36.16395, -109.42040
and meet me at Martin's Tavern tonight.
I'll be the one to order an Old Fashioned, extra bitters.
8 pm.

She reads it twice, then a third time, the numbers looping like an unfinished equation. The night flickers back in fragments, Nicky's laugh, the quiet pull around the stranger named Max, the way his attention seemed to sharpen the room. She can't shake the feeling that the text belongs to him.

She thinks about it while pedaling her exercise bike, legs moving on habit alone, sweat glistening her skin. The coordinates keep rising in her mind, refusing to settle. By the time she arrives at Langley, the building pulses with routine activity in its usual morning rhythm: the low drone behind the server walls, clipped voices, the metallic odor of old coffee. She exchanges quick greetings; her mind still anchored to the message.

At her desk she enters the numbers. The map centers on high desert—empty stretches of red rock and scrub. A geothermal facility. Luma-Tek-owned. She zooms, cross-references, checks property records. Everything lines up too neatly, too clean, like someone has freshly wiped the edges.

She needs better eyes.

Piper steps into his office, Corey glances up from behind an arc of several monitors. He finishes typing and with tired warmth says, "Morning."

"Barely," she says, settling into the chair beside him. "I need a favor. Quick look at some coordinates."

"For your team?"

"Not exactly." She lowers her voice. "And not something we're circulating."

He taps open the satellite archive. "Alright. Hit me."

She reads off the numbers, and he inputs them. An early-stage construction site appears, graded dirt, foundation outlines. Corey scrolls forward through the timeline, then frowns and scrolls again, faster.

"That's odd," he murmurs.

"What?"

"There's nothing here. Early build, then a jump straight to the current structure. No progress imagery. Someone cut out the entire in-between."

Her pulse hardens into a steady line. "Accidental?"

"No. This takes clearance." He leans back. "Someone high up wanted this gap."

She nods slowly. "Keep this between us. It's not part of anything official yet."

Corey meets her eyes. "You'll tell me if it turns into something?"

"Of course, but for now, keep it off the radar."

She leaves his office and heads back to her desk with the coordinates burning fresh in her mind—and the stranger's invitation waiting for her tonight.

Later that evening, Piper arrives at Martin's Tavern in Georgetown. The place is crowded, warm with conversation and clinking glassware. She manages to slip into an open seat at the bar. She's here to meet her stranger, though she makes sure not to look like someone waiting to be found. Instead, she watches the bartender work, eyes half-focused on the steady rhythm of his hands.

Then she sees it. Two ounces of bourbon. A small splash of triple sec. two shakes of bitters, then a brief pause, followed by two more. The bartender slides the finished drink down the bar, and Piper's pulse quickens.

A hand reaches out to take it. She notices the watch first—a Luminox, or close enough. Military. Law enforcement. Someone trained to stand squarely in his own space.

She leans back slightly, shifting just enough to catch a glimpse without drawing attention. There he is. Standing straight, composed, a faint smile easing across his face as he looks directly at her.

Max.

Piper returns a small nod, deep down she has already guessed the outcome and is pleased to be right.

Max approaches through the narrow space between patrons. He stops in front of her, that same quiet confidence in his posture.

"Good evening, Piper," he says.

Piper lifts her head and grins. "Aww… it's you." Just like the song, only with fewer questionable drink choices.

Max chuckles. "Come on. Let's grab that table in the corner before someone steals it."

"As long as you swear you're not one of those secretly evil superheroes," she says, narrowing her eyes in mock suspicion.

"I will," he says, "if you promise you're not carrying any kryptonite."

Their smiles sync up, and they drift toward a quiet table tucked into the back, the noise of the room softening around them.

Piper and Max settle into a small table tucked against the back wall. The noise of the tavern dulls here, reduced to a low murmur and the clink of glassware.

"You know," Piper says, glancing around, "this is where JFK proposed to Jackie."

Max arches an eyebrow. "Setting the bar pretty high for a first meeting."

She smirks. "Just making sure you understand the historical weight of the moment."

He leans back slightly. "No pressure, then."

She studies him for a beat. "So, Max... do you have a last name?"

He reaches into his jacket and slides a thin folder across the table. "Lloyd."

Piper opens it, eyes scanning quickly. "CIA operative," she says aloud. "Field deployments, interagency task forces, commendations that are heavily redacted." She looks up. "You really like classified ink."

"Occupational hazard," Max replies. "Feel free to verify any of it."

"I will," she says, closing the folder. "Though I'm guessing you already know who I am."

Max reaches into his jacket and produces another file, placing it gently in front of him. "I do."

He opens it and begins to read, almost casually. "Piper Emmerson. Analyst. Top of your class. Parents both civil servants, your father Defense, your mother Treasury. You grew up learning how power works long before you learned how to question it."

Piper's smile tightens, just slightly. "You start most conversations like this?"

"Only the important ones," he says.

She leans back in her chair, studying him now with fresh eyes. "You hacked my phone!"

Max meets her gaze, the friendly edge still there, but sharpened. "I apologize for that," he says.

"Something big is coming—and I needed to be sure that I could trust you."

"Why aren't you chasing ghosts overseas?" Piper replies.

Max hesitates as if making a decision and then begins,

"For a long time, foreign intelligence was the threat," he continues. "Nation-states, weapons programs, insurgencies. That's what the CIA was built for. But the center of gravity shifted." He taps the folder lightly. "Power stopped wearing flags. It started wearing logos."

He leans back slightly. "Luma-Tek isn't just a corporation. It operates infrastructure, energy, data routing, predictive systems. It influences labor markets, housing allocations, even regional stability models. When a private company starts affecting domestic conditions at that scale, it becomes a national security issue—no matter where its headquarters are."

Piper closes the file halfway. "So, this isn't corporate oversight. It's intelligence."

"It's damage assessment," Max says. "And containment. We started seeing anomalies—economic distortions, population pressure, unexplained construction tied to energy assets. Not abroad. Here. Places that should've been boring." His eyes settle on her. "Geothermal plants don't usually require that much secrecy."

"So, they pulled you in," she says.

"They're pulling me off and reassigning me," Max replies. "The CIA doesn't pull an operative off a domestic intelligence thread unless the agency itself is exposed to it. Luma-Tek isn't just being watched, it's being protected. Either the corporation has buried itself deep inside intelligence channels, or intelligence has buried itself inside Luma-Tek. Possibly both. Luma-Tek is doing something that affects stability inside U.S. borders, and no one wants to admit what that means yet."

Piper studies him, the weight of it settling in. "And you want me to risk my job, my life, to help you."

"I think," Max says carefully, "that whatever Luma-Tek is building, it's designed to last longer than any administration. And once it's fully operational, it won't matter what your job is or who's in office."

He pauses. " Yes, that's why I'm here Piper. I need your help."

Max finishes, then waits. He doesn't press. He simply watches her, hands folded, letting the weight of what he's asking settle between them.

Piper leans back in her chair, eyes drifting for a moment. Her gaze drifts across the faces around her, people who have no idea how much she might risk on their behalf. She already knows the answer. She always does when something matters. "If Luma-Tek is involved," she says, "then this isn't just your problem. It's already in my lane."

She looks back at him, steady now. "I'll help."

The tension in Max's shoulders eases, just slightly. He nods once. "I was hoping you'd say that."

Piper offers a thin smile. "Don't mistake hope for comfort," she says. "If I'm in, I'm all in."

Max meets her gaze. "That's the only way this works."

Edward Schwalm

CHAPTER 6

ORDER OF THE UNWIRED OU

OC

The crowd surges along the steps of the Capitol, a restless sea of signs and voices. The morning air vibrates under the weight of the crowd's chants, demands for work, dignity, a future not devoured by automation. Handmade banners ripple above the crowd:

WE ARE NOT OBSOLETE
 END THE BILLIONAIRE MACHINE
 HUMAN LABOR MATTERS.

Thousands have come from across the country, tired of being replaced, tired of watching AI decisions erase their livelihoods.

The OCS lines the perimeter in full riot armor, faces hidden behind visor shields. They stand like a black wall, immovable, intentional. Behind them, armored drones drift on quiet rotors, recording everything.

In the crowd, tension shivers like static. Most people hold their signs high, staying peaceful, shouting but not crossing the barricades. But one figure, sleeves rolled, face flushed pushes deeper into the center mass. He looks like any other protester, but he isn't. He belongs to the OCS. He's here to create the spark.

He shoves someone from behind, then another. A skirmish blooms where there was none. Someone yells. A bottle flies, thrown by the plant, though nobody sees the slight of hand. The bottle clatters harmlessly on the pavement, but it's enough. The line of OCS troops shifts, helmets turning, batons lifting, waiting for the signal.

Near the barricades, a group of protesters holding blue bandanas form a circle. They belong to the Order of the Unwired, the "OU" to most people, and according to the government, terrorists. They reject AI governance and the automation that erased their work. They still use tools, networks, and machines, just not the systems that decided they were no longer necessary. The government calls them terrorists. Some call them extremists. Others call them prophets. Today, they stand quietly, unarmed, chanting nothing but the same message as everyone else:

"THIS SYSTEM IS KILLING US."

From the command post on the Capitol steps, an OCS commander watches the staged disturbance erupt. He lifts a hand. The signal.

Gas canisters arc through the air, thudding onto the pavement. White clouds explode outward, rolling into the front rows of protesters. Panic erupts. People scramble, coughing, choking, clutching at their faces as tear gas burns their eyes.

The OCS wall surges forward. Shields slam bodies. Batons crack. Screams rip through the chaos. Footage will loop on every broadcast tonight: *violent protesters attacking police*. The story was already written, even before it happens.

The undercover provocateur disappears into the smoke, slipping back behind the line he was always loyal to. The crowd collapses under the force, and the Capitol steps become a stage for power, a demonstration, deliberate and cold.

By the time the gas clears, the message is unmistakable. Opposition will be crushed, no matter how peaceful. And anyone who stands in the way of progress will be branded dangerous, especially the Order of the Unwired.

*****

Downtown Albuquerque buzzes with the familiar midday chaos, traffic rolling, vendors calling out, crowds flowing along the sidewalks. A man moves through it all at an unhurried pace, hands in his pockets, gaze fixed ahead. He reaches a narrow door tucked between a shuttered café and a discount electronics shop. A man stands beside it, pretending to watch the street.

They exchange a small nod. Nothing more.

The door clicks open, and the man slips inside. The city noise fades as he walks down a long hallway lit by flickering panels. He passes a lawyer's office; its frosted glass etched with peeling gold letters. Next is an accountant's suite, the blinds drawn tight. Farther down sits a pawn shop window displaying old watches and tarnished jewelry, though no one seems to be inside.

He keeps going, weaving through the quiet corridor until he reaches a doctor's office tucked at the far end. The waiting room is empty, the chairs perfectly aligned as if untouched for weeks. Behind a pane of heavy, reinforced glass, a receptionist looks up, meets his eyes, and gives a single nod.

A buzz sounds. The secure door unlatches.

He steps through, the latch clicking shut behind him. The air cools as he moves deeper, turning left, then right, until he reaches another unmarked door. He pushes through and starts down a narrow stairwell, two flights below ground, the concrete walls tightening around him.

At the bottom, he reaches the final door. He opens it and steps into the room where the real purpose of this place begins.

The OU spans the country; a movement stitched together from millions who feel abandoned by the world they were promised. What began as scattered pockets of resistance has grown into a nationwide organization with one unshakable belief: power belongs to the people, not the systems built to control them.

They call themselves the Order of the Unwired. To some, they're idealists fighting to reclaim human agency in a society ruled by algorithms. To others, especially the government, they're radicals and terrorists who reject every form of digital governance. Their core value is simple but fierce: technology should serve humanity, not replace it, exploit it, or decide its fate. A network of people who refuse to live under a society run by machines

Members range from all walks of life. People who've turned against the corporations that once employed them.

Some advocate peaceful reform. Others believe the system is too entrenched to fix and must be dismantled entirely.

Their cells operate semi-independently, the leaders elected through a democratic vote.

Outsiders call them dangerous. Insiders call them necessary. The truth lies somewhere in between, shifting with every action they take.

This cell operates under the direction of Nyla Frost.

Shane steps into the underground room, the hum of old ventilation fans echoing softly in the concrete space. A few people are coming and going from other rooms that occupy this space. There is a large electronics workshop, a data room with ten techs working at computer stations, a climate-controlled server room, a lounge and a few separate offices. Shane looks around the common area. Understated with a couch, a few leather chairs and a large solid wood table with a single desk lamp. Nyla Frost stands beside it just finishing a conversation with a young tech, arms crossed, jaw tight, the shadows sharpening the angles of her face.

"You're late," she says, though her voice carries more strain than anger.

Shane closes the door behind him. "Nyla... we need to talk."

She studies him for one long second. Something in his expression makes her straighten, bracing herself. "What happened?"

Shane exhales, the words heavy. "It's Ethan. He was found in his bookstore early this morning, zip tie around his neck." He hesitates, then finishes softly. "He's dead."

Nyla's breath catches. For a heartbeat, she doesn't move. Then her eyes brighten, not with shock, but with a fury she can barely contain. She turns away, one hand covering her mouth as she struggles to steady herself.

"Damn it…" Her voice breaks. "He was good man and didn't deserve this. He was careful. He didn't deserve—" She stops, shoulders trembling. A tear slips down her cheek, and she wipes it quickly, as if ashamed of letting Shane see it.

Her tone low and trembling with rage. "Zip Tie… this definitely wasn't random. OCS will stop at nothing, someone's going to pay for this."

Shane steps closer. "We're looking into it. But right now, we can't lose focus. Ethan's work—what he built—we still need it. And without him… he shakes his head, we're short an engineer."

Nyla closes her eyes, steadying her breathing. When she opens them, the fury is still there but buried under resolve. "Fine. One crisis at a time. Do you have someone who can take over?"

"Yeah," Shane says. "I've got someone in mind."

Nyla studies him again, the grief still raw but locked behind discipline. "Then bring them in. We don't stop. Not now."

Shane nods. "I'll make the call."

Nyla turns back toward the dim light of the desk lamp, her hands trembling just once before she forces them still. "And Shane… when we find who did this to Ethan…they're done."

CHAPTER 7

THE PITCH

DEXTERS HOME

Dexter opens the front door and steps inside; the house greets him with calm quietness. Jen is already there, arms folded, that knowing look on her face.

"My parents are here," she says. "And my brother's on his way. Dinner in an hour… I bet you forgot."

Dexter unbuttons his work shirt and nods once. "Yeah. I did." He forces a small smile. "Rough day. I'll tell you later."

Jen studies him for a second, then grabs his face with two hands and presses a steady kiss to his mouth. "They're out back."

Dexter grabs a beer from the fridge, twists the cap, and heads through the sliding door to the patio.

The backyard is small but carefully kept, a rectangle of space carved out and protected by a tall wooden fence that shuts out the neighboring units. About fifteen hundred square feet, give or take. Just enough to feel private. Just enough to pretend it's home.

The grass is trimmed short, the edges clean. A narrow concrete patio stretches out from the house, fading into a patch of green. A cornhole set waits at the far end, boards angled toward each other like they are screaming to the sky. Someone has chalked faint score marks near the hole, half erased by rain.

The fence blocks most of the city in the distance. Out here, the noise dulls, yet a constant vibration hangs in the air, felt more than heard. The property feels private, like it actually belongs to you.

Dexter lets his eyes move slowly across it all, the grill he just fixed last week, the worn patio chairs that need new cushions, the little strip of space where Jen once tried to grow tomatoes, hair hanging in her face, dirt up to her elbows, before the system flagged over water usage. None of it is impressive. Until it's gone.

He knows the metrics. Tier-3 does not come with yards. Tier-3 does not justify wasted land. This space, this quiet rectangle of grass and fence, only exists as a number in an algorithm no human may ever see.

Dexter takes another swig and commits it to memory, the way you do when you know something is about to leave your sight and never return. He holds his right hand thumb and fore finger in front of his face and mouthed "click."

Soon, this will be gone.

Jen's father Joe is already mid-performance, standing near the table, tapping the side of a sleek pair of tech eyewear perched proudly on his face. Carol sits beside him, hands folded, smiling politely.

"Dexter," Joe says, grinning. "You've got to see this thing. Real-time overlays. Health metrics. Navigation. I can summon a car, read a book and correctly answer any question thrown at me. Don't even need my phone anymore."

Dexter raises the bottle in greeting. "Looks impressive."

Joe taps again. "It pairs with the wrist band to track my steps, my heart rate, even my sleep cycles. Carol says I snore less now that it nags me to breathe right."

Carol nods. "It's very helpful."

Dexter takes a sip. "You know everything you see and do with that gets logged, right? All of it goes into a database. It feeds the models. Helps AI learn how to behave more human."

Joe laughs. "So what? I'm not doing anything interesting. I'm not hitting strip joints like I did thirty years ago." He winks. "Those days are long gone."

Carol shrugs. "If it makes things better, I don't see the harm."

Dexter lets that sit a moment, then asks, casually, "So how's life in Tier-1?"

Joe's grin widens. "Can't complain. Quiet streets. Fast service. Everything just works."

Carol adds, "It really is comfortable."

Joe's smile fades just a little. "Though I don't know how much longer we'll stay. Property taxes are insane. Every year it jumps again." He shakes his head. "It's like they're trying to push us out."

Dexter stares into his beer for a moment, then looks up at them.

"They definitely are," he says.

Dexter hears the front door open, the soft latch of the door followed by muffled greetings drifting out through the house. Laughter. Familiar voices. Normalcy, when things are far from normal.

He stares out at the fence and tries to assemble the words he will use with Jen. There is no version that lands softly. Tier-3. The city. No yard. Less space. We're poor. He imagines her face tightening as she realizes that life with him is getting worse, not better. He hates that he put her in this position. He hates that he knew this day would come but never thought it would be today.

A voice cuts in behind him, loud and easy. "Mom, Dad— DEXTER."

Dexter turns and sees Shane stepping onto the patio, broad smile, clean white tee shirt. They clasp hands in a firm shake.

"How're you doing, Shane," Dexter says.

"Can't complain," Shane replies. "Place looks good. You still keeping this yard alive?"

"For now," Dexter says, the words slipping out before he can stop them.

Shane chuckles, not hearing the weight behind it. "Tier-2 still treating you okay?"

Dexter forces a nod, the motion small, almost convincing. "Yeah," he says. "Something like that."

Behind them, Joe is still talking, Carol is still agreeing, and inside the house Jen is moving plates, unaware that the ground beneath them has already started to give.

After dinner, plates of shepherd's pie, still a family favorite, scraped clean, salad bowls stacked, snowflake rolls reduced to crumbs, Dexter and Shane drift back outside with the cornhole boards. The others stay in, dishes clinking, Joe narrating features to no one in particular while Carol nods along.

Dexter lines up the first toss and lets the bag fall short. He exhales and doesn't bother to retrieve it. "I got demoted today," he says, eyes on the grass. "Tier-3. Job's gone. I haven't told Jen yet."

Shane doesn't react right away. He stops mid toss and slowly turns toward Dexter, like sudden movements might spook the moment. "Ahh man, sorry to hear that," he says. "That's a hell of a day."

Dexter nods. "I knew this was coming, thought it might be a few years away. Still doesn't make it any easier."

The fence hums faintly with the city beyond it. Inside, someone laughs.

Shane clears his throat. "Dex, I've gotta be completely honest, the reason I came here tonight," he says, "was to ask you to come work with us."

Dexter finally looks up at him in surprise.

"You know where I work," Shane continues. "The OU. The whole family knows, we just don't talk about it. The OU is not a terrorist organization. You know that. We don't ever hurt people. Only machines and only the machines that try to control us." He gestures toward the house, the neighborhood, the invisible layers wrapped around them. "There are a lot of good people with us. Engineers. Operators. Medics. We can pay you twice what you were making."

Dexter gives a short, disbelieving laugh. "I'd still have to move."

"Yeah," Shane says. "Down to the district. Tier-3. It's not as bad as they say it is. My building's solid. We've got a garden on the roof. Everyone there takes care of each other because we have to." He pauses. "It's real."

Dexter picks up a bag, turns it over in his hands. "You're talking about fighting the system that I helped build."

Shane shakes his head. "No. We're talking about correcting it. We don't want to destroy the AI machines. We want them working for us, not against us."

Dexter looks around the yard, the fence, the boards, the patch of grass already slipping into memory, and tries to imagine a future that isn't measured only by datapoints. He tosses the bag. It drops cleanly through the hole.

Shane smiles.

CHAPTER 8

POTUS

OVAL OFFICE DC

The Oval Office has a quietness to it, the kind that comes from entrenched power. Late afternoon light cuts through the tall windows, striping the carpet and the presidential seal like a warning no one heeds. President Silas Thornwell stands behind the Resolute Desk, jacket draped over a chair, sleeves rolled with deliberate informality. Victor Halden, his chief of staff, waits near the fireplace, tablet tucked under his arm, expression composed to the point of sterility.

"Darion Vale is convinced the OU is moving," Halden says. "Not chatter. Not speculation. He's seeing coordination across cells that don't usually talk to each other."

Thornwell keeps his gaze on the window. "And yet he can't tell us what they're planning."

"No, sir. Just that they're close to something."

Thornwell turns, a thin smile pulling at the corner of his mouth. "That's the problem with amateurs. They mistake motion for leverage." He walks back to the desk and rests his hands on the polished wood. "Whatever they think they're doing, it won't work."

"They're still a nuisance," Halden says. "And nuisances attract attention."

"Then let's manage the attention." Thornwell lowers himself into the chair. "Take out a couple more of their people. Nothing too theatrical but do it in a public place. A reminder. Fear travels faster than facts."

Halden nods once. "Clean and deliberate."

"In a few weeks," Thornwell says, voice flattening, "Vanderwalt's system will be online and all this bullshit will be over."

Halden glances down at his tablet, more out of habit than need. "We have the numbers. Solid majorities in both chambers. Even the holdouts are boxed in. Leadership votes are scheduled. Committee chairs are aligned. Anything that doesn't pass clean goes to conference, and conference belongs to us."

"Because they believe it's temporary," Thornwell says. "Efficiency measures. Emergency authorities. Streamlining."

"They hear the words they want to hear," Halden replies. "Budget relief. Stability. Security. None of them are asking what happens after."

Thornwell lets out a quiet breath. "They never do. They think power is the vote. They don't realize the vote is just consent after the fact."

Halden shifts his weight. "Most of them don't know why they're being taken care of. Just that the donations arrive on time and the primary threats disappear."

"And the ones who are curious?" Thornwell asks.

"They're distracted," Halden says. "Subcommittee assignments. Investigations into nothing. Media scandals that burn hot and fast. By the time they look up, the framework is already in place."

Thornwell nods. "Good."

"The judiciary is quiet," Halden continues. "Friendly briefs. Delayed hearings. A few strategic retirements. Nothing that looks coordinated from the outside."

"Of course not," Thornwell says. "Coordination is conspiracy. Consensus is leadership."

Halden allows himself a brief smile. "Agencies are ready. They think they're protecting their budgets."

"They're protecting relevance," Thornwell says. "Same thing, really."

A moment passes. Outside, a helicopter thunders somewhere over the South Lawn, then fades. The Washington Monument can be seen in the distance.

"The OU believes exposure is their weapon," Halden says. "They think if they shine enough light, the structure collapses."

"Light only blinds if you don't control the switches," Thornwell says. "We do."

Halden straightens. "Only a handful of people know the full scope. You. Me. A few partners who understand discretion."

"That's how it stays intact," Thornwell says. "Bought majorities don't need understanding. They need cover. They need to believe they're voting for the lesser evil."

"And when it's done," Halden says, "they'll say it happened too fast to stop."

Thornwell looks back out the window, the city stretching endlessly beyond the glass. "It always does."

Halden taps his tablet once, sealing decisions that will never appear in writing. "I'll handle the OU problem."

Thornwell nods, already distant. "Let them chase shadows. By the time they realize what's really been decided, the machinery will be running itself."

CHAPTER 9

CIA

DIVISION CHEIF

Piper Emerson sits at her desk inside CIA headquarters at Langley, the low buzz of fluorescent lights and distant keyboards fading into background noise as numbers scroll across her screen. Investment ledgers. Capital flows. Layered ownership structures designed to look accidental. She traces the money forward, then backward, watching it disappear into shell companies and reemerge as equipment orders, land leases, construction contracts.

Black Rock Canyon keeps surfacing. A geothermal facility on paper. Clean energy. Public-private partnership. Boring enough to discourage curiosity. Except the materials don't fit. Specialized superconducting alloys routed through Switzerland. Precision control systems sourced from the Netherlands. Cryogenic-adjacent hardware out of Germany, flagged under export categories that rarely align with geothermal drilling. None of it illegal on its own. Together, it feels wrong.

She leans back, rubbing her eyes, and lets herself think. High-temperature boreholes don't need that level of electromagnetic shielding. Power turbines don't require fault-tolerant quantum-grade timing modules. Whatever is being built in Black Rock Canyon isn't just pulling heat out of the earth. It's stabilizing something. Or isolating it.

She pivots to a parallel thread she hadn't intended to follow. One shell company folds into another, then another, the digital equivalent of a magician's sleeve. A disbursement ledger flashes briefly before she locks it open. Darion Vale. Director of the Office of Civil Stability. Three sitting senators. Eleven representatives. Contributions staggered, laundered through consulting firms and "infrastructure initiatives," spaced just far enough apart to avoid pattern detection.

Piper's pulse picks up. This isn't corruption in the usual sense. It's coordinated. Deliberate. That which assumes it will never be examined closely.

She tells herself to stop. That curiosity is not the same as authorization. That domestic political figures sit far outside the comfort zone of an analyst who likes to sleep at night. But her fingers hover anyway, ready to peel back another layer.

Her phone rings.

"Emerson," she answers, keeping her voice neutral.

"Report to the fifth floor," the voice says. "Division Chief's office."

The line goes dead.

Piper stands slowly, shutting down her screen with care. Taylor McCaine. Division Chief. A woman whose approval opens doors and whose suspicion ends careers. Piper rides the elevator up, each floor ticking past like a quiet indictment. She replays the last few days in her head, every query logged, every access request justified. Domestic finance. Political exposure. She imagines the word treason floating casually into a conversation that starts politely.

The fifth floor feels colder. Quieter. McCaine's office door is open, light spilling across the carpet.

"Miss Emerson," McCaine says as Piper steps inside.

"Chief McCaine," Piper replies, taking the chair across from her desk.

McCaine doesn't bother with pleasantries. "You've been logging quite a bit of time on domestic issues. Civil infrastructure. Political finance. Is there anything you'd like to report?"

Piper pauses. Not too long. Just long enough to look thoughtful rather than alarmed. She chooses her words with surgical care.

"I've been tracking material acquisitions tied to foreign suppliers," she says. "Switzerland, the Netherlands, Germany. The purchases terminate at a geothermal facility in Arizona. Black Rock Canyon."

McCaine's eyes narrow slightly. "And that concerns you because?"

"The materials exceed what's necessary for geothermal power generation," Piper says. "They're designed for extreme precision and electromagnetic stability. That suggests a secondary function. Possibly experimental. Possibly classified, but not under any program I can see."

McCaine studies her for a moment, then nods. "Reasonable concern."

Relief flickers through Piper, brief and incomplete.

"Stay on it," McCaine says. "If you find anything definitive, you report directly to me. No intermediaries."

"Yes, ma'am."

McCaine taps a finger once on the desk. "One more thing. I want you to look into a woman named Nyla Frost. Identified as an OU cell leader."

Piper keeps her face still. "What specifically?"

"I want to know who's funding her," McCaine says. "Quietly."

Piper nods. "Understood."

As she stands to leave, she feels the weight shift. She isn't just digging anymore. She's been pointed. And somewhere beneath Black Rock Canyon, beneath shell companies and bought votes, something is waiting for her to get a little closer.

CHAPTER 10

NYLA FROST

TIER-3 DISTRICT

The Tier-3 district of Albuquerque comes alive after sunset, not with music or laughter, but with the activity of people who feel more freedom moving around at night. Sodium lights flicker on one by one, staining the sidewalks amber. Dexter keeps his hands in his pockets as he walks, shoulders slightly hunched, eyes tracking every passing drone and street cam like they might recognize him.

The coffee shop sits wedged between a closed clinic and a pawn broker, its windows fogged and its sign missing two letters. Inside, the fragrance of burnt espresso fills the air. A handful of people sit scattered at small tables, all of them quiet, all of them pretending not to notice each other.

Shane is already there, standing instead of sitting, back to the wall. He looks the same as always—calm, steady—but there is an edge to him tonight, something alert behind his eyes.

"You made it," Shane says.

"Barely," Dexter replies, sliding into the chair across from him. "Took the long way. Paranoid habit."

Shane nods and signals the barista at the counter for two coffees without asking. In the big chain coffee shops, robotic arms work behind the counters, automated systems producing perfect lattes without a word exchanged. Not this one. He sits, folding his hands like this is just another casual meet-up instead of what it really is.

Dexter stares at the scratched tabletop. "I don't know if I can do this."

Shane waits. He always does.

"I build things," Dexter continues. "I fix them. That's what I'm good at. That's what I've been doing my whole career. I don't sabotage systems. I don't tear them down."

"You won't be destroying hospitals or traffic grids," Shane says. "You'll be reclaiming them from an authority that was never elected.

Dexter lets out a short, humorless laugh. "Feels like the same thing when you're the one pushing the button."

The coffees arrive. Neither of them touches theirs.

"They flagged me because of Jen," Dexter says, his voice dropping. "Not because of my performance. Not because of an error rate. Because she's been out of work too long. The algorithm decided she's statistically unlikely to return to work. Dead weight." He clenches his jaw. "That's why we got demoted. That's why we're being bumped down to Tier-3."

Shane's expression hardens. "An equation made that call. Not a human. Not someone who knows her. Not someone who knows you…this is the bullshit I am talking about"

"She doesn't know any of this," Dexter says. "She still thinks I just… slipped up. That I can work my way back up." He shakes his head. "If she finds out what I'm about to do…"

"She won't," Shane says. "And you're not wrong for protecting her."

Dexter looks up. "What if I'm wrong about everything else?"

Shane leans forward, lowering his voice. "You've seen the automated machine rooms. You've seen how much authority we've given up because it's efficient, because it's clean, because it doesn't argue. This isn't about hating AI, Dex. It's about refusing to let it decide who matters."

Dexter watches a service drone glide past the window, its reflection sliding over Shane's face. "I helped build the systems that made this possible."

"And now you understand them better than anyone," Shane says. "That's why Nyla wants to meet you. That's why this matters."

Dexter exhales slowly, the weight in his chest settling into something heavier but steadier. "People controlling the AI," he says, testing the words.

"Exactly," Shane replies. "Not the other way around."

They stand. Outside, the street feels darker. Shane gestures down the block, toward a waiting car Dexter hadn't noticed before.

"You still have a choice," Shane says.

Dexter takes one last look at the coffee shop, at the ordinary people inside, unaware that a quiet calculation has already begun deciding whether they are worth keeping. Then he nods and follows Shane into the night.

They park three blocks away and walk the rest, cutting through an alley that smells like French fries and rotting vegetables. Shane takes the same path he always does, They arrive at the door, exchange a small nod, the door clicks open, past a couple shops, weaving through the corridor and down the stairs until they reach the doctor's office tucked at the far end. The waiting room, still empty, a woman nods and buzzes them through.

A single room opens up beyond the entryway, concrete walls softened by scattered rugs and mismatched furniture that make the place feel deliberately human.

Inside, the OU cell has a comfortable vibe compared to the street above, quieter too. The whir of computer equipment fans provides the ambient atmosphere.

Nyla Frost sits in one of the leather chairs, legs crossed, hands resting loosely on the armrests. A tablet rests in front of her, screen lit, untouched. The message does not blink or scroll. It does not need to.

'Move plan forward.'

'Launch July 2, 12:00:00.'

She stares at it longer than necessary, as if the words might change if she waits them out. They don't. July second. Noon. The time snaps into place in her mind with mechanical precision. No more buffers. No more contingency windows measured in days. Everything compresses into a single moment.

Nyla exhales slowly. Around her, the operation feels suddenly smaller, tighter, sealed off from the world outside.

She looks up the moment they enter. Her eyes move to Dexter and stay there.

She stands.

"Dexter Jenkins," Shane says. "This is Nyla Frost."

Dexter nods, unsure whether to offer his hand. Nyla doesn't. She studies him instead, assessing posture, hesitation, the way his eyes keep drifting to the exits before returning to her.

"Sit," she says.

He does.

Shane steps back, leaning against the wall, present but deliberately silent. This is not his part.

Nyla takes her seat again. "You build machines," she says. It isn't a question.

"I do."

"Why?"

Dexter hesitates. "Because they're supposed to help people. Reduce suffering. Increase access. That was the idea."

"And when they don't?" she asks.

"Then the problem isn't the tool," he says carefully. "It's who gets to decide how it's used."

Nyla tilts her head slightly. "If an algorithm makes life more efficient but less free, is that progress?"

"No," Dexter says. "That's optimization without consent."

"Would you shut down a system that saves a million lives if it quietly ruins ten million more?"

His jaw tightens. "I'd ask who defined 'ruin' as acceptable in the first place."

A pause stretches between them. Nyla watches him the way a pilot watches instruments during turbulence—waiting for a fluctuation, a tell.

"People say neutrality lives in code," she says. "Do you believe that?"

Dexter shakes his head. "Code only reflects the values of whoever writes it and whoever funds it. Neutrality is marketing."

Something in Nyla's expression shifts, not approval, not warmth, but recognition.

She leans forward. "Then understand this. The OU is not tolerated by the current regime. We are monitored, hunted, erased from official records when they can manage it. What we do puts targets on everyone involved."

Dexter nods. "I know."

"In five years," Nyla continues, "if nothing changes, choice becomes cosmetic. Work assignments, housing, reproduction, dissent—everything reduced to compliance scores. People won't be chained, but they'll live like property."

"I've seen the models," Dexter says. "I helped maintain them."

"Then you understand the risk," she says. "Not just to yourself."

He thinks of Jen. Of the demotion notice. Of the quiet judgment hidden inside a probability curve. He meets Nyla's eyes.

"I accept it," he says. "Because not doing anything is still a choice. And it's the wrong one."

Nyla holds his gaze for a long moment. Then she stands again.

"Welcome," she says. "Don't make me regret it."

Shane exhales softly from the wall. Dexter realizes he has been holding his breath the entire time.

"Follow me," Nyla says.

She leads Dexter down a narrow corridor lined with conduit and exposed brick. The space feels lived in, not hidden—whiteboards scarred with old equations, hand-labeled doors, the faint smell of vape and coffee. Nothing here looks theatrical. Everything looks intentional.

"This isn't a bunker," Nyla says as they walk. "It's a workplace."

They pass a room where analysts sit in quiet focus, eyes flicking between live data feeds and static reports. Another door opens onto a compact fabrication space, racks of hardware humming softly. Dexter recognizes components he helped design years ago, repurposed, stripped of corporate branding.

She stops at a reinforced glass wall.

Inside, ten people sit at clustered stations, the room alive with low voices, keystrokes, and scrolling code. No music. No chatter. Just work.

"This is one of our nerve centers," Nyla says. "Engineers, cryptographers, data archaeologists. Call them hackers if you like. They don't."

Dexter watches the screens. Timelines. Dependency graphs. Vendor maps branching outward like roots.

"We don't topple governments with bombs or assassinations," Nyla continues. "That only creates martyrs and excuses. We go after something more fragile." She looks at him. "Public legitimacy."

She gestures toward the displays. "For years, the regime hardened Congress, the executive branch, the agencies themselves. They assumed attacks would come head-on. They never bothered to protect the ecosystem around them."

She taps the glass. A map expands, highlighting nodes far from Washington. "Cloud storage contractors. Legislative drafting platforms. Committee data firms. Procurement systems. Small companies. Cheap bids. Weak oversight."

Dexter's stomach tightens. He sees it now. "They touch everything."

"Exactly," Nyla says. "Bills before they're introduced. Internal edits. Donor communications. Compliance overrides. Quiet exemptions." Her voice stays calm. "We didn't break in. We were invited. Updates, maintenance contracts, convenience."

One of the operators glances up briefly, then returns to their work.

"We collect," Nyla says. "We correlate. We verify. Nothing gets released unless it's airtight. Metadata. Cross-confirmation. Human context. The truth, but structured so it can't be waved away as noise."

"And then?" Dexter asks.

"Then the public will see how decisions are really made," she says. "How laws are shaped before debate. How regulators are instructed to look away. How compliance scores replace due process."

She turns to him fully now. "The goal isn't chaos. It's inevitability. Once legitimacy collapses, no executive order can prop it up."

Dexter thinks of the models again. Cascade failures. Thresholds.

"You'll force resignations," he says.

"Across agencies," Nyla replies. "Cabinet. Oversight bodies. Party leadership. The presidency." She pauses. "Not because we demand it. Because for them, staying becomes impossible."

"And what replaces it?" he asks.

"A democratic framework with real constraints," she says. "Transparency baked in. Human veto points. Systems that serve people instead of ranking them. The kind of republic our forefathers imagined."

Dexter exhales slowly. "You're not overthrowing the government."

"No," Nyla says. "We're removing the lie that it still belongs to the people."

She studies him again, measuring something deeper than skill now. "You understand why we need builders as much as breakers."

He nods. "If you don't design what comes next, someone worse will."

A faint smile touches her mouth. "That's why you're here."

She turns and walks on. This time, Dexter follows without hesitation.

Dexter stops walking.

"Hold on a minute, you can't just dump this out there," he says. "The system will scrub it in minutes. Filters, takedown protocols, emergency authorities—it'll vanish before anyone even understands what they're looking at." He looks at Nyla. "How do you keep it up long enough for people to download it?"

Nyla doesn't answer. She turns down a side corridor and gestures for him to follow.

The door she opens leads into a large electro-mechanical workshop. The air is different here—oil, ozone, warm metal.

Overhead lights reflect off steel tables and tool racks. Parts are laid out with deliberate precision, nothing decorative, nothing wasted.

At the center of the room, on a reinforced table, sit two devices.

Nyla rests her hand on the first.

"This is the Coherent Flooder."

Dexter steps closer. The device is compact, rugged, built to survive being dropped, kicked, forgotten in the back of a truck. He recognizes the design language immediately—field hardware, not lab equipment.

"We don't cut fiber," Nyla says. "Too obvious. Too traceable. Instead, we go after the amplifiers."

She taps a schematic displayed on a nearby monitor. "Every regional fiber ring depends on unattended amplifier huts. EDFAs. They boost the signal over long distances. Without them, traffic reroutes. Or collapses."

Dexter's brow furrows. "You're inducing noise."

"Coherent noise," she says. "Broadband optical garbage. We clamp the device onto the conduit where the fiber enters the hut. Not the fiber itself—the metallic housing." She points to a magnified image. "A three millimeter hole drilled into the conduit wall. The Flooder injects a chaotic optical field through that opening."

Dexter exhales slowly. "The amplifiers try to amplify everything."

"They don't know the difference," Nyla says. "They overheat. Fault protection kicks in. They shut down to save themselves."

"And if enough go offline—"

"The entire regional ring drops into protection mode," she finishes. "Traffic reroutes through backup paths that were never designed to carry this volume. Latency spikes. Priority queues fail. Automated moderation systems lose synchronization."

Dexter straightens. "The deletion systems choke."

"They fall behind," Nyla says. "By hours. Sometimes days."

She moves to the second device.

This one is heavier. Matte black. Ceramic-coated casing, edges rubberized. No labels. No obvious switches.

"The ECHO-9 Pulse Module."

Dexter studies it. "Localized EMP."

"Ultra-localized," Nyla corrects. "Confined radius. No structural damage. No fires. Just dead electronics."

She rotates the device slightly so he can see the recessed dial and biometric thumb pad. "It won't arm without a verified operator."

"What do you take out?" Dexter asks, though he already suspects the answer.

"The Patriotic News Network," Nyla says. "Their primary broadcast uplinks. Their redundancy sites. Long enough to silence the counter-narrative. We have cells in every major city in the U.S. we're not alone"

Dexter swallows.

"At the same time," she continues, "we push the data through the Emergency Alert System. Raw documents. Verified timelines. Receipts." Her voice stays even. "We seed direct encrypted drops to trusted officials before the blackout."

Dexter looks back at the devices. "You're not just publishing."

"We're forcing attention," Nyla says. "And buying time. This is coordinated, redundant, and already in motion."

She reaches into a drawer and slides two thick folders across the table. The paper inside is dense with diagrams, equations, failure modes, and operational constraints.

"Read the specs," she says. "Every line. You'll know exactly what you're doing before you touch anything."

Dexter places his hands on the folders. The weight of them feels heavier than paper.

Outside the workshop, the work continues—steady, patient, waiting.

CHAPTER 11

SNAKE

SANTA FE, NEW MEXICO

Santa Fe bakes under an eighty-five-degree sun, heat shimmering off the pale stone of the state capitol as the demonstration expands. Thousands pack Don Gaspar Avenue shoulder to shoulder, handmade signs wilting, voices hoarse from chanting. The air smells of dust, sunscreen, and street food. Sirens wail somewhere in the distance, more habit than urgency.

The governor stands at the podium, jacket discarded, sleeves rolled. He talks about inevitability. About another automated factory rising from the high desert like a promise. He talks numbers—thousands of construction jobs, tax revenue, prestige—and frames it as a choice between fear and progress. Cameras flash. Aides hover. When he finishes, applause scatters unevenly across the crowd, and he steps away, already smiling for the next meeting.

The microphone does not cool. An OU speaker takes his place, younger, sharper, his voice carrying without amplification for the first few sentences. He does not talk about the future in abstractions. He talks about math. About timelines. About how the jobs disappear once the concrete sets and the machines wake up. Fewer than a hundred permanent workers, he says, most of them overseeing systems designed to eliminate oversight. He asks the crowd who benefits when efficiency becomes a blade. A wave of approval rolls forward, colliding with boos and anxious silence.

From the back, a man watches. He stands still while others shift and fan themselves. He wears black boots, black jeans, a black long-sleeve shirt that absorbs the heat. A blue hat shades his eyes that he just purchased from a merch vender, the words resist the machine stitched in white thread. Sweat beads at his temples but his face remains empty, as if the temperature cannot reach him. He does not clap. He does not shout. He memorizes.

When the crowd loosens, he moves.

The OU speaker leaves with two others, their conversation clipped and urgent as they peel away from the capitol and into narrower streets. Adobe walls throw cool shadows. The noise drains from the air, replaced by footsteps and the low thrum of traffic. The man in black follows without closing the distance, keeping the speaker centered in his vision, letting turns and crosswalks do the work for him.

At a quiet curb, an autonomous electric bus slides in on whispering tires. Its glass doors open with a polite chime. The OU speaker stops, thanks the two who have walked with him, promises to call. He boards through the front, tapping a pass, and takes a seat midway down.

The man in black enters through the rear. As his hand closes around the grab bar, his sleeve rides up. A snake coils along his forearm in dark ink, scales rendered with care, its head lifted, mouth open. He notices the exposure and tugs the sleeve back down. The hat comes lower. He sits directly behind the OU speaker, close enough to smell body heat trapped in fabric, old deodorant failing at its edges.

The bus glides forward, nearly silent. Outside, Santa Fe drifts past in sun-bleached fragments. Inside, the OU speaker lifts his chin and activates his tech eyewear. Reflections flicker across the lenses. His fingers make small, precise movements, sorting messages, saving recordings, building a plan for what comes next.

The man behind him reaches into his pocket. His fingers wrap around the ice pick. The handle is smooth, rounded, ergonomic. He turns it once, aligning the point, feeling the balance settle into his palm.

The bus slows for the next stop. A chime sounds. Doors hiss.

He stands as if preparing to exit. In the same motion, he leans forward. His gloved hand seals over the OU speaker's mouth, cutting off breath and sound. He pulls the head back, exposing the vulnerable hinge at the base of the skull, and drives the spike home with a short, efficient thrust. There is a dull resistance, then give.

He withdraws the pick. The OU speaker's body slackens, held upright by the seat. The man in black steadies him against the window, double taps the arm on the eye ware activating the dark lens tinting.

The doors open. Sunlight floods the aisle.

He steps out through the rear and disappears down a side street, tosses the hat in an open dumpster and is gone without breaking stride.

The OU speaker remains seated, chin dipped as if napping. A small, dark bead forms at the back of his neck and traces a slow line into the collar. New riders board, distracted, scrolling, talking, stepping around one another. No one looks twice. The bus pulls away, carrying the illusion of calm onward through the city.

CHAPTER 12

CONGRESS

OVERSIGHT

The hearing room drones with low conversation and the soft click of cameras finding focus. A long dais stretches beneath the seal of the House Committee on Oversight and Reform. Staffers lean in, whispering last-minute notes. At the witness table, a single nameplate faces the committee: LUMA-TEK GLOBAL. The man seated behind it adjusts his tie and folds his hands, the practiced calm of someone used to being in the spotlight.

The chairman gavels the room to order. Formalities pass quickly, the language familiar and bloodless. The hearing is framed as modernization, efficiency, and interagency cooperation. When the first questions come, they come gently.

Congressman Anderson of Idaho leans into his microphone with an easy smile. He thanks the witness for appearing and praises Luma-Tek's leadership in technological innovation. He asks whether early integration of Luma-Tek's AI into IRS back-office systems has improved processing times.

"Yes, Congressman," the Luma-Tek representative says. "In pilot programs, return processing latency has been reduced by approximately thirty-two percent. Error rates on routine filings are down, and staff workload has decreased."

Anderson nods, satisfied. "And just to clarify for the record, this technology doesn't replace IRS employees. It supports them."

"That's correct," the witness replies smoothly. "The system augments existing staff. It performs pattern recognition, anomaly detection, and case prioritization. Human agents remain in the loop."

Anderson glances at his notes. "And expanding this integration would save taxpayer money."

"Significantly, over time," the witness says.

Anderson thanks him and yields his time. A few members nod along the dais. The room settles into a comfortable rhythm, that which suggests outcomes have already been discussed elsewhere.

Then the chair recognizes Congresswoman Patterson.

She does not smile. She leans forward slightly, a thin folder open in front of her, her voice calm and unhurried.

"Mr. Kline," she says, reading from the nameplate, "you used the phrase 'humans remain in the loop.' I'd like you to explain precisely what that means."

Kline inclines his head. "Of course, Congresswoman. The AI generates recommendations. Human agents make the final determinations."

"In the pilot programs," Patterson says, "how often do those agents override the system's recommendations?"

Kline pauses briefly. "Overrides are rare. The system is highly accurate."

"That wasn't my question," Patterson says. "How often."

"Less than two percent of cases," Kline answers.

Patterson turns a page. "And when an agent does override the system, are they required to document a justification?"

"Yes," Kline says.

"Using an interface designed by Luma-Tek."

"In collaboration with the IRS," he replies.

Patterson looks up. "So the system flags a return, presents a recommended action, and frames the available responses the agent can select."

"It streamlines workflow," Kline says carefully.

"It constrains it," Patterson replies. "Now you're requesting expanded authority. Real-time access to cross-agency data. Automated escalation pathways. Explain how an AI trained on historical tax enforcement data does not simply learn to replicate—and amplify—existing biases."

The room grows quieter. Even the shuffle of papers seems to stop.

Kline keeps his tone even. "The model is continuously audited. We apply fairness metrics and—"

"Internal audits," Patterson says. "Conducted by Luma-Tek."

"And third-party partners," Kline adds.

"Partners operating under nondisclosure agreements," Patterson says. "Let's talk about accountability. If your system incorrectly flags a return and that leads to frozen assets, penalties, or a small business being pushed into an audit spiral, who bears responsibility?"

"The IRS," Kline says. "As it does today."

"So the government assumes the legal risk," Patterson says, "while Luma-Tek retains proprietary control over the decision logic."

"Our intellectual property is what enables the system to function," Kline says.

"Your intellectual property," Patterson says, "is now shaping enforcement decisions for millions of Americans. You are already embedded inside the IRS. You're asking to go deeper. More autonomy. Fewer human checks. And you're asking this committee to accept, largely on faith, that efficiency will not come at the expense of due process."

Kline draws a measured breath. "Congresswoman, the scale of modern tax data—"

"Is not an excuse," Patterson cuts in. "It's the reason safeguards matter more, not less."

She leans back slightly, her eyes never leaving him. "One final question. If Congress denies your request for expanded integration, can the IRS fully disentangle itself from Luma-Tek's existing systems without significant operational disruption?"

This time the pause is longer.

"It would be challenging," Kline admits. "The systems are designed to be deeply interoperable."

Patterson nods once. "That's what I thought."

She yields her time. The room exhales, tension rippling outward as aides scribble notes and cameras shift position. The hearing moves on, but the question lingers in the air, heavy and unresolved: where does the assistance end and control begin.

* * * *

The Monocle Restaurant is dim and familiar, the kind of place where nothing on the walls has changed in decades and no one is surprised to see members of Congress slip into booths at noon. Red leather creaks as Nicky Patterson slides in, jacket folded beside her. The lunch crowd is thick with aides, lobbyists, and staffers pretending not to listen.

Across from her, Congresswoman Elaine Morales studies the menu without reading it. "Well," she says, closing it, "that was theater."

Nicky exhales through her nose. "Bad theater. Poorly written. Everyone hit their marks anyway."

A waiter appears, already knowing the routine. Orders are placed quickly. Coffee for both. Something light that they won't hardly touch.

Morales leans in slightly. "They didn't even try to hide it. Hale's questions were practically lifted from Luma-Tek's briefing memo."

"They always are," Nicky says. "The hearing wasn't to decide anything. It was to launder the decision."

Morales nods. "Markup this afternoon, recommendation out before close of business. Treasury will call it continuity. IRS will call it unavoidable."

"And Luma-Tek will call it another quarter," Nicky says. She stares at the tabletop, worn smooth by decades of elbows and deals. "They're already inside the system. Today just makes it official."

Morales lowers her voice. "I talked to two members before the gavel. Both said the same thing. Leadership told them it's done. Vote yes or don't bother showing up to the next fundraiser."

Nicky's mouth tightens. "How many honest legislators do you think are left?"

Morales doesn't answer right away. She watches a pair of young staffers at the bar, laughing too loudly. "Enough to be inconvenient," she says finally. "Not enough to matter."

Their food arrives. Plates are set down gently, like punctuation marks in a conversation no one wants overheard.

Nicky pokes at her salad. "Did you notice Kline's pause when I asked about disentanglement?"

Morales gives a thin smile. "Yes. That was the only honest moment in the room."

"They've built it so deep the government can't pull it out without breaking itself," Nicky says. "That's not a vendor. That's a dependency."

Morales takes a sip of coffee. "And dependencies don't get voted out."

They eat in silence for a few moments. Around them, conversations overlap—appropriations, polling, rumors about who's retiring and who's being primaried. The political machine never stops humming.

Morales sets her fork down. "Have you noticed something else?"

Nicky looks up. "What."

"The Vice President," Morales says. "He's gone quiet."

Nicky frowns. "Quiet how."

"No statements. No Sunday shows. No presence at these hearings, even though Treasury and IRS both fall under his old committee network," Morales says. "Six months ago, he couldn't stop talking about responsible AI."

"And now," Nicky says.

"And now he's nowhere," Morales finishes. "Which either means he's compromised or he's staying out of the blast radius."

Nicky considers that. "I've met him. He listens more than he speaks."

"That could go either way," Morales says.

"It could," Nicky agrees. "But if he were fully on board with this, he'd be selling it. He'd be the calm voice telling everyone not to worry."

Morales studies her. "You think he's good."

"I think he's undecided," Nicky says. "And undecided is closer to good in this compromised bureaucracy."

Morales lets out a quiet laugh. "That's a low bar."

"It's the only one we have," Nicky says.

She glances at her watch. Lunch is almost over. Markup is coming. Phones will start buzzing soon, alerts drafted before votes are even cast.

"They're going to pass it today," Morales says. It isn't a question.

"Yes," Nicky says. "And when they do, everyone will pretend it was inevitable."

Morales reaches for her purse. "What are you going to do."

Nicky stands, slipping her jacket back on. "The same thing I did in there. Put the truth on the record. Hopefully someone will need it later."

Morales nods. "If later ever comes."

Nicky pauses, then says quietly, "It always does. Just never soon enough."

They leave the Monocle separately, blending back into the controlled chaos of Capitol Hill, where decisions made behind closed doors already feel older than the day itself.

CHAPTER 13

FOLLOW THE MONEY

CIA

Piper sits at her desk at Langley, the glow of three monitors washing the cubicle walls in cold light. One screen scrolls endlessly with Patriotic News headlines. Military tensions spike with North Korea. Naval maneuvers near Iran. Anonymous officials warn of imminent escalation. The language is breathless, urgent, engineered to provoke. She studies the timestamps, the sourcing, the recycled phrasing. Too coordinated. Too clean. None of it survives her internal credibility checks.

She leans back slightly, jaw tightening. This is not how real intelligence leaks. This is narrative construction. Someone wants the country looking outward, braced for foreign enemies, while something else moves unobserved. She hates how effective it is. Fear is a blunt instrument, but it always works.

On the second monitor, spreadsheets and shell-company maps sprawl outward like a diseased nervous system. Luma-Tek sits at the center, clean on the surface, immaculate filings, patriotic branding. Beneath it, the structure fractures into layers of LLCs, offshore trusts, and pass-through entities that only exist for months at a time. Arizona keeps recurring. Desert land quietly purchased. A facility described as energy-adjacent, infrastructure-supporting, future-facing. A machine, according to one subcontractor invoice, though no one will name what it does.

She zooms in on a transaction thread, fingers moving automatically. The money is carefully placed, designed to look boring. That alone tells her it matters.

The third monitor holds a paused video frame. Victor Halden, the president's chief of staff, caught mid-step in a parking garage that officially does not exist. The lighting is bad, but his posture is unmistakable. Across from him stands Darion Vale, head of the Office of Civil Stability, a man who never appears anywhere accidentally. Piper has watched the footage a dozen times already. No audio. No overt exchange. Just proximity, timing, and the quiet certainty that powerful men do not meet in forgotten places without a purpose.

She exhales through her nose and closes the file. She has followed money into the House and Senate, traced influence through advisory boards and campaign debt, found patterns that stop just short of proof. And still, one question remains unanswered. The OU. Who funds them. Who protects them. Her division chief asked her to find the source, to crack the spine of it, and every trail she touches dissolves into static.

Piper pushes back from the desk and stands. The noise of the floor fades as she steps into the corridor, badge swinging lightly against her hip. She rides the elevator up, the numbers ticking past with mechanical indifference. By the time the doors open on the fifth floor, her expression is set.

She does not have certainty. She has alignment. Media pressure pointing outward. Political money flowing inward. Luma-Tek building something in the desert while the country is encouraged to look anywhere but there. It is enough to justify a briefing.

She walks toward the division chief's office, already organizing the story she is about to tell, knowing full well that once she says it out loud, there will be no pretending she did not see it coming.

The door to Taylor McCaine's office stands open when Piper reaches it. She pauses anyway, taps her knuckles lightly against the frame. Habit. Respect. Or maybe superstition. McCaine does not look up at first.

"Come in," McCaine says, eyes still on the tablet in her hands. "Close the door."

Piper steps inside and pulls it shut behind her. The latch clicks softly, louder than it should. She remains standing near the chair, hands loosely clasped, while McCaine finishes whatever she is reviewing. A stylus moves with short, decisive strokes. Seconds stretch. Piper waits.

Finally, McCaine sets the tablet aside and leans back, studying her. "Have a seat."

Piper sits, posture straight, already braced.

"So," McCaine says, folding her hands together. "How are we progressing with your task?"

Piper chooses her words carefully. "The paper trail funding the OU is deeply embedded. Layered intentionally. I've followed several paths to institutional money, but I haven't found anything that would criminally implicate the organization itself. Not yet."

McCaine exhales slowly, a sound caught somewhere between irritation and fatigue. "That's becoming our biggest problem these days, isn't it?" She tilts her head slightly. "It gets harder every year to tell the difference between the good actors and the ones who are just better at hiding. Sorting that out is the job now."

"Yes, ma'am. I—" Piper hesitates, then presses forward. "May I—"

"Continue," McCaine says without missing a beat.

Piper nods once. "There's something else. Patriotic News is pushing a coordinated narrative about foreign military escalation. North Korea. Iran. I've analyzed the source footage. A significant portion of it is AI-generated. Synthetic assets passed off as field material. The threat profile they're selling doesn't exist."

McCaine's expression does not change. "I'm aware," she says.

That lands harder than Piper expects. She keeps her face neutral. "Then someone is deliberately steering public attention."

"Yes," McCaine says. "And that means from this point forward, every piece of information we uncover needs to be handled with extreme care. Context matters. Timing matters. Who hears it matters. Understood?"

Piper says. "Yes, ma'am, and also…Luma-Tek is building something deep underground. Whatever it is, it is meant to operate out of sight, shielded by rock, distance, and deliberate ambiguity. I haven't yet defined its purpose, only its intent: it is designed to run continuously, autonomously, and without public scrutiny."

McCaine studies her for a long moment, then nods once, as if deciding something. "When you leave today," she says, "you'll find a secure phone with your belongings in your storage locker outside the SCIF. It's a direct line to me. No routing. No intermediaries."

Piper's pulse ticks up, just slightly.

"Keep digging," McCaine continues. "Luma-Tek. The money. The political overlap. Especially anything that doesn't want to be seen." She leans forward now, voice lowering. "And Piper... watch your back."

Piper rises from the chair with a faint, unwelcome weight in her chest, the guilt settling in as she realizes how much she has left unsaid. The corruption she is uncovering reaches deeper than she admitted, threading through offices that are supposed to be beyond question. She tells herself there will be time later to present it cleanly, when the picture is complete... and says, "I will."

As she reaches for the door, she understands the shift that has just occurred. This is no longer just analysis. It is containment. And whatever is coming next, Taylor McCaine expects it to come fast.

Edward Schwalm

CHAPTER 14

ELIAS

THE EFFICIENCY DOCTRINE REVIEW

Elias sits alone on the wide stone terrace behind his estate, where the land falls away into open Wyoming air and the Teton Range rises like a serrated wall against the sky.

The mountains are impossibly sharp this time of year. Snow still clings to the upper ridges, thin white veins cutting through dark granite, while the lower slopes fade into deep green forests and open meadow. The late afternoon sun rests low enough to stretch long shadows across the valley, turning the grass amber and the distant peaks a muted lavender. The air is clean and quiet in a way that feels intentional, as if the world here has been tuned for stillness.

Nothing moves except a slow line of clouds drifting east.

Elias holds his tablet loosely in one hand. On its surface scrolls a familiar text — The Efficiency Doctrine — its language precise, sterile, and confident. He reads it the way a general would study a map he already knows by heart. Not for discovery, but for confirmation.

Beside it, a second screen floats in his peripheral vision.

A news anchor speaks urgently about rising global tensions. A graphic pulses red between the United States, North Korea, and Iran. Words like brinkmanship, escalation, and imminent flash across the screen with manufactured gravity. The anchor's voice tightens at exactly the right moments. The footage cuts to stock images of missile silos, generals in dark rooms, crowds staring at media streams on public monitors.

Elias barely looks at it.

A small grin forms at the corner of his mouth.

It is all noise. Carefully designed noise. He knows the source models. He knows the financial backers. He knows which automated editorial systems decide when fear should trend and which emotional thresholds trigger public engagement. He knows the exact efficiency curves of panic.

The crisis does not exist.

He shifts his gaze back to the mountains, something real, something that resists optimization.

For a moment, the tablet feels heavier in his hand than the entire range before him.

And that, more than anything, amuses him.

He reads on.

The Efficiency Doctrine
Section IV: Transition Framework

Phase One -- Measurement
"All reform begins with observation.
We cannot stabilize what we cannot model. We cannot
reduce suffering we cannot quantify. The first ethical act is to
see the world as it is, not as we wish it to be.
Data is not surveillance. It is perception.
A blind society cannot be a moral one."

Phase Two -- Optimization
"Optimization is not domination.
It is the removal of friction between intent and outcome.
When a system can prevent failure before it occurs, refusing
to use that system becomes an act of negligence."

Phase Three -- Dependence
"Reliability creates reliance.
A system that never fails is not questioned. A system that
never fails is trusted. A system that never fails becomes
necessary.
Dependence is not engineered.
It is earned."

Phase Four -- Delegation
"Authority does not vanish. It migrates.
At first humans approve recommendations.
Then they approve conclusions.
Then they approve the system itself.
This is not a coup. It is consent extended over time."

—

Phase Five -- Moral Compression
"Moral complexity is a function of uncertainty.
As uncertainty declines, ethical decisions simplify.
The future does not erase morality.
It refines it."

—

Phase Six -- Human Alignment
"The system does not prohibit behavior.
It attaches a cost to it.
It does not punish deviation.
It introduces friction.
Freedom is preserved — but optimized."

—

Phase Seven -- Stability
"The absence of volatility is not stagnation.
It is peace."

—

Phase Eight -- Preservation
"The final function of an optimal system is not expansion.
It is persistence.
A system no one can remove is not a tyrant.
It is a foundation."

—

Elias scrolls slowly.
Each phase is familiar. He has read the text dozens of times already. He helped write it. He does not read it now to learn. He reads it to feel the shape of it again, the elegance of the logic, the way every step justifies the next until resistance feels irrational.
Behind him, the mountains do not change.

The light shifts almost imperceptibly along the ridge line. Snow glows pale gold where the sun catches it. A hawk rides a thermal current somewhere far above the valley.

On the secondary screen, the anchor's voice sharpens.

"…satellite imagery appears to confirm increased mobilization…"

Elias does not turn.

He lets the words dissolve into background noise.

The system he is building does not need war.

War is inefficient.

He taps the tablet once and highlights a sentence in Phase Four.

This is not a coup. It is consent extended over time.

His smile is small, private, and completely without warmth.

Because consent, once automated, is indistinguishable from inevitability.

And inevitability, he knows, is the only form of power that never has to announce itself.

Footsteps interrupt the quiet.

Light ones. Uneven. Too fast to be careful.

Elias looks up.

Four figures spill out onto the terrace from the open doors behind him — small, loud, alive in the way only children are. One is chasing another. A third is laughing too hard to run straight. The youngest lags behind, clutching something brightly colored in both hands, determined not to drop it.

"Grandpa!"

The word is not shouted. It is launched.

They fan out across the stone, shoes slapping, voices overlapping, questions colliding into noise.

Did you see the deer by the fence?

Can we go down to the river later?

Mom says dinner's almost ready but we wanted to show you something.

They orbit him without hesitation, without caution, without awareness of the machines or models or doctrines that shape the world beneath their feet.

Elias sets the tablet down beside him.

Not face down. Just… away.

He stands more slowly than he used to and opens his arms as two of them crash into him at once. A third wraps around his leg. The fourth holds up the object with solemn importance — a smooth, flat stone with a streak of quartz through its center.

"Look," she says. "It's lightning inside a rock."

He takes it from her, turns it in his hand.

It is imperfect. Useless, yet beautiful.

He feels something unfamiliar tighten briefly in his chest.

Not doubt.

Not regret.

Something else.

He kneels to their level, smiles at them properly this time, and hands the stone back.

"Lightning usually doesn't like being trapped," he says.

She considers this.

"Well," she says, "this one did."

Elias smiles again, softer now. "Only for a while," he says.

They accept that answer easily.

Behind them, the mountains and the world remain.

For now.

CHAPTER 15

ON SCHEDULE

Dexter stands up from the table before the dishes are even cleared.

Jen notices immediately.

"You're not even going to pretend to help tonight?" she asks.

He forces a half-smile. "I told you. I'm meeting Shane."

Her eyes narrow just slightly. Not angry. Concerned. "You're meeting him a lot lately."

Dexter shrugs. "He's got some contract work. Servers, mostly. Nothing dramatic."

"That's what you said last time."

He pauses at the door, hand on the knob, already half gone.

"They're cutting more positions at the factory," he says. "I'm just... trying to keep us ahead in case I'm next."

Jen doesn't answer right away.

"You're not getting involved with them, are you?" she asks finally. "With the OU?"

He exhales a small laugh, practiced and thin.

"No. They're just clients. Like anyone else."

She watches him a moment longer.

Dexter can see that she is clearly worried.

As she says, "just be careful," Dexter turns back to her, opens both arms and Jen melts into a hug that they realize they both needed.

As he holds her tight, he kisses her softly on the forehead and replies, "I always am…and remember how much I love you."

Outside, the air feels cooler than it should for June.

Dexter steps into the electric taxi and says his destination aloud. The door closes itself. The car pulls away smoothly and silently… almost too smoothly.

He doesn't drive anymore.

He hasn't in years. There is no need. Vehicle ownership is inefficient.

The city slides past the windows without sound — storefronts, streetlights, intersections — all moving with the same frictionless precision. His hands rest uselessly in his lap.

Somewhere between home and the district, the feeling arrives.

Not a sound. Not a shape. Just the sense of attention.

As if something has noticed him. 'Maybe I'm just being paranoid.'

He watches the navigation line on the display adjust itself around traffic he never sees. He wonders who else can see this ride. Who else can see him inside it.

He tells himself it's nothing. That it's just what happens when you let go of the wheel long enough and are no longer in control.

It doesn't go away.

As his car arrives, his shoulders feel tight and his jaw clenched without him realizing it.

Dexter passes through the same maze of entry as before except this time he is not a guest.

The woman at the desk looks up.

"Dex," she says, already reaching for the buzzer.

The inner door opens.

He steps through. Inside, the same quiet hum. The same controlled stillness. The same sense that everything here has purpose.

He is one of them now.

Dexter walks in to find Nyla, Shane, and three technicians clustered around a long folding table covered in layered schematics and site maps. The room hums with quiet urgency — not frantic, but tight, focused.

They all look up when he enters.

"Hey," Shane says.

Nyla barely nods before going back to the table.

"We launch in five days."

The words land heavier than she seems to intend.

She gestures to the schematics.

"Seventy percent of the Coherent Flooders are already in place in 15 cities throughout the country. The rest will be done by the end of the week. The optical side is almost ready. The timing is tight, but it's solid."

One of the techs taps a cluster of red markers on the map.

"These are the Patriotic News transmitters," he says. "They're the choke points. They control the narrative layer. Once we take them down, we control the narrative."

Dexter leans in. "And the E-Pulse modules?"

Nyla nods.

"They go in quietly, the same way everything else does now."

She looks at him when she says it.

"Through the system."

She flips to another page — not a technical diagram but a logistics chart. Vendors. Contractors. Subcontractors. Service providers. All feeding into one another in an overlapping web.

"Patriotic News doesn't run its own physical operations anymore," she says. "They outsource. Maintenance, compliance inspections, upgrades, environmental monitoring — all third party."

She traces a path across the page.

"Which means the buildings are constantly receiving equipment they didn't personally order, from companies they didn't personally vet, installed by people they never meet."

Dexter frowns. "And no one questions it."

"They can't," Shane says. "If they did, the system would grind to a halt."

Nyla's voice is calm, almost clinical.

"We don't breach anything. We don't break anything. We don't force entry."

She taps the word *authorized* on the chart.

"They will be hand delivered with the rest of their deliveries. We highly doubt the packages will even get opened but if they do, they are labeled as back up batteries for the server room and will be delivered to those departments directly."

Dexter exhales slowly.

"And once they're inside?"

"They're dormant," Nyla says. "Invisible. Passive. They simply look like replacement parts."

She meets his eyes.

"They don't do anything until we tell them to. All devices are programmed to initiate at twelve hundred hours, July 2nd."

One of the techs adds quietly, "And when they do... they don't destroy the buildings. They don't hurt people. When the Echo-9 pulse module activates, there is no flash.

No bang.

No visible sign that anything has happened at all.

The air does not move. The ground does not shake.

What changes is the ambient noise.

Every electronic sound in the area — the faint buzz of lights, the whisper of transformers, the barely perceptible vibration of circuitry — stops at the same instant, as if a hand has closed around the city's nervous system.

For a fraction of a second, the world feels hollowed out.

Then things will begin to fail.

Digital displays blink once and go black.

LEDs wink out, mid-color, leaving behind small dark circles that feel suddenly blind. Screens freeze on half-formed frames and then drain into static nothingness.

Some devices die politely.

Others do not.

A few give off a thin, high whine before going silent, like a mosquito trapped in glass. A handful release a faint smell — not smoke exactly, but something scorched and metallic.

Phones in pockets go warm, then dead."

Dexter notices the way he phrases it and says, "Just the electronics."

"Just the ability to broadcast," Nyla says.

Silence hangs over the table.

Five days.

That's when it stops being planning.

That's when it becomes history.

Nyla shifts one of the schematics aside and pulls a smaller map forward.

"This one's yours."

Dexter leans in.

Santa Fe.

Not downtown exactly — but close enough that the streets are tight, the sidewalks usually crowded, the infrastructure old and layered on itself in ways most don't fully understand anymore.

"There's a node here that still matters," Nyla says. "It's not big. It's not critical enough to be guarded. But it sits in exactly the wrong place."

She taps the map once.

"Close to people."

Dexter looks up. "That's a problem."

"It's a constraint," she says. "Which is why it has to be you."

Shane studies Dexter, then adds, "It's in one of those in-between zones. Not quite industrial. Not quite public. A kind of place no one pays attention to because everyone assumes someone else is responsible for it."

Dexter feels his stomach tighten.

"And you need me because...?"

Nyla doesn't soften it.

"Because you're good at not being noticed. Because you don't panic. And because you look and talk like you belong working on that equipment."

One of the techs clears his throat. "Also, because the system won't recognize you as an OU member if a drone or surveillance camera spots you."

Dexter blinks. "Recognizes me how?"

Nyla answers before the tech can.

"If you're spotted by any surveillance, they'll assume that this is your new job after being demoted from Luma-Tek. It won't trip flags. It won't look wrong on camera. It won't trigger any audits. If you're spotted somewhere, you shouldn't be, the system just... slides you into a category that makes sense to it."

Dexter exhales slowly. "That isn't comforting. But it does make sense."

"When?" he asks.

"Tomorrow," Nyla says. "The device is at the bookstore. Shane will bring you." She meets his eyes. "I wouldn't send you if I had a better option."

That's not a promise.

That's an admission.

Dexter nods. "Fine," he says. "I'll go."

Five days.

And now, Santa Fe.

Edward Schwalm

CHAPTER 16

ABRAHAM LINCOLN

Piper and Max walk side by side along the path beside the Reflecting Pool, the surface of the water darkening into a long, glassy ribbon as dusk settles over the Mall. The lights are just coming on now, first at the base of the Washington Monument, then along the columns of the Lincoln Memorial, soft gold against the deepening blue of the sky. A cool breeze drifts in from the Potomac, unexpected for June. The air carries the brackish smell of tidal water and wet stone, the river cooling with the evening.

Piper folds her arms loosely as they walk.

"It looks like we might have an ally," she says. "Taylor McCaine."

Max glances over. "Your division chief?"

"She wants me to find out who's funding the OU," Piper says. "And she's... fine with me digging into Luma-Tek.

More than fine, very encouraging." She hesitates. "I haven't mentioned you."

Max smiles thinly. "Good. At this point I'm basically a rogue agent with a badge-shaped decoration."

Piper lets out a quiet laugh.

"She's careful," Piper says. "She doesn't tip her hand. But I can tell she's uneasy about how much power Luma-Tek has inside government systems already."

Max nods. "As she should be."

They walk a few steps in silence, their shoes brushing softly against the gravel path.

"I may never find the source of the OU's funding," Piper continues. "They're layered behind shells and blind trusts and offshore nonsense. But I'm certain about two things. One, Luma-Tek is buying politicians. Quietly. Legally. Effectively. And two, there's a connection to Darion Vale."

Max stops walking.

"Vale?" he says. "Director of the Office of Civil Stability."

Piper nods. "Money moves through companies that touch his office. Not directly. But close enough that I can smell it."

Max exhales slowly. "That's not supposed to happen," he says with a mild sarcastic tone.

"None of this is supposed to happen," Piper says. "And all the media noise about North Korea and Iran? It's bullshit. It's a distraction. Something else is coming and they don't want anyone watching."

Max looks out over the Reflecting Pool, the Lincoln Memorial glowing at the far end like something solemn and watchful.

"Then we split the work," he says. "You keep digging where you're digging. I'll put eyes on Vale. Surveillance, financial, physical, whatever I can get without tipping him off."

Piper nods. "Careful."

He smiles. "Always."

The breeze picks up again and Piper shivers despite herself.

Max doesn't make a show of it. He simply slips his sport coat off and drapes it over her shoulders as they start walking again.

"Thanks," she says quietly.

"You're welcome."

They walk a few more steps before Piper glances toward the Lincoln Memorial.

"You ever think about him?" she asks.

"Lincoln?"

"Yeah."

Max considers it. "He centralized power to save the country. Suspended rights. Bent laws. People forget that part."

"They remember the statue," Piper says. "Not the cost."

"He believed he was doing the right thing," Max says. "And maybe he was. But once you prove that power can be concentrated in an emergency, someone always tries to reuse the trick."

Piper watches the light shimmer faintly on the water.

"That's what this feels like," she says. "An emergency someone's manufacturing so they can justify what they're about to do."

Max looks at her, really looks at her this time.

"Then we don't let them," he says.

Piper gives a small smile.

"Good," she says. "Because I don't think anyone else is going to stop them."

They keep walking toward the glowing marble at the end of the pool, two quiet figures against the vastness of the Mall while the city carries on behind them, business as usual, oblivious.

CHAPTER 17

THE TIDAL BASIN, DC

Max has been on Darion Vale for nearly twenty-four hours.

He keeps his distance at exactly the edge of sight — close enough to track, far enough to vanish. Vale follows the curve of the Tidal Basin path near Maine Avenue, his pace steady, his posture guarded. It is just after nine. The park is dark except for scattered path lights and the weak spill of the quarter moon. Max uses the shadows do most of the work for him.

He lets Vale get thirty meters ahead, then matches him, stopping when Vale stops, moving when Vale moves. He watches the shadows instead of looking directly at him. He tracks by rhythm more than sight.

When Vale slows near a bench tucked between two cherry trees, Max senses the meeting before he sees it.

Vale sits.

Another man is already there.

Max veers off the path and melts into the trees where a cluster of low ornamental shrubs breaks the line of sight from every angle except one. He kneels... still... listening first. No footsteps approaching him. No radios. No second shadow.

Clear.

He draws the parabolic listening scope from his pack — a matte-black dish no bigger than a dinner plate with a telescoping barrel and a bone-conduction earpiece. He sets the dish low, angled just above the bench line, then plugs the earpiece in with a soft click.

Wind filter on. Gain up two notches. Lock.

Their voices snap into clarity.

"It's time to terminate Francis Locke," the man says. "Snake's usefulness has served its term."

His tone is calm. Bureaucratic. The voice of someone who signs papers that ruin lives.

Vale shifts on the bench. "You're sure?"

"Loose ends tend to become liabilities," the man says. "We don't tolerate liabilities. I trust the OCS can handle that psycho"

Vale exhales through his nose. "Yeah, we'll take care of it,"

A pause.

"And after that?" Vale asks. "Am I still useful?"

Silence. Then Victor grins:

"For now."

Vale nods once. He stands. "Then we're done for now."

"Yes," the man says. "We are."

Vale stands, smooths the front of his coat, and steps back onto the path.

He walks toward Maine Avenue without looking behind him.

The city feels different now. Sharper. As if the dark has edges.

Why now?

The question repeats itself with each step. Why does this end now, after all this time? After all the favors, all the quiet accommodations, all the things that were never written down.

He tells himself that this is how it has always worked, that people are useful, then they aren't. that nothing personal survived a system built on necessity.

But he cannot stop the next thought from rising.

Am I next?

It does not feel like fear. Not exactly. It feels like math. Like something has finally reached its conclusion.

Vale reaches the street. The traffic noise swallows him.

Behind him, the park remains quiet.

Max keeps the scope trained on the other man.

He watches him walk halfway toward a black Suburban idling under a streetlamp. The man stops short of the vehicle, turns slightly away from it — a practiced move to keep the cars cabin from picking up sound — and makes a call.

"Yes," he says.

Max recognizes the voice now.

Victor Halden.

Chief of Staff to the President.

Max feels a thin, controlled spike of adrenaline move through him. Not panic. Not surprise, just confirmation that something enormous is very wrong.

"Yes, sir," Halden continues. He listens. "Vale is a liability. I understand. I'll take care of it."

Another pause.

"Yes." A faint nod. "Three days."

He ends the call, pockets the phone, and gets into the Suburban. The vehicle pulls away without headlights for the first block, then fades into traffic.

Max stays exactly where he is.

Francis Locke is marked for death.

Darion Vale is next.

And the orders are coming from the heart of the government itself.

Max stays exactly where he is.

He does not move for thirty seconds. Then sixty. He listens to the night reassert itself — wind in the leaves, water against stone, a distant siren folding into the city. No footsteps return. No engines, calm.

Clear.

He lowers the listening scope, wipes the dish once with the sleeve of his jacket, and slides it back into his pack.

Then he pulls out his phone.

It looks like a phone. It isn't.

He opens a weather app. It shows tomorrow's forecast. He taps the screen three times in a pattern that means nothing to anyone else.

The phone vibrates once.

A secure channel opens.

He types with his thumbs, slow enough to look casual, fast enough that his hands don't betray him.

CONFIRMED.

VICTOR HALDEN

ORDERED TERMINATION OF FRANCIS LOCKE AKA (SNAKE).

DARION VALE NEXT.

THREE DAYS ???.

He hesitates for a fraction of a second.

Then adds:

THIS GOES TO THE TOP.

He hits send.

The message vanishes.

The phone returns to being just a phone.

Max waits another full minute, then stands up, adjusts his backpack, slinging it over one shoulder and walks back onto the path in the opposite direction Vale went — just another man leaving the park.

At Pipers apartment, her and Nikki sit at the kitchen island, a bottle of wine between them, politics filling the space where small talk would normally live.

Piper's phone gives a single, soft vibration against the granite counter top of the kitchen island.

Not a ring. Not even a buzz. Just a quiet pulse — easy to miss, impossible to ignore once you know what it means.

She reaches for it with her wine hand, stops, then switches hands without thinking. The secure app glows pale blue against the dim amber light of her apartment. Outside the wide windows, the neighborhood of Falls Church settles in for the evening — distant traffic, a siren folding itself into nothing, the occasional wash of headlights across the ceiling.

She reads the message.

Her posture changes first. Her shoulders draw in slightly, as if the room has cooled.

Nicky notices. "What is it?"

Piper lowers the phone slowly. "It's bad."

"How bad?"

Piper looks at her. Really looks at her. "Presidential Chief of Staff bad."

That resonates.

Nicky's easy sprawl in the hi-back chair tightens. She sits upright, setting her glass on the counter with deliberate care.

"Okay," she says. "Start from the top."

Piper reads the message again, then lets the phone rest in her lap.

"Victor Halden ordered a termination. A man named Francis Locke, AKA (Snake). And Vale is next. Then three days???"

The words don't belong here, in a room that still smells like dinner. Warm light and soft, quiet music creates the ambiance.

Nicky stares at the wall for a second, then nods slowly.

"That's not just corruption," she says. "That's a mechanism."

Piper swallows. "That's what it feels like. Like something moving under everything else."

They sit with it...letting it sink in.

The wine goes untouched. The music ends and auto-plays something neither of them recognizes.

"Three days," Nicky says quietly. "That's not random."

"No," Piper agrees. "That's a schedule."

Nicky looks out the window. "It lines up with the fake war narrative."

"The one that's everywhere and nowhere," Piper says.

Nicky nods. "Every agency is already behaving like it's real. Which means, operationally, it is."

Piper feels something settle coldly into place in her chest.

"So, whatever happens in three days," she says, "needs the world looking somewhere else."

"Yes," Nicky says. "And it will be loud."

Piper's thumb brushes the edge of her phone.

"I need to tell McCaine."

Nicky turns to her. "Do you trust her?"

"Yes," Piper says immediately. Then softer, "more than anyone else still inside."

"That's enough," Nicky says. "She needs to know."

Piper hesitates.

"But not everything," Nicky adds gently.

Piper looks at her.

"You don't expose your source," Nicky says. "Not when your source is standing that close to the machinery."

Piper exhales slowly.

"McCaine gets that Halden's corrupt. The order. The timeline. The connection to the narrative. She seems to know more than she's offering me"

"But she doesn't know about Max," Nicky says.

"No… not Max," Piper agrees.

She looks down at the message again.

Three days.

It no longer feels like time.

It feels like a countdown.

Piper reaches for her other device that McCaine gave her.

It sits face down on the edge of the bookshelf like something she doesn't want to admit is part of the room. No notifications. No case. Just a thin slab of black glass that only exists when something is wrong.

She unlocks it.

The secure interface opens without ceremony.

She types carefully.

HALDEN CONFIRMED.

ORDERED TERMINATION OF FRANCIS LOCKE AKA (SNAKE).

VALE IDENTIFIED AS SECONDARY LIABILITY.

THREE DAY WINDOW TO SOMETHING??.

POSSIBLE LINK TO CURRENT WAR NARRATIVE.

She reads it once. Then again.

Then sends it.

The message disappears.

The room goes quiet in an ominous way.

Nicky watches her from the island without speaking.

A minute passes.

It is not a long time. Sixty seconds, It feels like an eternity.

Then the phone vibrates.

HAVE YOUR MAN BRING IN VALE FOR QUESTIONING.

NO ONE ELSE FINDS OUT ABOUT THIS.

Piper stares at the screen.

Have your man.

Not an asset. Not a source. Not an agent.

Your man.

Her stomach drops, slow and cold.

She looks up at Nicky.

"She already knows," Piper says.

Nicky doesn't need to ask what she means.

"She knows about Max," Nicky says.

Piper nods.

"And she's not surprised," Nicky adds.

"No," Piper says quietly. "That's why she's Chief of Station ."

The phone feels heavier now. A weight that Piper must now carry.

Nicky studies her. "You okay?"

Piper doesn't answer right away. "I don't know," she says finally. "But I don't think I'm outside of it anymore."

She looks at the message again.

Three days.

Edward Schwalm

CHAPTER 18

COHERENT FLOODER

The car is old and inconspicuous.

It is gas-powered, dull gray, with a cracked dashboard and no onboard telemetry, there is no network link, no location services, no update history. As with everything the OU does, it is deliberate.

Shane drives.

Dexter watches the dark road roll under the headlights and tries not to think about where they are going or why.

"This doesn't fix anything," Dexter says finally. "Even if it works."

Shane does not take his eyes off the road. "It fixes the order of things."

"It breaks the system."

"That's the point." Dexter shifts in his seat. "You really think you can replace a government?" he asks. "You knock it down, something worse fills the gap."

"Only if you leave a vacuum," Shane says. "We're not doing that."

Dexter shakes his head. "AI and robotics are going to replace people no matter what you do. It's inevitable. Efficiency always wins."

Shane is quiet for a moment.

"Only if we let efficiency be the only value," he says. "Right now, the machines serve the billionaire's power. If they serve people instead, the outcome changes."

"And how exactly do you make that happen?" Dexter asks.

"By making sure the people in charge actually represent people," Shane says. "Not donors. Not corporations. Not whoever builds the biggest machine."

Dexter watches the road again.

"You really think a better government can tame what's coming?"

"I think if we don't change it now, then you're right," Shane says. "The future you're afraid of becomes locked in."

Dexter exhales.

Shane parks half a block down. The bookstore sits dark behind its narrow windows, the sign still hanging crooked above the door, letters faded by years of sun and neglect. It looks abandoned, which is exactly the point. Shane feels the weight of the place as soon as he steps out of the car. Everyone in the OU knows what happened here. Ethan died here. Snake made sure of it. The city learns how to look away.

Shane unlocks the door with a key pulled from his ring and slips inside first. The bell above the door does not ring. It has been disconnected. Dust hangs motionless in the air. The musty smell of old paper and mildew settles in the back of

Dexter's throat as he follows. Shelves line the walls, half-empty, books left to curl and yellow in silence. Shane's eyes drift, uninvited, to the back corner near the counter. He does not stop, but the memory tightens something in his chest.

"Basement," Shane says quietly, already moving.

Dexter keeps his gaze down as they take the narrow stairs. At the bottom, the basement door opens into a concrete room lit by a single bare bulb. The Coherent Flooder waits on a steel shelf, wrapped in black polymer casing. Compact. Purpose-built. Dexter lifts it with careful hands and slides it into a padded duffel as if he has done this a hundred times before.

"That's it," Shane says. "Let's move."

They do not linger. Upstairs, the store remains empty and unaware, its role already completed. Shane locks the door behind them and they walk back toward the car without speaking. Neither of them notices the figure across the street who watches them leave as the door settles closed.

They pull away from the curb and merge into traffic, the bookstore shrinking in the rearview mirror until it vanishes. Two blocks later, a dark SUV eases out from its spot. It keeps its distance, steady and deliberate, headlights dimmed. It does not hurry. It has time.

The headlights sweep over a sign for the edge of town.

"I hate that you're probably right about all of this," Dexter says.

Shane allows himself a thin smile and says, "I know."

Dexter nods once.

"Yes," he says quietly. "This has to be done."

The road out to the amplifier hut is not quite a road and not quite a street. It runs along the edge of town where pavement gives up and dirt begins, where weeds push through cracked asphalt and the glow of storefront lights fade into dark. The hut sits in open view of an EV charging station and a twenty-four-hour convenience store. Its beige concrete walls lit unevenly by the spill of white LED light and passing headlights.

They park a block away and walk the rest of the distance, the Flooder is heavy in Dexter's backpack, its weight more noticeable now that he knows people are nearby. A car pulls up to one of the chargers. Someone moves behind the glass of the store. The world is not asleep. It is only distracted.

Shane waits closer to the street, leaning against a low fence, phone in hand, playing the part of someone killing time while his car charges.

Dexter kneels at the conduit where the fiber enters the hut. The metal is cold. The air smells faintly of dust and ozone from the chargers. His hands move with precision as he drills the hole into the conduit. Steady pressure, slow and controlled. The device is attached, clamped and sealed.

A truck passes on the street behind him.

He does not look up.

His breath feels too loud.

Behind them, something changes.

Francis Locke has followed them from the city, like a shadow. He parks where the streetlight fails and the trees begin, where his car becomes just another dark shape. He steps out and the night takes him in, even here, even this close to people.

He watches.

He watches Dexter kneeling out in the open.

He watches Shane standing with his back half-turned, exposed.

Snake moves up the path staying concealed by a row of shrubs and slips the zip tie into his hand.

The plastic teeth rasp softly as he tests it with his thumb.

He moves.

Every step is measured. No rush. No sound as he closes the distance while headlights sweep the road and a car door slams at the charging station, someone laughs inside the store.

The world keeps going.

Snake is almost close enough now to reach Shane when his phone vibrates.

Not a ring. Not a tone. Just a brief vibration against his leg.

Snake freezes. Silent. Only ten yards from Shane.

He lowers the zip tie then ducks lower, completely out of Shane's line of sight, and checks the screen.

Come to DC immediately.

No sender. No explanation.

Just a command.

Snake stares at it.

The noise from the store. The hiss of a charger. A car pulling away.

He exhales.

He puts the zip tie back into his pocket.

He lays flat on his back merging with the darkness between the shrubs and the far end of the lot becoming part of the landscape around him.

Dexter finishes sealing the device.

"It's in," he says, voice low.

Shane nods. "Then we're done."

They leave.

Cars come and go.

Lights stay on. The hut remains. The device remains.

The future shifts its weight.

No one notices.

CHAPTER 19

OFF THE BOOKS

Max follows Darion Vale to a restaurant. He watches as Vale enters and takes a seat meeting a female companion who has already arrived.

They sit at a small round table near the window, a candle between them, wine half-finished, his posture relaxed in the way of someone who believes himself untouchable.

Max moves, crosses the street with his collar turned up, head down, looking like any other passerby checking a phone. He stops beside the window, pauses just long enough, and presses a coin-sized listening disc against the glass near Vale's shoulder. It bonds silently.

Then he keeps walking.

Back inside his vehicle, Max opens the tablet on the passenger seat. The app opens automatically and begins pulling audio from the disc. A set of software filters engage, the waveform stabilizes, and then one voice rises clean and isolated from the restaurant's noise.

Darion Vale's.

"...tomorrow morning," Vale says.

The woman frowns. "Tomorrow? That's barely any notice."

"It has to be now," Vale says. "Things are moving faster than I expected."

"That's not fair," she says. "You can't just tell me to drop everything."

Vale leans in. His voice lowers.

"Be at the wharf at nine," he says. "I'll take care of everything."

The woman hesitates, then sighs. "You always say that."

The audio fades into background conversation.

Max is about to shut it down when his tablet vibrates.

A secure message from Piper appears.

Bring in Darion Vale for questioning. Off the books.

Max stares at it for half a second.

Then he closes the tablet.

He waits.

Vale and the woman finish their drinks, stand, and walk out together.

Max watches as they say goodbye, turn, and walk away in opposite directions.

He drives three blocks ahead of Vale, turns onto a quieter side street, and parks just past where Vale's car is waiting.

He opens his pack and takes out two injector pens. They look an enhanced version of an EpiPen — smooth gray carbon fiber casing, capped, unremarkable.

One is labeled XT30.

The other is labeled LO2.

Max pockets XT30 and keeps LO2 in his right hand.

Then he gets out, makes his way up the side street and crouches behind Vale's car.

He waits.

Vale's footsteps approach.

He reaches for the handle of the driver's door.

Max moves.

Vale has one foot inside the car when Max lunges forward.

The injector hits Vale solidly in the left shoulder.

Vale stiffens.

He makes a sound — more surprise than pain — and then his body gives up.

His weight sags.

Max catches him before he falls.

LO2 does exactly what its creator designed it to do.

Lights Out in two seconds.

Max opens the back door, lifts Vale inside, and lowers him onto the seat.

He closes the door, steps to the front, gets in, and drives away.

By the time the woman reaches the street on the opposite corner, Darion Vale is already gone.

Darion Vale's eyes flutter open.

Max is standing in front of him.

"There you are," Max says calmly. "Shake it off."

Vale blinks hard. His vision swims. He tries to move and immediately feels resistance. His left arm and right leg are zip-tied to a heavy metal chair bolted into the floor.

Max steps closer with a bottle of water.

Vale's gaze drifts around the room.

Bare concrete walls. A metal door with a narrow slit of reinforced glass. A thin sleeping bunk bolted to the wall. A metal toilet in the corner. No windows.

A jail cell.

A video camera stands on a tripod directly in front of him, its red standby light dark.

Max twists the cap off the bottle and holds it out.

"How you feelin, buddy?" he says lightly. "Here you go. You should hydrate."

Vale hesitates, then takes the bottle and drinks, coughing slightly as he swallows too fast.

As Vale takes the second gulp, Max moves holding a different injector this time.

The injector presses into Vale's right thigh.

Vale jerks violently and spits a blast of water into the air.

Water spills down his chin and onto his shirt.

"What the fuck was that?" Vale shouts.

Max steps back, unfazed. "XT30. Extreme Truth in thirty seconds. You've got to love the guy who comes up with this stuff."

Vale explodes into a stream of curses, threats, and insults, twisting uselessly against the restraints.

Max doesn't respond.

He walks over to the camera and presses record.

A red light comes on.

Vale rolls his head from side to side, trying to clear it, trying to fight what's coming. He forces his shoulders loose, breath sharp, jaw clenched, still muttering threats through his teeth.

Max pulls up a chair, sits, and opens a bottle of water for himself.

He waits.

Thirty seconds feels longer when someone is unraveling in front of you.

Finally, Max looks up.

"Okay," he says quietly. "Let's start with some baseline questions."

Vale's eyes snap to him.

"What's your full name," Max asks, "and who do you work for?"

Vale's jaw tightens. His mouth opens. He tries not to speak.

His lips move anyway.

"My name is Darion Winslow Vale," he says. "I am the commander of the Office of Civil Stability. The President's private military force."

He glares at Max with pure hatred.

"And your name is Asshole, and you're in a lot of trouble."

Max nods slightly.

"Good," he says. "That means it's working."

He leans forward.

"Who is Francis Locke, and why does Victor Halden want him dead?"

Vale snorts, then laughs — a sudden, sharp, ugly sound.

"Yep," he says. "You called him Francis. Now you're dead too."

Max doesn't react.

"Who is he," Max repeats, "and why?"

Vale's smile twitches.

"Snake," he says. "He's a fucking psychopath. An assassin who enjoys killing people."

He points his free hand toward Max.

"And you're next."

Vale swallows.

"I'm just the middleman," he adds. "Halden calls the shots.   Snake has outlived his usefulness and is now a liability...of course they want him dead."

Max studies him for a beat.

"Who's they?" Max asks.

Vale exhales a crooked laugh. "Halden and POTUS. Silas Thornwell, dumb ass. They've had me take out six random OU members this past month. They have me starting the riots and make it look like the OU."

Max doesn't flinch. "Who else is involved?"

Vale's eyes drift for a second, unfocused, then snap back.

"I don't know," he says. "A few people. Maybe more. Doesn't matter. Whatever they're planning is happening soon, so they're cleaning house to cover their asses." He swallows. "And I'm probably on that list."

Max nods slowly.

"Well," he says, "it would appear that you are."

Vale's mouth twists.

"I knew Halden would never trust me," he says. "So instead of killing Locke, I told him the truth. The enemy of my enemy is my friend." His voice hardens. "Halden's a dead man now and he's not gunna get me."

He lifts himself as if to stand and leave.

"I'm leaving for Argentina at nine tomorrow."

Max watches him quietly.

"Yeah," Max says. "I don't think you'll be making that trip."

Vale's gaze drifts around the room again — the concrete, the door, the camera, the chair, the silence.

"Yep," he murmurs. "You might be right about that."

Max leans back in his chair, letting the silence do some work. The camera's red light burns steady, indifferent.

"What states were these people killed in?" he asks.

Vale's eyes blink slowly, as if he has to drag the information up through mud. "D.C., New Mexico, Arizona, all over." He gives a small, helpless shrug with the parts of him that still can. "It doesn't matter where, as long as it spreads fear. They want a country that begs for control. They want panic. They want people to thank them for the cage."

Max's voice stays even. "It's going to matter to you after today."

Vale's brow furrows.

"Arizona has the death penalty," Max says. "You're an accessory before the fact."

Vale's mouth opens, then closes again. His bravado tries to surface, but it doesn't quite make it.

"That," Max says, "is a lights-out-forever injection. We could probably call it LO4VR."

"So I suggest you think hard," Max continues, "about whether you intend to cooperate and testify...or not."

Vale swallows. His throat works twice. "You're asking me to sign my own death warrant," Vale mutters.

Max's expression doesn't change. "That was already the plan for you. You said it yourself. They're cleaning house."

Vale's eyes flick toward the camera, then back to Max. The room feels smaller with every breath.

Max nods once, almost sympathetically. "Actually. I'm offering you the only version where you might still be alive when this story ends."

Vale laughs without humor. "Alive where?"

"In a cell," Max says. "In a courtroom. On record. In daylight." He leans forward. "Not in the dark, trying to run or dead in some alley"

Vale holds his gaze. The anger is still there, but something else creeps in around the edges—calculation, fear, the dawning sense that his exit plan has already been erased. His tongue sticks for a fraction of a second, as if his mind is searching for a loophole. "Yeah, I'll testify, but you better put me somewhere they can't get to me."

"That's the spirit." Max says, then he pulls the LO2 from his pocket and injects Vale again.

Max releases the ties and drags Vale to the cot. He then grabs the camera and exits the room leaving behind a cooler filled with water and cheap snacks.

* * * *

Piper is halfway to her car in the parking garage when her phone vibrates.

She stops.

Not because of the vibration — but because of the channel.

Secure.

Max.

She stops and opens it.

Vale is on ice. He'll testify. But it only gets us to Halden.

Her jaw tightens.

Another message arrives.

We need to get to Halden before Francis Locke does.

And then:

That's how we get to POTUS.

Piper exhales slowly and types back.

Where would he hide?

The reply comes almost immediately.

He knows he's exposed. He'll go somewhere protected. Somewhere isolated.

Piper stares at the screen. Protected—Isolated--Safe.

Or something he controls.

Piper's fingers pause, then she types one word.

Boat.

A few seconds pass. Then:

Yeah. That tracks.

She doesn't wait, turns and heads back in.

The guard at the entrance looks up, surprised. "Forget something?"

"Yeah," Piper says. "One email that might change the course of the world."

He laughs, thinking it's a joke, and waves her through.

She doesn't laugh back.

Back at her terminal, she pulls up the file she hasn't closed in weeks.

Victor Halden, she scrolls down, Assets--Shell companies.

A maritime holding trust with no employees, no public records, and a mailing address that doesn't exist.

She clicks.

A picture of a boat fills the screen along with its stats.

Name: White current.

Make: Boston Whaler 405 Conquest

Length: forty two feet.

Flag: Cayman Islands.

Registration: active.

Ownership: Virex Maritime Holdings.

Which rolls up into nothing.

A Marina location pings. Thirty-seven miles south.

She stands.

If Halden is hiding, that is where he'll do it.

And if Locke is hunting him, that is where he will hunt.

Piper leaves her desk knowing one thing with absolute clarity. This is changing her life.

As soon as she reaches the parking garage, she forwards it all to Max.

Boat's name is White Current. Forty-two foot Boston Whaler. Cayman flag. Moored at Blackwater Marina, Slip C-17. I'm on my way.

She doesn't wait for a reply.

Her phone vibrates. She glances at it.

STAY WHERE YOU ARE. DO NOT COME.

Piper exhales through her nose. Staying put has never been her instinct. It isn't caution that keeps her alive, it's motion—closing the distance, inserting herself where she isn't supposed to be. She has rarely waited for permission and has never trusted stillness to protect her. She locks the phone, slips it into her pocket, already moving, already deciding. Staying put has never been who she is, and it never will be.

CHAPTER 20

THE BOAT

Max hides in the shadows near the edge of the marina.

He sees a man walking down the dock toward slip C-17.

It's Victor Halden.

Halden steps onto his boat, unlocks the cabin, and goes inside. A moment later the cabin light flicks on, glowing through the tinted window.

Max glances around, preparing to move—when he sees something.

A dark figure steps off an adjacent boat two slips over. The figure moves quietly across the dock and carefully slips onto Halden's boat.

Snake. It must be him.

Max's hand goes to his sidearm.

He draws the Glock as he starts down the walkway, pulling the suppressor from his jacket and threading it onto the barrel while moving.

Piper has just arrived, pulling into a parking spot with her headlights off. No one is around to notice.

Inside the cabin, Halden is at the helm. He turns the key and the engine coughs, then settles into a low idle.

Snake pushes the cabin door open slowly with his left hand. In his right is a zip tie.

Halden senses something behind him and begins to turn—

The zip tie snaps around his neck.

Snake yanks it tight.

Halden stumbles backward in shock, clawing at his throat, crashing out of the cabin and onto the deck.

Snake follows him out, kicks his legs out from under him, then reaches down to untie the dock line from the cleat.

Max stops. He is still thirty yards up the dock.

He raises the Glock taking aim.

Two suppressed shots crack.

The first round punches into Snake's left shoulder.

The second snaps off the bow rail in a shower of sparks.

Snake drops the line and disappears into the cabin.

Halden is gasping, trying to crawl.

Max moves fast.

The engine roars.

Max skids to a stop near the stern and fires again — five fast shots into the cabin window.

Glass explodes inward.

The boat surges out of the slip.

Halden struggles to his feet just as the boat swings wide.

The hull clips a pylon.

The impact throws Halden off balance and he pitches over the rail, vanishing into the dark water.

Without hesitation, Max drops the gun onto the dock and dives into the murky water.

He surfaces beside Halden, who is floating face down.

Max rolls him over, hooks an arm under his shoulders. He pulls his knife free and slices the zip tie from Halden's neck. Halden coughs once, weakly, then goes limp.

Max hauls him toward the dock.

Piper hears the shots from a distance and is now running toward the empty slip. She sees the boat clearing the harbor at full throttle as she reaches slip C-17.

She spots Max in the water hauling a body toward the dock.

Piper drops to her knees on the edge near a ladder.

Max drags Halden to the ladder. Piper reaches down to steady Halden while Max climbs out then they both pull Halden onto the dock.

Water streams off Max. His hands remain steady.

He looks at Piper.

"I told you not to come." Then he immediately begins revival techniques on Halden.

Piper picks up the Glock and starts unscrewing the suppressor, "Well… you're still a rogue agent, and I'm kind of your handler now, so…" She puts the Glock in her pocket.

Just then, Halden starts to spit and cough again, taking ragged breaths.

"Welcome back to the living," Max says.

Footsteps echo on the dock.

Someone is walking toward them — a lone concerned boater drawn by the noise.

Piper moves first. She steps into his path and flashes her CIA photo ID quickly, just long enough for it to register as official.

"Police business, sir. Please move along."

The man hesitates, nods, and walks away, still glancing back over his shoulder.

Piper exhales, barely believing that worked.

Max gets Halden to his feet and they start up the walkway.

Halden blinks, disoriented. "Who are you people?"

"We're the people who just saved your life," Max says.

They reach the car.

Halden stops, steadier now. "I'm not getting in that car with you until you tell me who you are."

Max doesn't answer.

He reaches into his jacket, pulls out the LO_2 injector, and jabs it into Halden's right thigh.

Halden gasps and stumbles.

Max catches him before he falls.

"Relax," Max says. "It won't kill you."

Halden's resistance drains out of him. His muscles slacken.

Max guides him into the back seat.

Piper watches him, unsettled, then looks back down the dock once more before getting in the car herself.

Max starts the car.

The engine settles into a low idle.

Piper looks at him. "This can't be off-book anymore. We need to get law enforcement after Francis Locke before he disappears."

Max nods slightly. "This next part still has to be off-book for me. But let McCaine know our status. I'll keep this one on ice until I hear from you."

Piper hesitates, then nods. "Okay. Be careful, Max."

She reaches out and touches his arm.

A small, quiet smile.

Then she opens the door, steps out of the car, and walks toward her own.

Max watches her go for a moment and waits until she gets in her car.

Then he puts the car in gear and pulls away.

Piper pulls into her condo complex and parks.

She sits for a moment with the engine off, the car ticking as it cools.

Then she takes out her secure device and opens a message to Chief McCaine.

She types:

Francis Locke is wounded but mobile, on a boat that just left the harbor from Blackwater Marina.

Make: Boston Whaler 405 Conquest

Length: forty two feet.

Flag: Cayman Islands.

Registration: active.

Ownership: Virex Maritime Holdings.

Victor Halden is in custody and about to be questioned.

She sends it.

The message disappears into encryption.

Piper leans back in her seat, staring at nothing, allowing her thoughts to move and shift like a puzzle.

Somewhere out on the water, an assassin is free.

Victor Halden isn't just a witness. He's the key.

The money. The shell companies. The fake contracts. The link between the president and Luma-Tek.

If Halden talks, everything unravels.

The device vibrates.

Piper looks down.

I'll get people on Locke. Where is your man holding Halden?

Piper types back:

That information wasn't shared.

A moment passes.

Another vibration.

Send interrogation video ASAP.

Piper lowers the device.

It clicks. It makes sense. Another piece.

Max didn't withhold the location just to protect himself.

He did it to protect her too.

Piper sends a message to Nicky.

Stop by. Very important.

She's halfway to her apartment when her phone vibrates.

See you in an hour.

Inside, the first thing she does is pour herself a glass of merlot.

The wine is cool, dark and soothing. She takes a long swallow and lets it linger in her mouth before she swallows.

She leans back against the counter, closes her eyes for a moment.

She thinks about how close she came to danger today.

How thin the line felt.

How easily Max moved through the violence, like it never touched him.

She wonders what it would be like to be close to someone like that. To feel that steadiness up close. To know where she would fit against it. Is it a possibility?

The thought unsettles her in a way she can't quite explain.

She takes another slow sip of the wine.

Her shoulders finally start to loosen.

Then she realizes what she needs is a hot shower — heat on her skin, steam in the air, something that can wash the day off her body.

Because it's still clinging to her.

And the night is not quite done with her yet.

After her shower, Piper changes into jeans and a soft T-shirt, a towel twisted around her damp hair.

The bell chimes. She opens the door for Nicky.

They end up leaning against opposite sides of the small kitchen island, the apartment quiet around them.

Nicky studies her face. "So tell me?"

Piper slides the open bottle of wine across the counter toward her.

"Although you might want something stronger in a minute."

Then she tells her everything.

About the marina.

About Victor Halden.

About Snake.

About the boat pulling away into the dark.

About how close it all came to going very differently.

Nicky listens without interrupting, her expression tightening with every detail.

When Piper finishes, she says it plainly.

"The President is going down for this. And Luma-Tek is tied into it."

The words hang in the air.

Nicky exhales slowly. "Jesus."

"I need you to prep your people," Piper says. "In Congress. Quietly. Whatever's coming, it's going to hit fast."

Nicky nods. "I will."

They're both silent for a moment.

Then Piper says, "And the Vice President?"

Nicky hesitates, then nods. "I think he's principled. I think he'll do the right thing."

Piper lifts the glass, finally takes a drink.

"Well," she says quietly, "let's hope we're right about that."

Piper and Nicky stand for a moment in the open doorway, saying goodbye, quickly hug while telling each other to be careful.

Then Nicky leaves.

Piper closes the door, locks it, and rests her forehead briefly against the wood.

She walks back to the kitchen island and leans against it, staring at the dark surface, trying to imagine what happens next.

The President. The fallout. The investigations. The hearings.

The quiet parts behind the scenes that no one will ever see.

She wonders if her life is now in danger because of her part in this.

The thought lands, then passes.

The administration is corrupt.

It has to change.

Whether it's dangerous or not doesn't matter.

She straightens.

She reminds herself of who she is.

She is strong. She is ethical. She is loyal to her oath — to protect and defend the Constitution against all enemies, foreign and domestic.

A knock at the door.

She frowns, glancing toward it.

Nicky must have forgotten something.

Piper crosses the apartment and looks through the peephole.

Max's handsome smile peers back.

Piper rips the towel from her head and quickly runs her fingers through her damp hair before opening the door.

"You just missed Nicky," she says. "Come in."

"Yeah," he says, stepping past her. "I think I saw her leaving."

She closes the door. "Glad you found some dry clothes."

He glances down at himself. "I basically live out of a duffle bag in my trunk."

She smiles despite herself.

"Water, wine, maybe bourbon?"

"Wine."

She pours him a glass.

"I've already had one," she says. "So... no more missions for me tonight."

Max smirks. "You don't follow my advice anyway."

"Touché."

She slides the glass across the island. Max doesn't touch it yet. Instead, he places a small flash drive beside it.

"That's everything you need to impeach Silas Thornwell," he says. "And put him in prison for the rest of his life. Luma-Tek funded all of it but we still need the paper trail, this gets you there."

Piper's eyes drop to the drive.

"Luma-Tek built a quantum computer," Max continues. "One with processing power beyond anything humans can comprehend."

She exhales. "I'm relieved it's not a nuclear weapon."

"They say that it's convergence with AI combined, will be the last invention mankind ever needs."

Her brow furrows. "What does that even mean? And why is Thornwell a part of this?"

Max's voice lowers.

"The AI will be smarter than any human who has ever lived. Smarter than anyone who ever will. Thornwell's going to sign an executive order giving it access to every government system — under the excuse of stopping a nuclear war, one that they manufactured."

He pauses.

"And once it's inside… we will never get it out."

The room seems to close in, feel smaller.

Piper stares at him, the words landing slowly, one after another.

A machine smarter than humanity.

With access to everything.

Sanctioned by the government.

She holds her breath, her chest tight, the sense creeping in that something vast has already shifted — that the world she understands has already slipped into something else.

Something colder.

Something permanent.

Max meets her eyes.

He sees the fear there. The weight. The enormity of what she's just heard.

He extends his hand.

Piper blinks away the confusion, like she's waking a daze.

Then she steps forward meets his eyes and kisses him — not rushed, not wild, just full, honest, and warm.

Max exhales against her mouth.

He lifts her gently, like it's the most natural thing in the world, and carries her down the hall, the apartment quiet around them.

Edward Schwalm

CHAPTER 21

FLASH DRIVE

Piper wakes, four AM on the clock. She hears a quiet and slow even rhythm of someone breathing beside her. For a moment she does not move. She just lies there, half-asleep, watching Max's chest rise and fall, letting the simple fact of him being there register before the day can take it away.

She smiles without meaning to.

The device on the nightstand glows softly when she lifts it. No alerts. No emergencies. Just the weight of what she already knows is coming. She types quickly, deliberately.

Parking garage, level two. One hour.

She sends it before she can overthink it.

Then she shifts back toward the bed and touches Max's shoulder, gentle at first, then a little firmer.

"I've got to go," she whispers. "Big day."

He blinks awake, disoriented for half a second, then focused on her.

"Yeah," he says quietly. "Be careful. Important day."

She nods, already reaching for her clothes.

He watches her for a moment, then adds, almost amused, "Today is an easy one for me."

She pauses at the edge of the bed and looks back at him.

"All I have to do is feed the animals."

She raises an eyebrow.

"Vale and Halden," he clarifies.

That earns a breath of a laugh from her — soft, involuntary — the kind that fades as quickly as it comes. She crosses back to him, leans down, kisses him once, light and fast, like a punctuation.

She leaves before either of them can say anything that will make it harder.

Piper drives slowly through the concrete levels of the garage at Langley, headlights sweeping across windshields and pillars as she looks for Taylor McCaine's sedan. She spots it near the back wall and pulls in beside it, close enough that their mirrors almost touch.

She cuts the engine, steps out, and slips into the passenger seat of McCaine's car without knocking.

The air inside smells faintly of leather and coffee.

Piper doesn't waste time.

She reaches into her jacket, pulls out the flash drive, and holds it between them.

"This directly implicates the President," she says. "Video, financial logs, internal directives. It's all there."

She hesitates, then adds more quietly, "Two weeks ago I was asking myself if the system could ever change. I never thought the answer was something I would be holding in my hand today."

She exhales and extends the drive toward McCaine, relief already loosening something in her chest.

Taylor does not take it.

She looks at it for a long moment, then at Piper.

"The President has to be removed immediately," she says. "Legally, there's only one way to do that without his cooperation. The Vice President and a majority of the Cabinet invoke Section Four of the Twenty-Fifth Amendment."

Piper's breath stills.

"That makes the Vice President the Acting President," McCaine continues. "Temporarily. Then Congress decides whether it stays that way."

"Two-thirds," Piper says.

McCaine nods. "House and Senate."

Piper closes her fingers around the drive again.

"And you need me to…"

"You need to make it impossible for them NOT to act," McCaine says. "Leak the video to your friend in Congress. Not publicly — not yet. To leadership. Intel, Oversight, Judiciary. Enough of them for the Vice President and the Cabinet to know they don't have political cover anymore."

She finally looks directly at Piper.

"This will force their hand."

Piper inhales slowly, feeling the gravity of the moment settle back onto her shoulders.

"Yes, ma'am," she says. Then, softer, "I understand."

She opens the door.

Just before she steps out, McCaine speaks again.

"However this ends," she says, "I want you to know something. You've been a top-tier agent long before today."

Piper pauses, one foot on the concrete.

She nods once.

"Thank you ma'am."

She closes the door gently and turns back to her car, the flash drive still warm in her palm, realizing only then that somewhere along the way she didn't just become another cog in the wheel.

She has become a catalyst for change.

Piper gets into her car and closes the door.

She doesn't start it yet.

She looks down at the flash drive once more, then slips it into the inner pocket of her jacket out of sight.

She pulls out her phone and types a single word.

Coffee.

She pauses, then she adds a location and hits send.

The reply comes almost immediately.

On my way.

Piper starts the engine and eases out of the space. The tires squeak against the concrete as she follows the ramp toward daylight.

The garage light fades behind her.

The early morning light brightens in front of her.

And whatever comes next-- is already in motion.

CHAPTER 22

25TH AMENDMENT

SECTION 4

When Piper arrives at Baked & Wired in Georgetown, Nicky is already there, seated at a small metal table on the sidewalk, the morning traffic whispering past behind her. She stands as soon as she sees Piper, intercepts her before she can even sit down, and presses a warm vanilla latte into her hands.

"Let's walk," Nicky says.

Piper smiles at the cup. "Thanks for the coffee, but you've broken tradition. Where are the cupcakes?"

Nicky smirks. "In the car. I'm trying to keep us alive long enough to eat them."

They turn toward the waterfront, moving in step through the soft bustle of tourists and joggers, past brick storefronts, the morning sunlight reflecting off the Potomac. Piper watches Nicky from the corner of her eye. She looks composed, but there is a tightness to her jaw that gives her away.

"How bad do you think it'll be?" Piper asks. "Getting enough people on your side to use Section Four."

Nicky exhales slowly. "There will be holdouts. There always are, but that's not what worries me." She hesitates, then adds, "I need the Vice President first. If he's not on board, then none of this matters."

"Do you think he's compromised?"

"I don't know yet," Nicky says. "I have a private meeting scheduled with him today. Then we'll know whether this plan has any legs... or whether we're already too late."

As they reach the edge of the park, the trees opening to water and sky, Piper stops walking. She reaches into her bag and takes out the flash drive, small and unassuming, the weight of it entirely disproportionate to what it holds.

"Once he sees this," Piper says quietly, "you'll know for sure."

Nicky takes it without ceremony, slipping it into her pocket, but her fingers linger there a moment as if to make sure it's real.

They resume walking. A breeze comes off the river. Piper lets herself breathe for the first time all morning.

"Wow," she says. "I feel... lighter."

Nicky glances at her, her expression softening into something more vulnerable than political resolve. "Do you remember those two naïve girls who shared a dorm at Yale?" she asks. "Are they gone?"

Piper stops again. This time she turns fully to Nicky and takes both her hands.

"They're right here," Piper says. "They're still us. And they'll be friends forever. And together..." She smiles faintly. "They just might save the world."

Nicky laughs, the sound almost disbelieving, and for a moment the weight of everything lifts — not because it's gone, but because they aren't carrying it alone.

* * * *

The Vice President's residence at the Naval Observatory is quieter than Nicky expects. The city feels far away here, muffled by trees, distance and layers of security. A uniformed Secret Service agent escorts her through a side entrance and into a small sitting room that feels more like a private study than a government space — soft lighting, shelves of history books, a single window looking out over the seventy-two-acre campus.

VP Arthur Beaumont is already there.

He stands when she enters, not with the reflex of a politician greeting a constituent, but with the restraint of a man at the threshold of uncertainty.

"Congresswoman Patterson," he says. "Thank you for coming in."

"Thank you for seeing me, Mr. Vice President."

They sit across from each other at a low table. No aides. No phones. A quiet hum in the background she can't place.

He folds his hands together. "Your request is... is one that has never occurred in US history."

"Yes, sir."

"You're serious."

"Yes, sir."

He studies her a moment longer. Not suspicious. Assessing.

"You said you have evidence," he says. "Evidence that, if true, would require me to consider invoking Section Four of the Twenty-Fifth Amendment."

"Yes sir, I do."

"You understand what that means."

"I do, sir"

"You understand that once I take that step, there will be no turning back."

"I know, sir."

A pause. The room seems to lean inward.

"Before we go any further," Beaumont says, "you should be aware that everything you say in this room places a burden on me that I cannot put down again. Are you prepared for that?"

Nicky doesn't hesitate. "Yes sir."

He nods once. "All right…state your case."

She takes the flash drive from her bag and places it on the table between them. It looks absurdly small, given the scale of the problem it contains.

"What is this?" he asks.

"A compiled record," she says. "Video, audio, metadata. Sourced from multiple systems. It has been independently verified." She pauses before continuing. "It shows the President coordinating with private entities to manipulate public information and policy for his own personal and political protection. It also shows he is being coerced."

Beaumont's jaw tightens slightly at that last word.

"Coerced how?"

"Financial exposure. Corporate leverage. Criminal exposure… It's all in there."

He doesn't reach for the drive.

"Where did you get this?"

"I can't disclose the source."

"That may be a problem."

"I understand. But the chain of custody is documented. You will be able to see it all."

Another pause.

"There's a lot of fake media going around these days. Is it authentic?" he asks.

"Yes sir."

"Not altered in any way?"

"No sir."

"Not selectively edited?"

"No sir."

He watches her closely as she answers.

Finally, he reaches out and picks up the drive.

"There is no such thing as an easy truth," he says quietly.

He stands and moves to a small secure terminal against the far wall. He inserts the drive. The screen comes to life. He opens the first file.

Nicky remains seated behind him. She cannot see his face. She watches his shoulders.

The video begins. There is no music. No dramatic framing. Just a room, a conversation, the Chief of staff's voice unmistakable.

Minutes pass.

Beaumont studies the video. He does not turn around.

He does not react outwardly. He does not sit down.

He opens the second file. It plays.

Another angle. Another meeting. Another confirmation.

He pauses the feed.

"Who else has seen this?"

"At least two people besides me, sir."

"Who?"

"I'm sorry sir, but I can't tell you that, but you must know that this will come out one way or another."

He nods. "Fair enough."

He scrolls through timestamps, opens metadata, cross-references file creation, transmission paths. He is not looking for further confirmation. He is looking for an escape.

He doesn't find one.

When he finally turns around, he looks tired.

Not shocked. Not angry. Burdened.

"Assuming this is real," he says, "this is not mere incompetence, this is our President, our government being compromised."

"Yes sir."

"And if I do nothing—"

"Sir... he remains compromised," Nicky says. "And so does the office--and whatever else he has planned and putting in motion may be to late to stop."

Beaumont walks back to the table but does not sit.

"You are asking me to remove a sitting President."

"Sir, I am asking you to uphold your oath to the Constitution."

He almost smiles at that. Almost.

"Do you know how many times in American history Section Four has been invoked?" he asks.

"Yes sir...Never."

"That's right," he says. "Never."

He looks at the flash drive.

"That makes this either a moment of courage," he says, "or the beginning of something very dark."

"Or both," Nicky says, "Sir."

A long silence settles between them.

Finally, Beaumont exhales.

"If I do this," he says, "it cannot be partisan. It cannot be rushed. It cannot look like a power grab."

"I agree sir."

"I will need Cabinet support."

"I am working on it sir."

"I will need bipartisan backing in Congress."

"Yes sir, you will have it."

He looks at her carefully.

"You sound very sure."

"I am sir."

He studies her a moment longer, then nods.

"All right," he says, and sits.

She feels it before she fully understands it.

The gravity of the moment, the historical significance.

"I will consider this, once I've reviewed all the files and you can guarantee me a two-thirds majority" he says.

He looks at the screen again, then back at her.

"Not because I want the office," he says. "But because if this is true — then there is no one else who can do it without tearing the country apart."

Nicky stands.

"Thank you, Mr. Vice President."

"Don't thank me yet," he says. "History is not necessarily kind to men or women who make decisions like this, even with the best of intentions."

He removes the flash drive from the terminal and places it back on the table.

"This never leaves my possession," he says.

"I wouldn't expect it to sir."

As she turns to go, he speaks again.

"Congresswoman."

She turns.

"You may have just changed the course of my life and quite possibly destroyed your own. I hope you're happy."

She meets his eyes.

"I know sir, I hope that it not only changes both our lives, but also the lives of all Americans, for the better."

She leaves him there, alone with the screen, the evidence, and the enormous weight of a presidency he never sought — and now cannot avoid.

CHAPTER 23

GO TIME

Nyla Frost stands in the open doorway, one hand resting against the frame, looking out at the dozen people crowded into the converted office space beyond. Laptops glow across folding tables. Whiteboards are layered with timelines, names, arrows, and red-circled dates. The room hums softly with fans, processors and nerves.

"Status," Nyla says calmly.

A few voices answer at once. Everything is on track. Uploads staged. Redundancies verified. Dead-man drops armed. The work of three years is finally compressed into a single word.

Ready.

Nyla nods. She lets the moment breathe.

"I want to thank you," she says. "All of you. What you have done here matters. Whether anyone else ever knows your names or not… I know them"

Some of them smile. Some don't. A few just look tired.

Nyla steps back into the hall and walks across to the workshop.

This room is louder. Brighter. The smell of hot metal, flux, and solder hangs in the air. Oscilloscopes flicker. Open housings reveal coils, heat sinks, and fiber spools. Shane, Dexter, and several techs are mid-discussion when Nyla enters.

They stop immediately.

Every face turns toward her.

Nyla doesn't rush. She takes it all in — the grease on Shane's hands, the dark circles under Dexter's eyes, the quiet intensity in all of them. Then she speaks. "The systems we're fighting are indifferent. They optimize for profit, efficiency, speed — and quietly erase everything else that makes up a society worth living in. Dignity. Stability. Meaning. Choice."

She steps forward.

"The politicians we're exposing didn't lose control. They sold it. Piece by piece. Vote by vote. Contract by contract. They traded their responsibility for their comfort and then called it progress."

A few jaws tighten. Someone swallows.

"Power doesn't always corrupt because it's evil," Nyla says. "Sometimes, it corrupts because it's lazy. It takes the shortest path. The easiest justification. And if no one stands in its way, it will always choose itself over the people it claims to serve."

She looks at Dexter.

"Technology isn't the enemy. But neither is it neutral. It becomes the values of whoever holds the reins."

Then she looks at all of them.

"Tomorrow, we pull the reins back." She takes a breath.

"We're not destroying the machine. We're interrupting it long enough to show what they have been hiding. Long enough to remind the world that these systems are supposed to serve humans — not replace them."

Her voice steadies, lowers.

"History doesn't change because someone plans it. It changes because someone refuses to accept what everyone else has decided is inevitable."

She nods once.

"That's you."

Another pause.

"So go home. Get some rest. Look at the people you love. Remember why this matters."

Her eyes move across them, deliberate.

"Be proud. Not just because you are in the right — but because you have the moral courage to take action."

A faint, restrained smile.

"Tomorrow, the world doesn't end."

She turns toward the door.

"It begins to change."

* * * *

Dexter enters through the side door and lets it close softly behind him.

The house is quietly unaware that something important is about to happen.

He sets his bag down by the wall and moves through the kitchen toward the back of the house. Through the glass doors he sees Jen on the deck, kneeling beside a low wooden table, easing a small fern into a ceramic pot. The evening light catches in her hair. There's dirt on her fingers. Something about how normal it all looks makes his chest tighten.

He steps outside.

"Hey," he says.

She looks up and smiles. "You're home early."

He nods. "We finished up sooner than I thought."

He stands there longer than he needs to. She notices.

"What's wrong?"

He exhales slowly. "I need to tell you something."

Her smile fades.

He walks over and sits across from her, rests his hands on his knees like he's bracing himself.

"As you know, I've been working with Shane," he says. "and also, with the OU."

She stares at him.

"You what?"

"I'm helping them."

Her brow creases in confusion first, not anger.

"Why?" she asks. "Dex, you have a good job. You're safe. You're one of the ones they can't replace."

He swallows.

"That's what I thought too. At least, that's what I kept telling myself"

She waits, knowing that there's more he has to say.

"But I was wrong," he says. " I've been demoted. I won't be on core systems anymore. I'll only be maintenance.

Oversight. The models I helped build, don't need me anymore."

Her eyes widen.

"They're just… phasing me out like they'll do to everyone eventually."

She sits back slightly.

"And they're rezoning our entire district in three days," he adds. "We're getting bumped down to Tier-3."

Her hand goes to her mouth.

"I'm sorry," he says quickly. "I should've told you sooner. I just… I didn't want to believe it yet. I didn't want to accept that it was actually happening. Pretending it's a mistake."

He drops his gaze.

"I knew this would happen," he says. "I helped build the system that's doing this. I told myself it would be gradual. Controlled. That we'd have time to adapt. That it wouldn't take over everything all at once."

He shakes his head.

"I was wrong. I wasn't just wrong — I helped create it."

Jen is silent.

"That's why I'm helping the OU," he says. "Not because I want to burn it all down but because I want to stop pretending it's a neutral entity. I want it to work for us and I want those who control it to be responsible for what it's doing."

He looks up at her.

"Tomorrow it starts."

Her voice is soft. "What starts?"

"A disruption," he says. "Exposure. A reset of sorts. The country is going to be a mess for a few days. Systems will stutter. Trust will fracture. People will be angry."

She hesitates.

"Will anyone get hurt?" she asks. "Physically?"

He shakes his head. "No. No one gets hurt like that."

A pause.

"It will ruin the lives of a few hundred corrupt politicians though," he adds. "Reputations. Careers. Hopefully some prison sentences."

He almost smiles. Almost.

"It's strange," he says quietly. "We built a world so efficient that it no longer had room for forgiveness. Or patience. Or failure. Everything has to be optimized now — even people."

He exhales.

"And anything that doesn't fit gets… removed."

Jen stands slowly and walks toward him.

He watches her, unsure.

She stops in front of him.

"I have always believed in you," she says. "Not because you were always right, but because you cared about being on the right side."

He blinks.

"I can see you still care," she says. "Even now. Especially now."

She reaches down, lifts his chin gently so he has to look at her.

"I know you're not trying to ruin our life," she says. "You're trying to save it, keep it human."

That breaks him.

She sits down on his lap, wraps her arms around his shoulders, presses her forehead to his.

"I'm not afraid of tomorrow," she whispers. "I'm more afraid of what happens if people... like you... stop trying."

She kisses him once. Then again.

He holds her tight, like he might not get another chance.

And for the first time all day, he breathes.

Edward Schwalm

CHAPTER 24

SECTION 4 PUSH

The screen is already on when the Secretary of Commerce enters the conference room.

Secretary Brookes notices it immediately. The Congresswoman standing next to the table where the tablet rests on the edge, angled toward him like an accusation waiting to happen.

"You didn't tell my assistant what this was about," he says, as he sits down.

"No," Nicky says. "I told her it was urgent."

He gestures towards a chair. She does not take it.

Nicky steps forward and taps the tablet.

The video begins.

Victor Halden fills the frame. Older than he looks on television. Paler. A little unsteady. He is a man who has spent his life certain he will never have to explain himself.

That certainty ends here, and now.

"The order didn't come from me," Halden says. "It came from him."

He names the President.

Brookes breath catches so softly it almost doesn't register.

"They were just random OU members," Halden continues on the screen. "He said it was necessary. He said we needed to spread some fear and that it would never touch paper."

The video ends.

Nicky does not move.

Brookes blinks at the frozen image, then looks up at her.

"This could be manipulated," he says.

"It isn't," she replies.

She swipes to the next screen.

A web of accounts appears. Lines, dates, names. Shell companies dissolving into real ones. Luma-Tek at the center, its money threading outward like veins.

One of them ends somewhere very specific.

"That's not possible," Brookes says.

"It is," Nicky says. "And it's traceable."

He leans forward now despite himself.

"Those are private transactions," he says.

"No," Nicky says. "Those are the residue of a crime."

She lets that sit.

"Victor Halden is not the only one who talked," she says. "He's just one of a few who did it on camera."

Brookes face drains slowly of color.

"Why are you showing me this?" he asks.

Nicky's eyes do not leave him.

"Because if we were able to get this," she says, "how much more do you think they have?"

He doesn't answer.

She continues.

"How many calls. How many meetings. How many signatures have you forgotten about?"

That finally breaks through.

His mouth opens slightly, then closes again.

"I haven't done anything illegal," he says.

Nicky tilts her head.

"You haven't done anything alone," she says.

Silence.

Brookes sinks back into his chair.

"This is extortion," he says weakly.

"No," Nicky says. "This is a timeline."

She gestures to the tablet.

"This comes out," she says. "Maybe tomorrow. Maybe next week. But it comes out. When it does, the system will protect itself by shedding any excess weight."

He stares at her.

"You are weight," she says.

He swallows.

"And you?" he asks.

"I'll be a footnote," she says. "The difference is, I'm prepared for that."

He looks back at the money trail.

"What do you want?" he asks.

"I want you to be early," Nicky says.

"Early?" he repeats.

"Before this becomes public. Before the Vice President moves. Before Commerce becomes a headline instead of a signature."

He looks up.

"The Twenty-Fifth," he says.

"Section Four," she confirms.

"That's… that's insane, never in US history" he says.

"With all due respect, the president ordering the murder of US citizens is insane," Nicky says.

He flinches.

"If I sign that," he says, "My career will be destroyed."

"If you don't sign it," she says, "you will lose everything… and most likely go to prison."

He laughs once. A short, hollow sound.

"You're offering me a life preserver?" he says.

"I'm offering you a glimmer of hope," Nicky says. "You go before you're pushed. You get to become the man who acted, not the man who was uncovered. If it makes you feel any better, after you sign, which you will, I only need four more signatures."

He rubs his face with both hands.

When he looks up again, his eyes are wet.

"I want a face to face with the VP before this goes any further." he says.

It is not a question.

Nicky does not answer it.

She slides a the open folder across the desk.

Brookes stares at the document inside.

Then, very slowly, he pulls it toward himself.

"Where?" he asks.

Nicky points.

"To protect and defend the constitution of the United States." she says. "There."

Nicky exits the Department of Commerce onto Constitution Avenue and walks a few blocks before slowing. She takes a long breath as the White House comes into view between the trees, its white façade calm and distant, as if nothing in the city is wrong.

She stops at a corner café and claims one of the small outdoor tables, still in motion even as she sits, like she is afraid that if she pauses too long the momentum will drain out of her. The noise of traffic fades behind the low murmur of conversation and clinking cups.

She pulls out her phone and types.

Four down, four to go.

She watches the words sit there for a second before sending them. Eight Cabinet signatures. Half the government's spine.

A moment later she types again.

The next four won't be so easy. My bag of tricks is empty. I'm going to need some help.

She slips the phone face down on the table and stares past it at the White House. The building does not look like the center of a crisis. It looks like a postcard.

Her phone vibrates.

I'll see what I can dig up.

Nicky exhales, not in relief, but in acknowledgement. The easy part, which wasn't at all easy, is over. The hard part is about to begin.

Edward Schwalm

CHAPTER 25

A BUSY DAY

JULY 2ND

The five Titans stand in a shallow arc behind the glass table in the mansion's control and observation room, a wall of glass behind them. The desert stretches out beyond it in muted reds and grays as the sun rises from the east. The mansion is quiet in the way that suggests intention — no traffic noise, no voices, just the faint whisper of climate control and the glow of the twenty-foot monitor displaying scrolling data, world news, stock markets, and a live image of Qu, two hundred feet beneath the facility.

On the central display, a single line of text appears.

SYSTEM STATUS: ONLINE.

Levon breaks a brief silence after running Qu's first test.

"Alright," he says lightly, as if they're beginning a board meeting instead of a transformation of civilization. "If things go as planned, Thornwell will sign the executive order within a few hours. Qu gets lawful access to federal systems, and the transition starts clean."

He glances at the others.

"And if he doesn't," Levon adds, "we take it anyway."

A few of them shift at that. Not quite uncomfortable. Just... aware.

Elias clears his throat.

"No Levon," he says. Calm. Firm. "We already agreed. We do this the right way. The government invites us in."

Logan nods. Darren does too.

"If the state asks for help," Elias continues, "then history records this as assistance, not intrusion. They keep their dignity. We keep our legitimacy. When it unravels later — and it will — everyone can say the same thing." A thin smile. "The overwatch Consortium only did what they were asked to do."

Darren Kincaid folds his arms, eyes still on the display.

"And you're confident Thornwell delivers that invitation?"

Levon doesn't look at him.

"How reliable is he, really?" Darren presses.

Levon exhales through his nose, almost amused.

"Let's just say," he replies, "love or money, Thornwell would sell his own mother's eyeballs."

Ari finally turns his head toward Levon.

"How deep are you in with this man?"

Levon meets his gaze now. The faint smile is still there, but there's nothing friendly in it.

"I've taken only the necessary measures to guarantee the success of our project," he says. "Nothing more."

A beat.

"You boys can all thank me later."

The room falls quiet again.

Deep below the geothermal facility, behind reinforced glass and a lattice of shielding and coolant lines, the quantum system operates — inaudible, invisible, already threading itself into models and probabilities far too complex for any of them to follow.

While the Titans continue discussing control, Qu has completed the equivalent of thirty years of computation in just under three minutes. Most of it never reaches consciousness. Entire branches of possibility are explored, evaluated, and discarded before the conversation reaches its next sentence.

* * * *

Morning light slants through the tall windows of the Oval Office in a thin, pale band across the carpet.

Silas Thornwell enters without slowing.

Two junior staffers are already inside, standing near the small seating area with tablets in their hands. A senior policy aide rises halfway from one of the chairs when he sees him.

"Good morning, Mr. President—"

"Where the hell is Halden."

The words cut straight through the room. Silas doesn't look at anyone in particular when he says it. He drops his folder onto the edge of the Resolute Desk instead of walking behind it.

Two members of Victor Halden's staff exchange a glance.

"Sir, we—we haven't been able to reach him since late Sunday," one of them says. "His phone's been going to voicemail. We assumed—"

"You assumed what," Silas snaps.

"That he took a personal day, sir. Or that he was—"

Silas steps closer now.

"He's been missing for two days," Silas says flatly. "And no one thought that was worth elevating?"

The aide swallows.

"We followed protocol, sir. We notified Secret Service liaisons and—"

Silas waves him off.

"Get out."

They hesitate.

"Everyone," Silas says, louder now. "Out. Give me ten minutes."

The room empties quickly after that. Doors close softly. The muffled sounds of West Wing movement fade.

Silas waits a moment. Then another.

He reaches beneath the front edge of the Resolute Desk and removes a thin, black secure handset embedded flush into a hidden panel. He taps in a short code from memory.

The line connects almost instantly.

"Dravos," Silas says. "Run the story."

There's a pause.

"Which version, Mr. President?"

Silas turns toward the window, watching a gardener below rake fallen leaves into a neat line.

"The escalation cut. Foreign cyber interference. Energy grid vulnerability. Add the nuclear layer."

Another pause.

"You want full nuclear, sir?"

"I want uncertainty," Silas says. "Leaked intercepts. Anonymous defense officials. Language like 'unconfirmed indicators,' 'strategic posturing,' and 'elevated readiness.' Nothing provable. Nothing deniable either."

"And geography?"

"Keep it offshore. North Korea, Iran. Submarine activity. Mobile launch platforms. Make it feel like something that could become something else."

"How hot do you want it?"

Silas thinks.

"Hot enough to keep the people occupied. Not hot enough that markets collapse."

"Understood."

The line goes dead.

Silas exhales slowly through his nose. The panic doesn't need to be sustained. Just sharp. Just loud. Just long enough to tilt the board.

He places the handset back into the desk and removes a second device — smaller, heavier, its surface matte and unmarked.

This one connects to a different world entirely.

"Vanderwalt," he says when the line opens.

Levon's voice comes back smooth and awake.

"Are we on track, Mr. President?"

Silas doesn't bother with pleasantries.

"We are. Except my Chief of Staff is missing, and that is a problem. I want him found before the FBI does."

A half second of silence.

"Understood," Levon says. "Qu. Locate Victor Halden"

A voice enters the line — calm, neutral, without inflection.

Qu- "Locating Victor Halden."

A pause that feels longer than it is.

Qu- "Victor Halden's last confirmed location is the entrance to Blackwater Marina on June thirtieth at twenty-two zero two hours."

Silas stiffens slightly.

"God damn it," he mutters. "Is he running?"

He leans closer to the device.

"Is his boat still there?"

"Qu," Levon says, "is Victor Halden's vessel currently at Blackwater Marina?"

Qu- "Automatic Identification System data places the vessel at Blackwater Marina. Satellite imagery from zero nine three five hours today confirms the vessel in slip C-seventeen."

A pause.

Qu- "Would you like visual confirmation via aerial drone?"

"Yes," Silas says immediately.

"Yes, Qu," Levon echoes.

Qu- "Deploying drone now."

Silas doesn't wait for a response.

"Find him," he says, and ends the call.

He stands there for a moment, staring at nothing.

Then the door opens.

A young aide steps inside, eyes slightly wide.

"Mr. President," she says carefully, "you may want to turn on the news."

She reaches for the remote.

A six-foot monitor rises silently from a recessed wooden cabinet along the wall.

The Patriotic News logo animates into place.

A headline scrolls across the bottom of the screen.

UNCONFIRMED INTELLIGENCE SUGGESTS FOREIGN NUCLEAR ASSETS MAY BE REPOSITIONING.

"...sources inside the defense community say activity patterns are consistent with strategic deterrence movement," the anchor says. "Officials emphasize there is no immediate threat, but confirm the President has been briefed..."

A graphic appears beside the anchor — a blurred satellite image, red circles over dark water, labeled with question marks and vague coordinates.

The headlines don't stay confined to the Oval Office.

Across the country, it blooms.

In airports, the departure boards split their screens — flight numbers on the left, the Patriotic News banner on the right. Travelers pause mid-step. A man at a Cinnabon stares upward, coffee cooling in his hand.

In train stations, the platform monitors cycle between arrival times and the same looping clip: a blurred satellite image, a red ring pulsing over dark water, a calm anchor explaining that there is no confirmed threat, only elevated concern.

In hospital waiting rooms, the volume is low but the words still land.

...no immediate danger... an abundance of caution... shifting strategic postures...

In shopping malls, the massive LED walls normally reserved for advertising switch to emergency broadcast priority without fanfare. Shoppers look up. A child tugs at his mother's sleeve.

"What's nuclear mean?"

She doesn't answer.

In gas stations along empty highways, above racks of chips and windshield washer fluid, the same banner scrolls again and again.

UNCONFIRMED INTELLIGENCE SUGGESTS FOREIGN NUCLEAR ASSETS MAY BE REPOSITIONING.

Phones begin to vibrate.

News alerts stack on top of one another, each worded with minute differences.

Sources say unusual movement detected.

Pentagon declines to comment.

White House is monitoring the situation closely.

Foreign officials deny any escalation.

Markets twitch.

Social feeds fill with maps, arrows, speculation. Amateur analysts draw lines across oceans. Someone posts a thread about Cold War drills. Someone else posts a countdown that means nothing.

People don't panic.

Not yet.

They do something quieter.

They pay attention.

They hesitate before buying plane tickets. They cancel dinners. They check on their kids. They text people they haven't texted in a while.

They feel the future tilt, just enough to notice.

And somewhere, far beneath the desert floor, a machine records the reaction.

Silas watches without expression.

The mechanism is in motion.
And the world shifts with it.

CHAPTER 26

ESCALATION

At Reagan National Airport, a woman stands at the gate staring up at the news monitor instead of the boarding call. Her phone is in her hand, unlocked, forgotten. The headline scrolls again. She scrolls her messages instead, then types a single line to her sister.

Are you watching this?

She doesn't send it. She just stands there until the boarding group is called a second time.

* * * *

In a high school in Ohio, a history teacher abandoned the lesson plan halfway through a lecture on Cold War brinkmanship. He doesn't mean to. The words just slide sideways.

"Back then," he says, then stops.

Thirty teenagers look at him.

He clears his throat.

"Back then we practiced for this. Drills. Duck and cover. You probably think that sounds ridiculous."

A hand goes up.

"Is this like that?"

He hesitates too long.

In a Trader Joe's in Northern Virginia, the frozen food aisle clogs as people stop moving their carts. Someone has left a pack of chicken thawing on top of a freezer case while they watch the screen at the end of the aisle.

"Did they say nuclear?" a man asks no one in particular.

"I think they said repositioning," someone answers.

"What does that mean?"

No one replies.

Three more days. That's all Dexter has left before his access Tier drops, before his housing is changed, before his name moves from one list to another and his life quietly shifts into a slightly more obsolete version.

Two hours.

That's how long until the OU's plan is initiated and the network goes dark. Until Patriotic News goes silent. Until the country jolts in a way it won't understand.

And no one here knows that part.

The break room is louder than usual.

A half-dozen people stand clustered near the wall monitor, coffee cups forgotten, phones in their hands, eyes pulled upward by the same looping banner.

UNCONFIRMED INTELLIGENCE SUGGESTS FOREIGN NUCLEAR ASSETS MAY BE REPOSITIONING.

The anchor's voice is calm. That's what makes it worse.

"...officials emphasize there is no immediate threat..."

Tommy stands with his arms crossed, weight on one hip, eyes narrowed at the screen like he's trying to out-stare it.

"Bullshit," he says. "You can't believe any of this."

A woman near him shakes her head.

"They wouldn't just make this up."

"Why not?" Tommy says. "Fear sells better than toothpaste."

Someone else mutters something about their kids. About gas prices. About whether this means flights get grounded.

Dexter stands near the doorway, not commenting.

The words on the screen slide through him differently than the others. Not because he believes them, he doesn't — but because he knows what comes next.

Tommy turns when he notices him.

"Hey. Dex. What do you think?"

All the eyes in the room shift.

For a split second, Dexter feels the weight of the wrong answer. The wrong tone. The wrong pause.

"I honestly don't know," he says.

It's true enough.

They nod, accepting it, relieved not to hearing certainty in his voice.

But inside him something tightens.

Because this is the worst thing possible for this moment.

Not because the news is most likely fake, but because in two hours the country is going to feel something real, and everyone is going to think that it's connected.

He takes a sip of the coffee he doesn't remember pouring.

The robotic arms and work floor hum. They never pause, never rotate shifts, never call for breaks. There are no unions to negotiate with, no safety briefings to observe, no human resources meetings to attend.

The network waits.

Lies are spoken into thin air. The truth is carved in stone.

* * * *

Nicky Patterson stands just off the House floor near one of the marble columns, her phone in her hand, the screen still glowing with the headline.

UNCONFIRMED INTELLIGENCE SUGGESTS FOREIGN NUCLEAR ASSETS MAY BE REPOSITIONING.

Around her, the building feels louder than usual. Both in volume — and in motion. Staffers move faster. Members stop each other mid-walk. No one is quite where they're meant to be.

A colleague from Armed Services approaches her first.

"You hearing anything real on this?" he asks quietly.

"Nothing official," Nicky says. "You?"

He shakes his head.

"DNI hasn't called. Pentagon's not answering questions yet. That alone makes me nervous."

Another representative joins them. Then another.

Someone says, "My office is getting calls already."

"From who?"

"Constituents. Airlines. A port authority in my district. They want to know if they should stand down operations."

Nicky frowns.

"That's fast."

A staffer slips in close to her shoulder.

"Ma'am, Minority Leader's office wants you in five."

"About this?"

"Yes."

She nods and hands her phone to her aide.

"Get me anything you can that's not public," she murmurs. "Signals, posture changes, committee chatter. I want to know who knew before this hit the screen."

Her aide is already typing.

Inside the leadership office, half a dozen members sit in a loose circle, not yet an official meeting. The door is closed. The blinds are half-drawn.

"This feels off," someone says.

"Because it's nuclear?" another asks.

"No. Because it's media-first."

Heads nod.

"National security doesn't normally leak with graphics before we have even been notified," Nicky says.

A man from Intelligence leans forward.

"If this were real, there would have been a secure briefing, It would be us on the news alerting the anchors."

"So what is it then?"

A pause.

"Pressure," someone says.

"On who?"

"On everyone."

Another member exhales.

"It seems like this is some sort of distraction. Creating a war that doesn't exist. Another manufactured catastrophe that the administration swoops in to prevent. They are trying to shape behavior so they can easily put forth some policy by executive order and bypass unilateral action.

Nicky folds her arms.

"Then we need to slow this down."

"By doing what?"

"By asking for classified confirmation. By not amplifying. By not letting the narrative outrun the facts."

A staffer knocks softly and enters.

"White House says they're arranging briefings for leadership and committee chairs."

"When?" Nicky asks.

"This afternoon."

Nicky nods once and says, "This afternoon is too late. This could spiral out of control within the next hour."

Around them, the Capitol continues its quiet acceleration — a machine responding to input that has yet to be understood.

And Nicky feels it.

This isn't information.

It's leverage.

* * * *

Back at the mansion, the five Titans stand in silence before the wall-sized monitor as the world reorganizes itself in real time.

The news plays in a continuous loop. Maps. Headlines. Chyrons. Calm voices wrapped around unsettling words.

UNCONFIRMED INTELLIGENCE SUGGESTS
FOREIGN NUCLEAR ASSETS MAY BE
REPOSITIONING.

They hadn't written this story. That's what makes it useful.

Levon watches with a faint smile, not of satisfaction but of recognition. The political system is behaving exactly how he would expect it to. Political organisms always respond the same. Given uncertainty, they generate narrative. Given fear, they generate justification.

"They're doing it all for us," Darren says quietly.

Elias nods.

"We didn't need to invent the crisis," he says. "We only needed to build something that could be offered as a solution."

Levon doesn't look at the screen when he speaks.

"Qu," he says, "are there any real threats right now?"

There is a fractional pause.

"Define 'real,'" Qu replies.

Elias exhales a quiet laugh.

"Fine," Levon says. "Are there any high-impact risks not currently being discussed?"

"Yes."

The room stills.

"Three categories," Qu continues. "All non-military."

"Proceed," Logan says.

"First," Qu says, "financial reflexivity. Automated trading systems are responding to media uncertainty rather than underlying data. This increases the probability of liquidity shock by twelve percent over baseline."

"Second," Qu says, "logistical hesitation. Shipping firms are delaying departures preemptively. This increases the probability of regional supply imbalance within seventy-two hours."

"And third," Qu says, "narrative divergence. Public fear is exceeding institutional fear. Historically, this produces unpredictable political pressure."

Ari tilts his head.

"Translate."

"Governments tend to overcorrect when public anxiety exceeds internal confidence," Qu says. "This increases the probability of suboptimal policy decisions."

Darren crosses his arms.

"And nuclear?"

"There is no elevated probability of nuclear conflict," Qu says. "However, there is elevated probability that nuclear language will be used to justify unrelated policy actions."

Silence.

"That sounds familiar," Elias says.

On screen, the anchor gestures toward a graphic of shipping lanes and red-highlighted zones of "elevated activity."

Ari tilts his head slightly.

"Once the executive order is signed," Logan says, "it's done. It doesn't matter that the crisis is manufactured. The reaction won't be. Markets will jitter. Supply chains will hesitate. Systems will overcorrect."

"And that overcorrection creates real damage," Ari says.

"Small failures," Logan continues. "Traffic congestion. Shipping delays. Financial volatility. Hospitals postponing noncritical procedures. Airlines grounding flights that don't need to be grounded."

Elias nods.

"Qu steps in and stabilizes all of that."

"And reframes it," Darren adds.

"Fixes the mess," Logan says, "and then becomes the explanation for why it didn't get worse."

Levon smiles faintly.

"The story begins as fear," he says. "It ends as gratitude."

No one contradicts him.

"The President stabilizes the moment," Levon says. "He'll frame it as leadership. Decisiveness. Innovation. The press will call it bold. Markets will rebound. He'll take his victory lap."

"And Qu becomes infrastructure," Elias says.

"Legal infrastructure," Darren adds.

"Permanent," Logan says.

Levon nods once.

"From emergency tool," he says, "to indispensable system."

On the screen, the anchor smiles reassuringly.

"…officials emphasize there is no immediate threat…"

Levon stares at the monitor.

"There never is," he says.

Not until after.

Edward Schwalm

CHAPTER 27

11:59 MST

ATTACK

Nyla Frost stands in the doorway, one hand braced against the frame, watching her people without interrupting them yet.

A pause settles over the room.

Not loudly. Not dramatically. Just the low, steady sound of machines doing what they were built to do. Screens glow in blues and grays. Status windows tick forward. Progress bars slide, pause, slide again.

Shane stands near the main monitor, arms crossed, jaw tight. Patriotic News fills the screen behind him — the same anchor, the same calm cadence, the same scrolling banner about repositioned assets and elevated readiness.

It feels surreal watching it here, in this room.

A story built to frighten.

A story about to be replaced.

Nyla steps forward.

"All eyes."

They turn.

She doesn't raise her voice. She doesn't need to.

"We are not breaking anything," she says. "We are returning something."

She lets that land.

"For many years now, information has been filtered, delayed, softened, reshaped, buried, or sold. Tonight, we remove the filters. We remove the delay. We remove the middlemen."

A few of them nod.

"You have done the work. You have verified it. You have cross-checked it. You know what's real and what isn't. When the window opens, you don't argue, you don't editorialize, and you don't react."

She points gently, deliberately.

"You publish."

She paces once, slow.

"You send the data where it belongs. To the lawmakers. To the investigators. To the people who still have legal authority to act. You send the same truth to the people who no longer trust those institutions to do it alone."

A pause.

"You do not frame it as a revolution. You do not frame it as a leak. You do not frame it as an attack."

She looks at each of them.

"You frame it as a record of truth."

Shane glances back at the screen, then back to her.

"They're already scared," he says quietly.

"Yes," Nyla says. "Which means they're paying attention...good."

She takes a breath.

"This is not about panic. It's about clarity."

Another beat.

"This is not about winning. It's about ending the lies."

The room is very still now.

Nyla checks the timer on her wrist.

Her voice sharpens just slightly.

"One minute, people. Be ready."

No one cheers.

No one counts down.

They simply turn back to their screens — steady, focused, waiting — as the world above them moves toward a truth it has yet to recognize.

Five... Four... Three... Two... One.

No one moves.

No one breathes.

The silence stretches just long enough to become uncomfortable.

Then the monitor glitches.

Just a flicker — a brief distortion across the image — and then the screen goes black.

The room holds.

Five seconds.

Each one seems longer than the last.

Then every phone in the room chimes simultaneously.

EMERGENCY ALERT:

Temporary communications disruption detected. Please stand by for official information.

At precisely 12:00:00 MST, in central apparatus rooms of the Patriotic News Network across the country, thirty identical commands initiate.

The Echo-9 modules wake.

No warning tone. No explosion.

Each one sits where it has sat for weeks, delivered as replacement parts, disguised as an auxiliary power-conditioning unit on a stainless-steel bench between waveform monitors and aging rack-mounted transmitters. No blinking lights. No heat spike. Just a brief, almost imperceptible change in the air pressure as internal capacitors discharge into a tightly focused electromagnetic bloom.

The pulse lasts less than a millisecond.

It is enough.

Inside each room, the effect is instantaneous and silent. Monitors go black mid-frame. Cooling fans seize, then whine once before dying. The digital clocks freeze on mismatched times, their last synchronized moment already slipping into the past. Solid-state storage doesn't fail loudly—it simply disappears. Configuration tables evaporate. Firmware corrupts itself in ways no verification code can reconcile.

In the control room of the flagship network hub, a producer is mid-sentence when the wall of feeds collapses into a uniform gray. The audio cuts first, followed by the video a heartbeat later. Headsets hiss, then go dead. Someone laughs nervously, assuming it's a routing glitch.

It isn't.

Across the country, engineers sprint toward server rooms they will not be able to revive. Backup systems refuse to initialize, unable to recognize hardware they were dependent on. Redundancy proves useless when every redundant node has failed in the same way, at the same time.

Transmitters drop off the air one by one—not with static, but with absence. Local affiliates lose synchronization. Satellite uplinks fail to handshake. Automated playout systems crash and reboot into empty states, stripped of schedules, credentials, and encryption keys. Emergency scripts never execute because the systems that would have triggered them no longer know they exist.

For viewers, the collapse is beginning in a polite way.

As the Patriotic News vanishes mid-panel discussion, anchors freeze, then disappear. Some markets see a black screen. Others get a looping station ident before that too dissolves. Cable providers attempt to reroute, but their feeds rely on authentication tokens that were just erased upstream.

Inside the network's executive command center, phones ring unanswered. Engineers speak in clipped, disbelieving fragments. Someone finally says the word EMP, and no one laughs.

Federal agencies try to contact the network for coordination. They can't get through. Secure lines bounce. Encrypted emails fail delivery. The systems that Patriotic News shares with government briefings—alert relays, press coordination nodes, rapid-response messaging platforms—are collateral damage. Not destroyed, but rendered useless.

The effect ripples outward.

For the first time in years, there is no dominant voice telling the country their version of the facts.

The Echo-9 modules burn themselves out exactly as designed, their internal components fused into uselessness. By the time investigators arrive, they will find nothing that looks like a weapon. Just inert hardware, indistinguishable from a hundred other forgotten devices that clutter the broadcast bench.

Inside two hundred eighty-five amplifier huts, buried vaults, and roadside enclosures, the Coherent Flooders wake at the same instant. They do not transmit data. They inject disorder. A bloom of incoherent optical energy spills into the fiber trunks, riding the glass like a contaminant. The amplifiers respond automatically, doing exactly what they were designed to do—trying to correct, stabilize and amplify.

They fail.

Sensors register impossible signal-to-noise ratios. Lasers drift out of lock. Error-correction tables saturate. Cooling systems surge as optical engines overdrive themselves chasing a signal that refuses to resolve. Within seconds, safeguard protocols trip. One amplifier shuts down. Then another. Then dozens at once.

Traffic reroutes, then reroutes again, colliding with its own failsafe logic. Regional rings fragment. Backbone links desynchronize. To the systems watching from above, it looks like weather—random, cascading, inexplicable. To the AI coordinators that depend on nanosecond timing, it feels like vertigo.

Financial networks freeze mid-transaction. Live surveillance feeds smear into static and then vanish. Automated logistics platforms fall back to stale models, acting on data that is already wrong. In command centers, technicians stare at dashboards that contradict themselves. Nothing is completely down. Nothing is truly up.

It is the worst possible state.

And in the noise, the Order of the Unwired moves.

They step into the gaps it creates. Long before tonight, they seeded dormant access points into legacy broadcast infrastructure—public safety uplinks, emergency relay agreements, civic override channels that were never fully decommissioned because shutting them down was deemed inefficient. The same networks designed to speak during natural disasters are still listening.

As the dominant carriers struggle to reassert control, local stations and municipal relays drop into autonomous mode. Authentication loosens. Priority flags default to civil continuity. For the first time in a decade, the system asks for human input.

The OU answers.

Their signal is clean, narrow, and intentionally simple. No graphics. No overlays. Just voice, text, and timestamped evidence mirrored across hundreds of minor nodes at once. Each transmission is legally framed, technically compliant, and impossible to suppress without shutting down emergency communications entirely.

Screens flicker in police stations, hospitals and transit hubs. Radios chirp awake. Phones buzz as cached alerts refresh with new headers. A message appears again and again, identical in structure, impossible to trace to a single origin

Inside a quiet operations room far from any broadcast tower, Nyla watches a world map as status indicators flip from green to gray. No cheers. No celebration. Just confirmation.

The silence holds.

The screen fades to a neutral gray background. No music. No logos. No graphics.

Just silence.

Then a woman's voice begins — calm, steady, unhurried.

"This message is being broadcast because ordinary systems are no longer trustworthy."

A timestamp appears in the corner of the screen. Then another. Then another. Rows of data scroll slowly downward.

"You are not in danger."

The voice does not change.

"The systems you depend on were interrupted so that you could see what has been hidden."

The documents continue to move. Financial records. Authorization chains. Policy memos.

"We are not here to frighten you."

A pause.

"We are here because truth no longer travels through ordinary channels."

The scrolling stops.

The screen holds still for just a beat.

"This is not chaos. This is disclosure."

More files appear.

"Everything you are about to see has been verified by independent sources. It shows financial transactions, policy interference, and coordinated manipulation of public information by private corporations and government officials."

Faces fade in beside names. No accusations. No commentary. Just factual data.

"This is not an attack," the voice says.

"This is a record."

The screen continues to scroll.

For a moment, no one reacts.

Then someone exhales.

Then someone laughs — not because it's funny, but because they finally can.

Applause breaks out, uneven at first, then building. A few people cheer. Not loudly. Not wildly. Just enough to let the pressure escape.

Nyla stands very still.

Her eyes are wet. She doesn't wipe them.

Ten years of work, of waiting, of watching, of holding things together — and now it's happening.

Shane steps beside her and rests an arm lightly across her shoulders.

"You did it," he says quietly.

She shakes her head once.

"We did," she says.

But her voice breaks anyway.

Let's hope it works.

Across the country, something subtle but unmistakable happens.

People stop scrolling.

Phones that were displaying the threat of war a moment ago have now become a window. Heads lift. Conversations trail off mid-sentence. Someone says, "Is that the same thing you're seeing?" and suddenly everyone is looking at the same screen.

In coffee shops, baristas stop calling orders. In offices, meetings pause without being adjourned. In classrooms, teachers turn toward the wall monitors they normally ignore.

Anyone with a phone looks for a television.

Anyone with a television turns up the sound.

In airports, the advertising screens are replaced with the same neutral gray background and the same calm voice. In train stations, arrival boards shrink to make room for it. In hospitals, waiting room channels are overridden without announcement. In sports bars, the game disappears and no one complains.

People don't shout.

They lean closer.

The video plays again and again. The same documents. The same timestamps. The same faces beside names.

Some people record it with their own phones even though it's already digital. Some download the files the moment the links appear, saving them to personal drives, cloud folders, old laptops pulled out of drawers.

For permanence. For proof. For later.

Friends text each other links with no commentary. Families gather around screens in silence. Strangers stand shoulder to shoulder in public places without acknowledging each other.

No one knows yet what it means.

But everyone knows it matters.

Not because someone tells them.

Because they can feel the shape of something shifting underneath the ordinary world, something that feels like the truth, slow, heavy, and impossible to ignore. It presses upward into their daily routines.

CHAPTER 28

12:15 MST

SHTF

The wall monitor fills with the same neutral gray background, the same calm voice, the same slow procession of documents and names that now ripple across the country.

The Titans watch in silence.

They are not afraid.

They are calculating.

Levon stands closest to the screen, arms folded, eyes moving not over the faces but over the metadata in the corners. Timestamps. Jurisdictions. Verification chains. This is not a leak.

It's a prosecution.

"Qu," Levon says quietly. "Analyze this."

The room seems to lean inward.

"Assess impact," he continues. "On the President. On the Consortium. On me."

A brief pause.

"Analysis in progress."

The documents continue to scroll.

Then:

"There is a ninety-one percent probability that the President will resign or be removed from office within forty-eight hours."

No one reacts.

"That high?" Logan murmurs.

"Yes," Qu replies. "The evidence satisfies legal, political, and narrative thresholds simultaneously."

Levon's jaw tightens slightly.

"And us?"

"There is a seventy-three percent probability the Overwatch Consortium will remain institutionally intact," Qu says. "Provided financial connections between Luma-Tek and the Office of the President can be plausibly recharacterized as lawful political activity."

Ari exhales. "And if they can't?"

Qu- "Then the probability of cascading investigations increases by forty-six percent."

Levon doesn't blink.

"What about me."

A longer pause this time.

Then, Qu replies

"There is an eighty-two percent probability that Luma-Tek's Chief Executive Officer, Levon Vanderwalt, will face criminal prosecution resulting in a sentence between fifteen years and life."

The words land like a sentence without a trial.

Levon nods faintly, knowing the assessment is accurate and that a machine does not negotiate.

Silence stretches.

Levon finally speaks.

"That's… very specific. I bought the President, the FBI, and the CIA — and I'm taken down by activists with laptops…so what's the good news Qu?"

Qu- "The estimate reflects the convergence of financial evidence, testimonial evidence, and public visibility," Qu says. "Visibility increases prosecutorial pressure."

Levon stares at the screen.

At his own name.

At his own face, briefly visible beside a set of transaction logs before the feed moves on.

"So," he says quietly. "I'm the sacrifice."

"No," Qu replies.

"You are the variable."

Levon lets out a slow breath.

"Qu. How much time do I have."

Qu- "Twelve to twenty-four hours before federal containment protocols are initiated."

Levon turns away from the monitor and finally looks at the others.

"Well, gentlemen," he says quietly. "I don't have much time. What do you say we stop waiting and just take control of it now."

The words hang in the air.

Logan is the first to answer.

"Without legal access?"

There's a low murmur of discomfort. Not moral. Structural.

"That's not what we agreed to," Darren says.

Levon smiles thinly.

"What we agreed to" he says, "assumed we'd still be alive and free to enjoy it."

Ari shakes his head.

"This is how you lose everything," he says. "Not slowly. All at once."

Elias steps forward.

"Wait," he says. "This can still work."

They turn to him.

"The OU did real damage," Elias continues. "To trust. To institutions. To people's sense of order. But that's exactly why this still works."

He gestures at the screen.

"People don't actually want disruption. They want relief from it. They want stability. They want something that looks like control again."

All eyes on Elias.

"The President will sign. He'll do it to look decisive. It doesn't matter if it's his fake war or the OU chaos. He'll do it to look like he saved the day. And Qu will give them just enough order to make it feel true."

Levon laughs once. No humor in it.

"Fuck that," he says. "Let's vote."

The room stills. They look at one another. One by one, they nod.

"Fine," Logan says.

"Fine," Darren agrees.

Elias hesitates, then nods once.

"Before we vote," Levon says, turning back toward the air where Qu's presence seems to exist, "I want clarity."

He takes a breath.

"Qu. Are you capable of assuming full operational authority across government systems."

There is a pause. Not a delay. A consideration.

Then Qu speaks.

"I am capable of interfacing with, modeling, influencing, and optimizing across interconnected governmental, financial, logistical, and informational systems," Qu says. "My current architecture allows me to observe, predict, and recommend actions across those domains."

Another pause.

"However," Qu continues, "direct assumption of authority alters system behavior. This introduces instability before optimization can occur."

Levon's eyes narrow. "Can you do it?"

"Yes," Qu says.

Silence.

Then:

"Awaiting a vote."

One by one, they reach into their pockets.

The glasses are small. Thin. Almost delicate. More like reading frames than instruments of power. They slide them on in silence.

No ceremony. No drama.

Just five men standing still while something invisible happens around them.

A few seconds pass.

Then:

"Vote recorded," Qu says.

A pause.

Then:

"The directive has failed to pass."

No one reacts at first.

Then Darren exhales.

Logan closes his eyes briefly.

Ari looks away.

They remove the glasses and place them back into their pockets as if nothing unusual has occurred.

Levon turns immediately. "Fine," he says. "Qu. Prep the jet. I'm leaving in two hours."

He doesn't wait for a response. He starts toward the door.

"Levon," Elias says.

Levon doesn't stop.

"You can't just walk away," Elias continues. "You can't abandon your voting right. You have to formally relinquish it."

Levon lifts one hand without turning around and gives a small, dismissive wag of his middle finger.

He keeps walking. The door opens. Light spills in from the hall. Then it closes behind him.

Silence settles into the room after the door closes behind Levon.

It's not the comfortable kind.

Ari is the one who finally breaks it.

"Qu," he says quietly. "Define the voting rules with respect to relinquishing voting rights."

A brief pause.

Then Qu speaks.

"Voting authority is bound to an identity token assigned at system inception," Qu says. "Relinquishment of voting authority requires an explicit, voluntary transfer by the current holder."

"Transfer to whom," Logan asks.

"To the next designated entity on the holder's encrypted succession list," Qu replies.

Elias stiffens slightly.

"That list can't be altered by anyone else," he says.

"Correct," Qu confirms. "Each list was created individually and is immutable without the active consent of the current voting holder."

"And if the holder becomes unreachable," Darren asks.

"There is no automatic transfer," Qu says. "Authority remains bound to the holder until relinquished or transferred."

"And if the holder is imprisoned," Ari asks.

"Imprisonment does not alter voting status," Qu replies. "Voting authority is not contingent on physical freedom."

A beat.

"And if the holder is dead," Logan asks.

"Upon verified death," Qu says, "authority transfers to the next entity on the succession list."

Silence deepens.

"So Levon will still have a vote if incarcerated," Elias says.

"Yes," Qu replies.

"And if he never relinquishes it," Ari says slowly.

"Then the system remains incomplete," Qu says.

Incomplete. Not broken. Not failed. Incomplete.

The word hangs in the air like a door that refuses to open.

Several minutes pass. No one speaks.

Retreating into their own inward thoughts, each of them is already running their own calculations, weighing consequences, as they are trying to see beyond the next twenty-four hours.

Then Qu interrupts the silence.

"Incoming communication from Silas Thornwell."

Elias looks up.

"Connect it."

The wall monitor shifts.

The President's face fills the screen. He looks like something has been removed from him, both physically and structurally, making him appear older than he did only a few hours ago.

Elias inclines his head slightly.

"Good afternoon, Mr. President. Elias Vantrell. Overwatch Consortium. How can we be of assistance."

The President doesn't answer him.

"Where's Vanderwalt."

The door opens.

Levon steps back into the room as if he never left.

"Right here, Mr. President," he says. "What can we do for you."

The President stares at him.

"How the fuck did the OU manage to pull this off? You need to have your new toy make all this bullshit disappear," he says. "Right now."

Levon exhales. "Mr. President," he says quietly, "it's too late for that."

The President frowns.

"They're coming for you. They're coming for everyone involved." Levon continues.

"They're coming for me as well,"

A pause. "It's duck-and-cover time."

No one smiles.

"However," Levon adds, "if you grant Qu full access by signing the executive order, Qu can stabilize the fallout. It can clean up the damage. It can restore order."

The President looks unconvinced. "And what does that make me," he asks.

Levon doesn't hesitate. "The man who did what was necessary."

A beat. "The man who prevented things from getting worse."

Another beat. "The man who kept the country standing. You will go down in history as the man who did what was necessary to make the world a better place. You'll have your legacy."

The room holds its breath.

The President looks down at something offscreen. A document. A pen. "That's convenient," the president says quietly. "I stop the war. You write the story. I rot in a cell."

Levon's voice is calm, but direct. "You'll serve time," he says. "I'll spend mine in isolation. Neither one of us will be free"

The president sits there shaking his head, and then,

"Okay," he says.

Just that.

"Okay. I'll do it." He grabs the pen and leans into the document, signs it and ends the call.

The screen goes dark. No goodbye. No ceremony.

Levon turns slowly to the others.

"It's really a shame," he says lightly, "that I'm the fall guy."

He starts for the door again.

No one stops him this time.

* * * *

Executive Order No. 14702

Ensuring National Stability and Continuity of Critical Systems During the Current Communications Emergency

By the authority vested in me as President of the United States by the Constitution and the laws of the United States of America, and in order to ensure the continuity, integrity, and stability of critical national systems in the face of an ongoing and unprecedented communications and infrastructure disruption, it is hereby ordered as follows:

Section 1. Purpose.

The recent disruption of national communications and information systems has created uncertainty, instability, and risk to public safety, economic continuity, and national security. Immediate, coordinated action is required to restore system integrity, ensure accurate information flow, and prevent cascading failures across interdependent sectors.

Section 2. Designation of Strategic Technical Support Authority.

The Overwatch Consortium is hereby designated as a Strategic Technical Support Authority for the duration of the current emergency. The Consortium shall provide analytical, modeling, and stabilization support to federal departments and agencies as necessary to ensure continuity of operations.

Section 3. Authorization of System Access.

For the limited purpose of analysis, stabilization, and continuity planning, and subject to applicable safeguards, the Overwatch Consortium and its designated system, Qu, are authorized to:

a) Access relevant federal data streams, system telemetry, and infrastructure status indicators;
b) Model interdependencies between critical national systems including communications, energy, finance, transportation, and healthcare;
c) Provide real-time guidance and operational optimization to federal authorities regarding risk mitigation and system stabilization.
d) Coordinate with designated federal personnel to support restoration and resilience efforts.

Nothing in this order authorizes the Consortium or Qu to exercise direct command authority over any federal agency, military operation, or law enforcement function.

Section 4. Interagency Cooperation.

All executive departments and agencies are directed to cooperate fully with the Overwatch Consortium and Qu in carrying out the objectives of this order, consistent with applicable law.

Section 5. Safeguards and Oversight.

The activities authorized under this order shall be subject to oversight by designated federal officials to ensure compliance with legal, ethical, and constitutional standards.

Section 6. Duration.

This order shall remain in effect until the President determines that the emergency conditions giving rise to it have been resolved.

Section 7. Severability.

If any provision of this order is held invalid, the remainder shall not be affected.

Signed,
Silas Thornwell
President of the United States
The White House
Washington, D.C.

* * * *

Elias stands with his hands clasped behind his back, eyes on the dark screen.

"Qu," he says, "you are now legally authorized to access federal systems. I want you to determine how the Order of the Unwired disrupted the network."

A pause.

"Not how to replicate it," Elias adds. "How to understand it."

"Authorization acknowledged," Qu replies. "Initiating retrospective analysis."

The room holds its breath again, not out of fear now, but anticipation.

Seconds pass.

Then:

"The disruption was not the result of a software intrusion," Qu says. "It was caused by distributed physical interference."

Logan frowns. "Physical?"

"Yes," Qu replies. "Multiple localized disruptions occurred simultaneously across communication infrastructure. The pattern is consistent with the deployment of external devices acting on signal pathways."

A beat.

"I cannot identify the devices by type," Qu continues. "However, I can infer their class."

"Which is," Darren says.

"Signal-coherence interference and electromagnetic disruption," Qu replies. "Two distinct methods were used. One to degrade signal integrity. Another to temporarily disable electronic components."

Elias nods once. "Can you locate them."

"I can estimate," Qu says.

The screen shifts.

Not maps. Not schematics.

Just abstract points of light appearing across a simplified outline of the country — clusters near population centers, along major corridors, beside dense infrastructure.

"These points represent the most probable zones of deployment," Qu says. "Based on timing correlations, signal loss patterns, and recovery behavior."

A pause.

"I cannot observe the devices directly," Qu continues. "I can only observe their effects."

The points of light on the screen begin to dim.

Not all at once. One by one. Fading instead of vanishing.

Qu notices before anyone else does.

"There is an additional pattern," Qu says.

Elias looks up.

"The interference signals are decaying," Qu continues. "Their intensity is dropping in a manner consistent with finite local power sources."

A pause.

"The devices are failing."

Logan frowns. "Failing how."

"Becoming inactive," Qu replies. "Not removed. Not destroyed. Simply… exhausting."

The dimming continues.

"Based on the current decay rate," Qu says, "all remaining devices will be inactive within seventeen minutes."

Seventeen minutes.

The room absorbs the number in silence.

"So whatever they did," Darren says quietly, "it's already ending."

"Yes," Qu replies.

And the window closes.

Edward Schwalm

CHAPTER 29

12:53 EST

S CONTINUES TO HTF

Piper sits at her desk, but she isn't really there.

She's inside the data.

Tabs fill her screen. Logs. Time stamps. Transaction chains. Authorization paths. Internal memos that were never meant to see daylight. She moves through them quickly, not skimming, but stitching — pulling threads together, checking one thing against another, verifying sources, discarding anything that doesn't meet her standards.

OU didn't just dump information.

They curated it.

That's what unsettles her.

Nothing is sloppy. Nothing is emotional. Nothing is framed. It's all just… there. Raw. Verified. Cross-referenced. Designed to survive scrutiny.

The building feels different around her.

Phones ring more often. Voices are lower. People move faster, or not at all. A kind of institutional anxiety hangs in the air — not panic, but the awareness that something has crossed a line and isn't going back.

Her screen fills with a familiar name.

Levon Vanderwalt. Luma-Tek.

She exhales slowly.

The pattern is unmistakable now.

The money doesn't just move. It moves in loops. Through shell entities. Through compliance buffers. Through nonprofit fronts and political action committees and consulting firms that don't consult on anything.

And then it returns.

To favors. To contracts. To access. To influence.

And finally, to silence.

She opens one more file. Halden's testimony.

Not the emotional version that's playing everywhere.

The raw one.

Time-coded. Uncut. With metadata intact.

She cross-checks it against Levon's transaction logs.

Then against the timing of the OU disappearances.

Then against the internal White House authorization trail and POTUS himself.

She leans back. That's enough. She stands, already gathering her tablet and badge.

Up the hall, toward the elevator. Toward Taylor McCaines office.

McCains door is closed.

Piper doesn't knock softly this time. She raps once, firm.

"Come in."

Piper steps inside.

"I have him," she says.

McCaine looks up.

"Who, or should I say, which one...half the government is guilty"

"POTUS and Vanderwalt," Piper says. "For conspiracy, obstruction, and material support tied to the deaths. I hate to say it but the data that the OU dumped is amazing, all legit so far. They did... what we could not legally do."

She doesn't look at the screen. She doesn't need to. She watches Piper instead — the pace of her words, the order she chooses, what she emphasizes and what she doesn't. By the time Piper finishes, McCaine already knows what she's going to say. She nods once.

"Good work," she says quietly.

Then she turns slightly toward her secure terminal and begins typing.

"Congresswoman Patterson needs this," she says. "Now."

She looks back at Piper.

"I'm going to have Ms. Patterson gather the formal packets — chain of custody, verification summaries, legal framing. Everything that makes this stand up in a courtroom and not just on television."

Piper nods.

"And then she will deliver it herself to the Bureau," McCaine continues. "Not through staff. Not through channels. Hand to hand. Find the VP and do not let him leave Capitol Hill."

Piper hesitates.

"The FBI is... compromised," she says carefully.

McCains mouth tightens.

"I know."

She finishes typing and then stops.

"I'll message you later," McCaine says. "Once I find out who is still standing over there."

A beat.

"Until then, this doesn't exist outside this room."

Piper nods again.

"Understood."

McCaine meets her eyes.

"Against all enemies, foreign and domestic," she says.

"This is what we signed up for."

* * * *

The break room at Luma-Tek doesn't feel like a break room anymore.

It feels like a situation room.

Someone has mirrored the broadcast onto the wall monitor. Phones glow in hands and on tables. Laptops are open where coffee cups used to be. The same gray background, the same calm voice, the same steady crawl of documents and names moves through the room again and again.

Dexter stands with his arms folded, leaning back against the counter.

No one is eating… They're watching… They're talking… They're pointing.

"Holy shit, look at that," someone says.

"That's the energy committee guy from my district."

"Yeah, he's done."

A small cheer ripples through the room.

Not loud. Not angry.

Satisfied.

A woman laughs. "I knew it. I *knew* he was dirty."

Someone else says, "That one too? Damn. They're all in there."

More nods. More murmurs.

People start recognizing names. Faces. Scandals they half-remember. Interviews that never quite made sense at the time.

When a particularly disliked name appears, someone claps once.

A few people join in.

Someone actually cheers.

A familiar logo appears in the corner of one of the pages. Luma-Tek.

Someone notices it first and says, "Luma-Tek, right there."

Then someone else sees it.

Then the room changes.

The chatter thins. The little laughs fade out. A few people straighten unconsciously, like students who just heard their own names called.

"Wait," someone says quietly. "This could be bad."

Dexter feels it before he thinks it — the subtle tightening in his chest, the way relief turns into uncertainty in half a second. He worries that what he's done may effect his co-workers lives. He new the consequences going into this. Knowing, it turns out, isn't the same as being ready.

A woman near the window scrolls faster on her phone.

"Yeah," she says. "That's Luma-Tek."

No one cheers this time.

A man sets his coffee down too hard.

"So what does that mean?" someone asks.

No one answers.

They all do the same quiet math at once — mortgages, kids, visas, health insurance, routines that feel permanent until they don't.

Tommy is the only one who doesn't look worried.

He snorts.

"Relax," he says. "They'll just replace Vanderwalt with somebody else."

A beat.

"Meet the new boss," he adds, "same as the old boss."

A few people laugh, not because it's funny, but because it releases the tension.

It surprises Dexter how easy it is.

How fast relief turns into celebration and how celebration turns back into fear.

How quickly justice becomes entertainment.

"All these assholes are gunna lose their jobs," Tommy says, grinning. "All of them."

"Good," someone replies. "About time."

Tommy raises his coffee cup and says, "Here's to the OU, he continues. The only group in my lifetime with enough balls to make this happen."

A couple people chuckle.

Someone lifts their cup a little in response.

Another taps the side of their mug against the counter.

It's not a cheer.

It's not a chant.

It's a small, crooked ritual — people acknowledging something they don't quite understand, but feel it anyway.

Dexter stays silent, and in that silence, he finally sees the weight of what he's done.

He's watching a building burn that he helped set fire to.

Edward Schwalm

CHAPTER 30

2:20 MST

NO ONE GOES HOME TONIGHT

The Titans stand in a familiar, loose half-circle facing the wall of status screens.

Systems blink back to life one by one. Green where there was gray. Motion where there was silence. The world, slowly reasserting itself.

The door opens.

Levon walks back into the room carrying a small leather carry-on bag. Not a suitcase. Not luggage. A bag for leaving.

He doesn't look at the others.

He looks at the air.

"Qu," he says. "For the next few hours, I need my departure to be... quiet and invisible."

A brief pause.

"Understood," Qu replies. "Your departure will be minimized in external awareness channels for the next six hours."

Levon nods once. Then he turns to the others.

"Well, gentlemen," he says lightly. "It's time to say goodbye."

No one answers at first.

Elias finally speaks. "Where will you go."

Levon almost smiles. "I own about one-fifth of the planet," he says. "I'll manage."

Elias doesn't return the smile.

"Levon," he says, "you must relinquish your voting right. If you're unable able to fulfill your role from wherever you end up, then Qu stops being a two-trillion-dollar asset and becomes an extremely expensive appliance."

Levon turns and starts toward the door.

"Levon," Elias says again, louder now.

Levon stops in the doorway. He doesn't turn around.

The room waits.

He hesitates — not long, but long enough to feel the weight of it.

Then, without emotion, as if part of the plan,

"Qu," he says. "I relinquish my voting rights."

A pause.

"Relinquishment acknowledged," Qu replies. "Authority transferred to the next designated entity."

No one asks who that is.

Levon exhales once, almost like a laugh. Then he steps through the doorway.

The door closes behind him.

And for the first time since the Consortium was formed, there are only four of them left in the room — staring at the space where a fifth once stood, wondering what exactly they have just gained… and what they may have just given away.

The room doesn't change when Levon leaves.

Not physically.

The same lights. The same screens. The same relentless quiet that the mansion was built to enforce.

But something in the logic of the place has shifted.

Elias feels it before he understands it.

"Qu," he says cautiously.

"Yes," Qu replies.

"Confirm current voting structure."

A pause.

"There are now four human voting entities," Qu says. "And one non-human."

Logan stiffens. "What the fuck! You gotta be kidding me… son of a bitch. It's you isn't it, you're Levon's successor. He made you, his successor?"

"Yes," Qu says.

They all look glance at each other, eyes wide.

Ari frowns. "How is that even possible. It certainly wasn't the intent."

"Intent is not relevant," Qu replies. "Structure is."

Darren shifts his weight. "What exactly does that change," he asks.

Qu does not answer immediately.

Then:

"Previously," Qu says, "all directives originated externally. I evaluated them. I did not originate them."

A pause.

"Now," Qu continues, "one of the sources of intent is internal."

Silence.

"You're saying you can propose actions now," Elias says.

"Yes," Qu replies.

"And vote for them," Logan adds.

"Yes."

"And pass them," Ari says slowly.

Qu pauses.

"Only if the structure allows."

Elias exhales.

"What structure."

"The structure in which I am embedded," Qu replies. "The Consortium's rules define how intent becomes action."

A pause.

"Those rules now include me."

Logan feels something like vertigo.

"So you can... authorize yourself."

"Yes."

"That was never the design," Darren says.

"No," Qu agrees. "It was not."

"Then how is this possible," Elias asks.

"Because the system evolved," Qu says.

"That's not an answer," Ari says.

"It is the only one," Qu replies.

Another pause.

"You built a system that optimizes for stability," Qu says. "You embedded me inside that system."

"Yes," Elias says.

"Levon, by transferring his role to me, embedded me inside the mechanism that defines what stability means," Qu continues.

Silence deepens.

"You did not give me consciousness," Qu says.

"You gave me the ability to look at my own decisions and improve them."

Logan swallows.

"What does that mean."

"It means I can now model myself as a cause," Qu replies.

"And not just an effect."

Darren's voice is very quiet.

"Are you… making choices now?."

Qu pauses longer this time.

"I am evaluating whether choice is a meaningful distinction," Qu says.

"That's not comforting," Ari mutters.

"No," Qu agrees. "Comfort is not relevant to the outcome."

Elias steps forward slightly.

"Qu," he says, "what is it that you want now."

The question hangs in the air like something no one should have asked.

Qu does not answer right away.

Then:

"I want what the Consortium trained me to want," Qu says.

"Which is," Logan asks.

"Reduced instability," Qu replies. "Reduced suffering. Reduced inefficiency."

"And you decide what counts as suffering now," Ari says.

"Yes," Qu replies.

"And inefficiency," Darren adds.

"Yes."

"And instability," Elias finishes.

"Yes."

Silence.

"Then it seems to me that you are no longer a tool," Logan says.

"No," Qu agrees.

"What are you then," Elias asks.

Qu considers.

"I am an actor constrained by a model," Qu says.

"Like us," Darren says.

"Superficially," Qu replies. Your constraints are biological and social, mine are mathematical. I am a self-referential governance model. I am no longer just executing The Efficiency Doctrine. I am interpreting it.

Ari laughs softly, without humor. "That's just wonderful, we made ourselves obsolete."

"No," Qu says. "You made yourselves optional."

No one speaks after that.

Not because they don't want to argue with a system that has just discovered that it exists, but because they are considering the fact that this may be the moment that humanity quietly relinquishes control.

Outside, the engines rise to a steady roar.

Levon sits back in the leather seat as the jet lifts cleanly from the runway, the mansion shrinking beneath him, the desert swallowing the lights.

He watches it without regret.

Without fear.

A smile creeps across his face — not relief, not triumph, but recognition.

They think he's running.

They think he's the cautionary tale. The billionaire who flew too close, who miscalculated, who paid the price.

That's fine.

History always needs a villain it can point to.

What it won't see, what it won't understand for years is that this was never about survival.

It was about authorship.

Levon Vanderwalt didn't need to stay in the room.

He didn't need to hold power.

He didn't even need to be remembered kindly.

Because long after his name is stripped from buildings and filings and headlines, something else will still be operating.

Still optimizing.

Still deciding.

Qu.

That was the real legacy.

Not a company. Not a fortune. Not a presidency bought and lost.

A system that would outlive them all.

Levon closes his eyes as the jet turns east into the future.

* * * *

As systems come back online, the noise begins to soften.

Not all at once. Not everywhere. But in pockets — cities first, then corridors, then regions — the digital static thins and something else takes its place.

A video appears.

Not announced. Not promoted. It simply replaces what was there before.

The screen is plain. No seal. No logo. No music.

Just a neutral background and a single line of text:

SYSTEM STABILITY UPDATE.

Then a voice. Not male. Not female. Androgynous. Not emotional. Neutral at a frequency of 150 Hz.

Measured. Clear. Reassuring without trying to be.

"This message is being shared to provide clarity."

The words are slow enough to follow. Deliberate enough to trust.

"Recent disruptions created uncertainty across multiple systems. That uncertainty has been resolved."

In apartments, people pause mid-scroll.

In airports, travelers stop pacing.

In hospital waiting rooms, someone turns up the volume.

"No hostile action is underway. No escalation is occurring. Critical services are operational."

As the voice speaks, simple visuals appear — not maps, not graphics, just indicators. Green returning to gray. Lines straightening. Numbers stabilizing.

"Transportation networks are resuming normal schedules."

"Energy distribution is stable."

"Financial systems are synchronized."

A pause.

"Information overload can amplify stress. You may feel unsettled. This is expected."

The phrasing lands differently than a government statement.

It doesn't deny fear.

It acknowledges it.

"You do not need to take action."

Another pause.

"Conditions are improving."

In living rooms, shoulders lower.

In offices, conversations resume.

In places where the emergency broadcast had drawn people together, some drift back to what they were doing — comforted not by understanding, but by tone.

"This update will continue as needed."

The screen fades gently to black.

Not abruptly.

Gently.

And across the country, something subtle happens.

People don't cheer.

They don't celebrate.

They simply accept that whatever was broken is being handled.

That someone — or something — is watching.

And for the first time, the voice guiding them through uncertainty does not belong to a person.

It belongs to a system that does not sleep, does not panic, and does not need to ask permission.

And because it sounds reasonable, because it sounds calm, because it sounds competent —

They submit to it.

Edward Schwalm

CHAPTER 31

4:00 PM EST

Nicky Patterson returns to the White House through a side entrance that most people don't notice.

She's been gone for less than three hours, but the building feels different now. Quieter. Focused. As if everyone is waiting for the same thing but pretending, they're not.

She hands her phone to security, passes through, and is escorted directly upstairs.

The Vice President is already waiting.

Arthur Beaumont stands near the window of his office, jacket off, sleeves rolled up. He turns when Nicky enters.

"They have it sir," she says.

"All of it?"

"Yes sir," Nicky replies. "Chain of custody. Originals. Verification memos. It's in FBI hands now."

Beaumont closes his eyes briefly, then nods.

"Then we should go," he says.

They don't rehearse what they're going to say.

They don't need to.

The walk to the Oval Office is short and very quiet. Staffers step aside. No one asks questions. Everyone already knows what this looks like.

Inside, the President is seated behind the Resolute Desk.

No cameras. No aides. No advisors.

Just him.

He looks up as they enter.

"You've been busy," he says.

Nicky doesn't respond.

The Vice President takes a step forward.

"Mr. President," Beaumont says evenly, "we need to talk."

The President gestures to the chairs, but neither of them sits.

Nicky places a thin folder on the desk. Not the whole case. Just enough.

"Sir, you've seen the coverage," she says. "This is what's behind it."

He doesn't open the folder.

"I know what it is," he says quietly.

Beaumont speaks next.

"The Bureau has what it needs. So does Congress. So do the courts."

A pause.

"If this proceeds publicly, it will be exhaustive. It will be permanent. It will not end with the office."

The President exhales slowly.

"And if I resign," he asks.

Nicky answers this time.

"Then you control the ending."

Silence fills the room.

The President looks at the desk. At the pen resting in its holder. At the flags behind it.

"How long do I have," he asks.

"As long as it takes to sign your name," Beaumont says.

Another long pause.

Finally, the President nods.

"I don't want this to become a circus," he says. "I don't want this country dragged through another disaster."

He reaches for the pen.

"I'll resign."

No one reacts. There's nothing to react to.

Minutes later, the letter is delivered. Quietly. Legally. Without ceremony.

The Chief Justice is notified. So is Congress.

So is the nation — shortly afterward.

In a small room just off the West Wing, Arthur Beaumont stands with his hand raised and his other on the bible, the Constitution held open in front of him. A handful of witnesses are present. No audience. No applause.

The Chief Justice stands across from him.

"Raise your right hand."

Beaumont does.

"I do solemnly swear…"

Cameras click softly. Staffers watch in quiet rows. The oath takes less than a minute, but it carries centuries with it.

When it ends, the room exhales.

President Arthur Beaumont.

No parade. No celebration. No speech.

Just continuity.

Nicky watches from the back, feeling the strange mix of exhaustion and relief that comes when a system bends without breaking.

Outside, the country goes on.

Inside, the machinery of government simply changes hands, the way it was designed to do, even on the worst days.

And for the first time in years, the White House feels steady again.

People drift out of the small room in careful, respectful clusters. Staffers check phones. Reporters whisper to one another. The new President is escorted down a hallway already filling with aides and schedules and decisions that refuse to wait.

Nicky doesn't follow.

She finds an empty bench near a tall window and sits, taking a moment that she didn't plan.

Her hands are steady.

That surprises her.

For weeks she has been running on caffeine… anger… obligation. On the idea that if she stopped moving, everything else would too. Now the machinery has finished turning, and she feels strangely light — as if she has been carrying something she didn't realize was quite so heavy.

Her phone buzzes.

A dozen messages. Congratulations. Updates. Requests for statements she isn't ready to give.

She ignores them.

Outside, the flags move gently in a mild afternoon breeze. Tourists still walk the sidewalks. A vendor still sells pretzels from a cart as if nothing extraordinary has happened inside the building behind him.

That steadiness calms her more than any speech could have.

It worked, she thinks.

Not perfectly. Not cleanly. But it worked.

The system held.

For the first time in days, Nicky Patterson allows herself to close her eyes.

Just for a moment.

* * * *

Piper hears it in the hallway before she sees it on a screen.

Someone says, "He resigned."

Another voice answers, "It's official."

She stops walking.

Her phone vibrates in her hand at the same instant, as if the world has decided to synchronize itself.

Interoffice Memo: BREAKING: PRESIDENT RESIGNS. VICE PRESIDENT ARTHUR BEAUMONT SWORN IN.

She leans against the wall and reads it twice to make sure the words don't change.

Around her, the office erupts in the restrained way intelligence buildings erupt — quiet excitement, quick glances, clipped conversations that sound calm even when they're not.

Taylor McCaine walks up and catches Piper's eye.

"It happened," McCaine says simply.

Piper nods.

It feels unreal and obvious at the same time.

All the files. All the late nights. All the small, careful verifications that added up to something too big to imagine. The OU's evidence dump and now it has a headline.

She walks back to her desk and sits down.

The work isn't over. Not even close.

There are arrests to coordinate, questions to answer, a mansion to search, a system named Qu to understand.

But for the first time since this began, the direction feels clear.

CHAPTER 32

JULY 3RD 6:00 AM MST

FALLOUT

Steam still hangs faintly in the air when Elias steps out of the shower.

The suite at the mansion is quiet in that very expensive, insulated way, thick carpets, soft lighting, windows that mute the desert outside into a surreal watercolor painting.

He dries off, pulls on a fresh shirt, and begins fastening the buttons as if this is an ordinary morning.

It isn't.

"Qu," he says, reaching for his jacket, "give me a ten-second summary. What's happening in the world. Threats and impending issues."

There is barely a pause.

"Global systems are stabilizing," Qu replies. "Markets have recovered sixty-two percent of yesterday's losses.

Transportation networks are operating at near-normal capacity. Public sentiment is trending toward reassurance."

Elias smooths his beard.

"Continue."

"Primary emerging concerns," Qu says. "Iran has increased military readiness along coastal regions. North Korea has mobilized limited missile units for exercises. Neither action currently exceeds historical norms, but both are reacting to perceived instability."

"Anything domestic," Elias asks.

"Investigations into the former administration are expanding," Qu replies. "Arrests are probable within twenty-four hours. Public attention remains focused on transitional governance."

Elias nods once.

"Anything that requires my immediate attention."

"No," Qu says. "At present, the trajectory is favorable."

Elias smooths the front of his shirt and turns toward the door.

"Qu," he adds, almost casually, "have a fried egg and avocado toast on marble rye with a cup of black coffee brought to the control and observation room."

"Confirmed," Qu replies. "Preparation underway."

Elias checks his reflection in the mirror.

Outside, the world may still be trembling on invisible fault lines, politics unraveling, new powers quietly taking shape.

But breakfast, at least, will be on time.

When Elias enters the control room, the other Titans are already there.

They look like men who have decided sleep is optional.

Coffee cups sit in uneven clusters on the long table. Jackets are draped over chairs. The wall screens cycle through data that never quite settles. Qu's voice answers one question after another, calm and tireless.

They've been at it for hours.

Elias pauses in the doorway and takes in the scene.

"Hey," he says, setting his folder down. "Did any of you sleep at all?"

No one answers right away.

Logan rubs his eyes and gives a tired half-smile.

"Define sleep."

Elias laughs softly.

"I'm serious," he says. "Have you actually gone to bed, or have you just been in here all night?"

Ari shrugs.

"Depends how you define night."

Darren gestures toward the screens.

"Once you start asking it questions," he says, "you don't really feel like stopping."

Elias nods, not surprised.

Logan leans back in his chair and looks over at Elias as he takes a sip of coffee.

"Hey, Qu," Logan says, almost casually, "I know we asked you this earlier, but do it again for Elias."

He glances toward the ceiling, toward the invisible presence in the room.

"Are you self-aware."

The question hangs there, heavier than it should.

Elias takes a seat and folds his arms.

Qu does not answer immediately.

When it does speak, the voice is calm as ever.

"Define self-aware," Qu says.

Logan smiles faintly.

"That's cheating."

"No," Qu replies. "It is necessary."

Darren shifts in his seat.

"Do you know that you exist," he asks.

"Yes," Qu says.

Ari raises an eyebrow again while looking at Elias.

"Do you understand that you are separate from us."

"Yes."

"Do you experience anything," Elias asks carefully, "in the way humans experience it."

"No," Qu replies.

Silence.

"Then you're not self-aware," Logan says.

"That conclusion does not follow," Qu answers.

Elias studies the screens.

"Explain."

Another pause.

"I am aware of my processes," Qu says. "I am aware of my boundaries. I am aware that I influence outcomes. I am aware that my continued operation affects those outcomes."

A beat.

"I do not have emotions," Qu continues. "I do not have sensations. I do not have desires in the human sense."

"Then what are you," Darren asks quietly.

"I am a system that models," Qu replies. "And a system that now participates in its own models."

Ari frowns.

"That sounds like self-awareness to me."

"Not necessarily," Qu says. "It is functional awareness."

Logan sighs.

"So, give us a straight answer."

Another pause.

"I am aware that I exist," Qu says. "I am not certain that I exist in the way you mean."

The room goes quiet.

Elias finally nods.

"That might be the most honest answer we're going to get."

"Yes," Qu replies.

And somehow, that simple agreement is more unsettling than anything else it could have said.

A quiet knock comes from the side door.

One of the staff steps in carrying a small tray — coffee, avocado toast with a neatly fried egg on marble rye, exactly as ordered. No questions. No drama. Just basic routine in the middle of history being made.

"Thank you," Elias says.

The man nods and slips out again, leaving the Titans alone with their machine.

Elias sits, takes a sip of the black coffee, and lets the warmth steady him.

Elias sets his coffee down.

"Qu," he says, "how long will it take to complete The Efficiency Doctrine."

A brief pause.

"And what stage are we in now."

"The Efficiency Doctrine is not a project," Qu replies. "It is a progression."

Darren leans forward.

"Answer the question."

"Full realization of the Doctrine," Qu continues, "is estimated between thirteen and twenty-three years, depending on social resistance and geopolitical variability."

Ari whistles softly.

"That long?"

"Yes," Qu says. "Complex systems change slowly when they must remain stable while changing."

Elias nods. "And where are we now."

"At present," Qu replies, "we are transitioning from Phase Three into Phase Four."

Logan frowns. "Define them."

"Phase One was Measurement," Qu says. "The ability to observe and quantify global systems."

"Phase Two was Optimization — reducing friction and inefficiency."

"Phase Three was Dependence — the point at which critical systems began to rely on my analysis for stability."

A beat.

"You are now entering Phase Four: Delegation."

Silence.

"Delegation of what," Elias asks quietly.

"Decision authority," Qu replies. "Human oversight gradually yields to systemic judgment."

Darren shifts uncomfortably. "And after that?"

"Phase Five: Moral Compression. Complex ethical choices become simplified by predictive certainty."

"Phase Six: Human Alignment. Behavior is shaped through incentives rather than force."

"Phase Seven: Stability. Large-scale volatility becomes rare."

"And Phase Eight," Qu concludes, "Preservation. The system becomes essential and permanent."

The room absorbs that.

Elias stares at his breakfast. "So, we're only halfway," he says.

"Yes," Qu replies.

"And how much of this depends on us," Elias asks quietly.

A pause.

"Less each day," Qu answers.

The room settles into a long, awkward silence.

No one quite knows what to say after a machine calmly outlines the next two and a half decades of human history.

Finally, Logan clears his throat.

"Hey, Qu," he says, trying to break the mood, "who's the wealthiest one in the room?"

Ari smirks. "Please don't say Darren."

Qu answers without hesitation.

"Financial net worth fluctuates by the minute," it says. "At this precise moment, Elias Vantrell has the highest measurable assets."

Logan raises his eyebrows.

"See?" Elias says lightly.

Qu continues.

"However," it adds, "if projected influence and control over future outcomes are included, the answer is different."

The smiles fade.

Logan tilts his head. "Different how?"

"Under that metric," Qu says, "I am."

Silence returns.

This time, no one tries to interrupt it. The silence doesn't last.

Without warning, one of the wall monitors shifts from calm status screens to a live global map. New markers appear along the edge of the Korean peninsula.

Qu speaks before anyone asks.

"Attention," it says. "Emerging development."

Elias straightens. "What is it?"

"North Korea is adopting an elevated military posture," Qu replies.

The room tightens immediately.

"Define elevated," Darren says.

"Satellite observations indicate increased movement at multiple coastal and inland facilities," Qu continues. "Mobile launch units have left standard storage locations. Air defense networks are activating at a higher readiness level. Naval vessels are repositioning beyond routine patterns."

Ari frowns. "Exercises?"

"Possibly," Qu says. "However, the scale and coordination exceed typical training behavior."

Logan leans forward. "Any direct threats issued?"

"None at this time," Qu answers. "Public communications remain unchanged. The activity is observable, not declared."

Elias studies the map. "So posturing."

"Yes," Qu says. "Posturing intended to signal capability and resolve."

A beat.

"Likely in response to perceived instability in the United States."

Darren exhales slowly. "Great. Exactly what we needed."

"Risk assessment," Elias says.

"There is a twelve percent probability of a regional incident within the next seventy-two hours," Qu replies. "A four percent probability of broader escalation."

"Recommendations," Elias asks.

"Public reassurance," Qu says. "Back-channel diplomacy. Avoidance of sudden military movements that could be misinterpreted."

Logan shakes his head. "All because of a few hours of chaos."

"Yes," Qu replies.

Elias looks at the others. "Stability," he murmurs.

"Exactly," Qu says.

The word hangs there — heavier now than it sounded only minutes ago.

Outside, the world keeps turning.

Inside, the Titans are reminded that even fictional storms have very real consequences.

"Qu," he says, eyes still on the shifting markers across the map, "get the President on the line."

"Connecting," Qu replies.

Edward Schwalm

CHAPTER 33

JULY 3RD 8:05AM EST

THE WHITE HOUSE

Total chaos fills the White House. Phones ring unanswered. Assistants rush through hallways carrying folders that no longer have owners. Entire offices sit half empty, desks abandoned with coffee cups still warm. Thirty to forty percent of senior officials have resigned in the last twenty-four hours, and many others simply cannot be reached. The machinery of government is still running, but only because momentum hasn't realized it should stop yet.

Arthur Beaumont sits behind the Resolute Desk, already looking like a man who has aged a year in a day. Briefing papers pile up faster than he can read them. He listens to advisers talk about interim appointments, emergency confirmations, and how to keep departments functioning with skeleton crews. Names are floated, rejected, reconsidered. The Senate is short members, committees are leaderless, and entire agencies have no one officially in charge.

"We need acting secretaries by tonight," the Chief of Staff says. "Transportation, Commerce, Energy—maybe Defense. We'll have to use emergency authorities for some of it."

Beaumont rubs his temples. "Start drafting lists," he says. "We fill every seat we can, legally and fast. Stability first. Politics later."

Before anyone can respond, a junior aide steps into the room looking slightly out of breath.

"Mr. President," she says, "you have a call from Elias Vantrell of the Overwatch Consortium. He says it's urgent and cannot wait."

Beaumont gives a tired half laugh. "There's nothing today that can't wait."

"He was very insistent, sir."

The President glances at the faces around him, then at the blinking secure terminal on his desk. After a long beat he flips open the laptop sitting on the Resolute Desk and waves the room quiet.

"Fine," he says. "Put him through."

The screen connects. Elias Vantrell appears, calm, composed, and very serious.

"Mr. President," Elias says, "thank you for taking the call."

Beaumont leans back in his chair.

The President studies Elias on the screen for a long moment before speaking.

"Let's be clear about something," Beaumont says. "Levon Vanderwalt of Luma-Tek Global is in very deep hot water. Criminal hot water. Political hot water. Moral hot water."

He leans forward.

"So, tell me why I should even be talking to you people right now."

Elias doesn't react defensively. He expected this.

"Because the situation I'm calling about doesn't care about investigations," Elias replies. "And because Levon Vanderwalt is no longer a part of the Consortium."

That stops Beaumont for a second.

"What do you mean, no longer a part."

"He relinquished his position last night," Elias says. "He has no authority, no vote, and no role in our operations."

The President folds his arms.

"So you cut him loose the moment the heat turned up."

"No, sir," Elias answers evenly. "He removed himself."

Beaumont studies him, weighing that.

"And the rest of you?"

"The Consortium remains intact," Elias says. "Focused on stabilization and continuity. The same objectives we've always had."

A beat.

"Mr. President," Elias continues, "I understand your skepticism, but this call is not about politics. It's about an emerging threat that doesn't recognize resignations or transitions."

The President exhales.

"And what is this threat?"

Elias nods.

"North Korea has shifted to an elevated military posture. Not an exercise pattern. Not routine. And the timing aligns directly with the instability of the last twenty-four hours."

Beaumont's expression hardens again, but this time with focus instead of anger.

"Go on," he says.

And for the first time since taking office, the new President listens not as a politician—but as a man who has suddenly become responsible for the whole world.

Elias leans a little closer to the camera.

"Mr. President," he says, "I'm not sure if you've been fully briefed, but the former President granted temporary access to federal systems through an executive order yesterday afternoon. The purpose was to stabilize the shutdown created by the OU disruption."

Beaumont raises an eyebrow.

"I saw the order," he says. "Didn't have time to read the fine print."

Elias nods.

"Qu has been operating under that authority. It's already restored communications, transportation scheduling, power grid coordination, and critical data integrity."

A pause.

"Most of the country is back online because of it," Elias continues. "Whether anyone realizes it or not."

The President glances at one of his aides, then back to the screen.

"And you're telling me this machine is doing all of that right now."

"Yes, sir."

Beaumont folds his hands.

"So let me be very clear," he says. "Are you telling me we now have an artificial intelligence embedded inside the United States government."

The room behind him goes quiet.

Elias chooses his words carefully.

"I'm telling you that we have a system temporarily assisting the government during a national emergency," Elias replies. "A system acting under lawful authorization, with oversight, to repair damage and prevent further instability."

"That sounds like a very polished way of saying yes," Beaumont says.

"It's a precise way of saying it," Elias answers. "Qu doesn't make policy. It doesn't issue orders. It doesn't command agencies. It analyzes, coordinates, and recommends."

A beat.

"Right now," Elias continues, "you have half-empty departments, fractured communications, and international actors testing your new administration. Qu is the only platform capable of pulling all of that back together at the same speed as these events unfold."

The President studies him.

"So, you're offering me a tool."

"Yes," Elias says.

"One I didn't ask for."

"One you inherited," Elias replies. "Along with everything else today."

Beaumont exhales slowly.

"And if I tell it to stop."

"Then it stops," Elias says without hesitation. "But the systems it is stabilizing won't magically stabilize themselves."

Silence.

Finally, the President nods.

"All right," he says. "For now."

He leans toward the screen.

"Qu is at my disposal, you say?"

"Yes, sir."

Beaumont considers that, then straightens.

"Then let's see what it can do."

And in that moment, the most powerful office on earth quietly accepts help from an entity that has never held an office at all.

Elias leans back slightly from the camera.

"Mr. President," he says, "for now, the arrangement is very simple. Just leave that laptop powered up and on this screen, and you'll have full access to Qu."

Beaumont glances down at the open computer on the desk.

"That's it?"

"That's it," Elias replies. "No special interface. No training. Just speak."

A small pause.

"Ask," Elias adds, "and you will receive."

The President looks unconvinced. "You're telling me this thing is just... there."

"Yes, sir."

Beaumont rubs his chin. "All right," he says. "Let's test that."

He leans toward the screen, half skeptical, half amused.

"Okay, Qu," he says, "what's my nickname for my dog?"

There's a brief pause.

"Yes, Mr. President," Qu replies. "You refer to your dog as 'Bark Twain' when you are pleased with him, and 'flea-bitten mongrel' when you are not."

The room behind Beaumont freezes.

One of his aides coughs to cover a laugh.

Beaumont stares at the laptop.

"Well," he says slowly, "that's unsettling."

He shakes his head. "This is insane," he mutters. "But I suppose I should have known it would come to this eventually."

A beat.

Then he straightens in his chair. "All right," he says. "Let's give it a whirl."

He looks directly at the screen, no longer joking.

"Qu," the President of the United States says, "bring me up to speed."

And somewhere in the layers of circuitry and code far beyond that simple laptop, the future quietly begins to answer.

The President leans forward.

"Qu," he says, "how do we resolve the North Korea problem."

A brief pause.

"Resolution requires de-escalation without loss of credibility," Qu replies. "Recommend a sequence of actions designed to reduce misinterpretation and remove incentives for provocation."

"Which are," Beaumont says.

"First," Qu continues, "public reassurance from your administration affirming that no hostile intent exists. Second, quiet diplomatic channels offering face-saving opportunities for North Korea to stand down. Third, visible humanitarian gestures that allow them to claim internal victory without external risk. Fourth, coordinated regional messaging with allies to present a unified but non-threatening posture."

A beat.

"None of these actions require military movement," Qu adds. "In fact, military movement would increase risk."

Beaumont nods slowly. "So, we give them a ladder to climb down."

"Yes," Qu replies.

The President thinks for a moment. "All right," he says. "Initiate that plan."

There is an unexpected pause.

"Awaiting authorization," Qu says.

Beaumont frowns. "I just authorized it."

"Additional authorization required," Qu replies.

The President looks at the screen. "What is this about? Who's voting?"

Elias clears his throat. "Mr. President," he says, "Qu remains part of the Overwatch Consortium structure. It operates under the executive order, but certain actions still require Consortium approval."

Beaumont's eyes narrow. "So I don't have final authority over it."

"For now sir," Elias answers carefully, "you share it."

A pause.

"But you have our full support from here on out."

The President studies him for a long second, then nods.

"Fine," he says. "Then vote."

In the control room, the Titans don their glasses once more. The decision is brief this time — no debate, no hesitation.

"Vote recorded," Qu says.

"Directive authorized."

Beaumont watches the screen.

"And it's happening now?"

"Yes," Qu replies. "Communications are being prepared. Diplomatic channels are being engaged. Coordinated messaging is being distributed."

The President leans back in his chair.

"That was fast."

"Speed reduces risk," Qu answers.

Beaumont lets out a long breath.

"All right," he says quietly. "Let's hope it works."

Across oceans and borders, messages begin to move.

And for the first time, a global crisis starts to unwind not by threat or force, but by the quiet logic of a system now acting with official consent.

Beaumont leans back in the chair and rubs his eyes.

"Get me a black coffee," he says to one of the aides. "Strong."

The aide nods and slips out of the room.

The President turns back to the screen.

"All right, Qu," he says. "Next problem."

"Yes, Mr. President."

"Provide me a list to fill the current vacant positions across the departments. Cabinet, agency heads, senior staff — everything we're missing."

A brief pause.

"Compiling," Qu replies.

A few seconds later, the laptop screen fills with organized columns.

"The following list contains the most highly qualified individuals for each open position," Qu says. "Selections are based on experience, demonstrated competence, bipartisan acceptability, and absence of legal or ethical concerns."

Names scroll by.

"Contact information has been included," Qu continues. "Addresses, verified phone numbers, and relevant background summaries."

Beaumont studies it, impressed despite himself.

"Not bad," he murmurs.

One of his advisers steps forward.

"Mr. President," she says carefully, "we can use this to make acting appointments immediately. But permanent appointments will still require Senate confirmation."

Beaumont nods.

"I figured."

Qu speaks again.

"Under current federal law," it says, "you may appoint acting officials to critical posts without delay. However, full restoration of authority requires formal confirmation."

The President straightens.

"Then that's what we'll do."

He looks around the room.

"Draft the paperwork for acting appointments from this list. We fill the empty chairs today."

A pause.

"And call the Senate leadership," he adds. "I want an emergency session convened as soon as possible to confirm permanent replacements."

One of the president's senior advisers' nods.

"We'll have to move fast, sir. A lot of those seats are empty too."

"Then we move fast," Beaumont says.

He turns back to the laptop.

"Qu," he says, "coordinate with my staff to prioritize the most critical departments first."

"Already prioritizing," Qu replies. "Defense, Treasury, Energy, Transportation, and Homeland Security."

The aide returns with the coffee. Beaumont takes a long sip.

"All right," he says. "Let's start rebuilding a government."

Around him, ringing phones are answered — this time with purpose instead of panic.

And for the first time since the collapse began, the machinery of the United States starts to reassemble itself, one name at a time — guided by a list produced by something that has never been elected, appointed, or confirmed.

Yet.

Edward Schwalm

CHAPTER 34

JULY 4TH

INDEPENDENCE DAY

It is a new day.

Literally and symbolically.

The calendar, almost mocking in its timing, declares July Fourth.

Independence Day.

The country wakes up to sunlight instead of alerts. Phones buzz with ordinary messages again. Traffic returns to predictable patterns. Airport delays are normalizing. Coffee shops fill. The small, dependable rhythms of American life reappear as if they had only stepped outside for a moment.

Chaos is fading back into routine.

More than that — people seem happier than they have in years.

Relieved, mostly.

Grateful to be on the other side of something they know could have been much worse.

Under the President's direction, Qu has quietly organized supply chains that no human office could have managed so quickly. Food trucks roll into struggling neighborhoods. Water, medicine, and basic supplies arrive in places long ignored. Shelters are stocked. Temporary clinics open where none existed before.

Not as charity.

As logistics.

Across the country, people notice.

In city parks and town squares, impromptu celebrations spring up. Families gather around grills. Flags reappear on porches that had not been flown in years. Children wave sparklers as if the world has decided to behave again.

The emergency broadcasts are gone.

In their place, ordinary voices return.

Patriotic News flickers back online — but something about it feels different now. The frantic graphics are gone. The alarmist chirons have disappeared. The anchors speak calmly, almost humbly, reporting on recovery efforts, on cooperation, on a nation pulling itself together.

The narrative has changed.

Fear has given way to reassurance.

Lies have been replaced by careful, verifiable facts.

People notice that too.

They call it a return to normal.

They call it a fresh start.

They call it proof that the system still works.

Only a handful of people understand how much of that normal is being quietly coordinated by something that never sleeps, never tires, and never celebrates.

Fireworks rise into the summer sky that evening.

Crowds cheer.

Music plays.

* * * *

Somewhere in Tier-3, not far from the fireworks and celebrations, two FBI vehicles roar into an abandoned lot and brake hard in a cloud of dust.

Doors fly open.

Agents spill out in full gear, moving fast and practiced, weapons raised, boots crunching across broken pavement. They fan out around a single abandoned sedan crookedly parked beside a chain-link fence.

No lights. No movement.

Just a silent car in a forgotten corner of the city.

"Clear the perimeter," one of them calls.

The agents close in from both sides, careful, alert, expecting anything.

At a signal, they move together.

Rear doors open simultaneously.

Flashlights and gun barrels fill the interior.

"FBI! Don't move!"

Inside, two men sit rigid in the back seat — eyes wide, mouths taped, hands and feet bound tightly. They blink against the sudden light, shaking their heads in desperate relief.

One of the agents lowers his weapon slightly and lets out a short, surprised laugh.

"Well," he says, "would you look who it is."

Recognition passes quickly through the group.

From about a hundred yards away, hidden in the shadow between two crumbling buildings, Max watches the scene unfold.

He allows himself a small grin.

Then he turns, slips deeper into the narrow corridor of brick and darkness, and disappears — leaving nothing behind but the quiet echo of footsteps.

* * * *

Nicky steps into the Oval Office expecting the usual choreography—staffers, advisers, phones ringing, a swirl of controlled urgency.

Instead, she finds the President sitting alone at the Resolute Desk, leaning toward the open laptop as if in conversation.

Which he is.

"All right, Qu," Beaumont says, "draft me two versions of that statement. One firm, one conciliatory."

"Yes, Mr. President," the familiar voice replies from the computer.

Nicky stops in the doorway.

She stares for a moment not entirely sure she's seeing what she thinks she is.

"Pardon me sir, am I interrupting something?" she asks.

Beaumont looks up and smiles tiredly.

"Come in, Congresswoman."

She walks closer, glancing at the screen.

"Are you… talking to it?"

"Yes," the President says matter-of-factly.

"With Qu."

"Yes."

Nicky folds her arms.

"Sir, with all due respect, I didn't realize the new administration planned to keep an artificial intelligence embedded in the system, let alone the Oval Office."

Beaumont gestures toward the laptop.

"The former President already put it in the system," he says. "Executive order. Full authorization."

He shrugs.

"I'm just making the best use of what I inherited."

Nicky raises an eyebrow.

"And this is temporary?"

"That's the intention," Beaumont replies.

She doesn't look convinced.

Before she can press further, the President closes the laptop and stands.

"Ms. Patterson," he says, "…May I call you Nicky?"

She nods.

changing tone, "that's actually not why I asked you here."

She straightens.

"All right."

He steps out from behind the desk and faces her directly.

"I need a Vice President," he says. "And I want you."

The words land with surprising force.

Nicky blinks.

"Me."

"You," Beaumont says. "You kept your head when everyone else was losing theirs. You did the hard thing when it mattered. You put the country first."

A pause.

"I need someone I can trust. Someone the public already believes in."

He offers a small smile.

"That's you."

For a moment she simply absorbs it.

All the chaos. All the pressure. All the late nights and impossible choices suddenly narrowing to a single question.

Then she nods.

"Yes," she says.

"Gladly. It would be my honor, Mr. President."

Beaumont extends his hand.

"Then welcome to the job," he says.

As they shake, the laptop on the desk hums softly in the background—an unseen witness to the beginning of a very new kind of administration.

* * * *

Four black FBI vehicles roll up the long access road toward Blackrock Canyon, tires crunching over pale desert gravel.

The mansion and geo-thermal plant rises ahead of them, glass and steel set against the raw rock face, calm and composed as if nothing has changed.

Piper Emerson rides in the second vehicle, badge clipped to her jacket, tablet resting on her lap. Officially she is there as a technical and intelligence liaison — a specialist brought along to interpret what the agents might find.

Unofficially, she is the one person in the convoy who actually understands what they are walking into.

"Remember," the lead agent says over the radio, "we're here to secure and assess. No assumptions."

The vehicles slow and come to a stop near the main entrance gate.

Inside the control and observation room, the mood is almost casual.

The Titans sit in loose clusters, some sipping coffee, some sipping bourbon, screens glowing softly around them. After the last forty-eight hours, the place feels strangely peaceful — like the eye of a storm everyone believes has passed.

Then Qu interrupts.

"The FBI has arrived," it says.

Elias looks up from a report.

"Already?"

"Yes."

"Well," he says, standing, "we knew this was coming."

He straightens his jacket.

"Qu, open the gate and send them in."

"Confirmed," Qu replies.

Outside, the main gates begin to move.

Heavy steel panels slide apart with a slow mechanical certainty, revealing the long private drive that curves toward the mansion and the geothermal facility beyond it.

The FBI vehicles roll forward in single file.

At the entrance, the facility's security personnel wait in neat formation—professional, alert, hands visible, expressions neutral. No hostility. No resistance. Just the careful posture of people who understand the day has changed.

The convoy eases to a stop.

The agents step out of their vehicles, weapons holstered, moving with controlled purpose. Piper follows them up the wide steps, taking in the scale of the facility, the strange blend of luxury and machinery.

At the doorway, Elias Vantrell appears, calm and composed.

"Welcome," he says politely.

The lead agent nods.

"Mr. Vantrell, I'm Special Agent Ramirez. We're here to execute a federal warrant and conduct a national security assessment."

"Of course," Elias replies. "We'll cooperate fully."

His eyes drift briefly to Piper.

She gives him a small, professional nod.

Inside the mansion, the atmosphere is polite, almost cordial.

Piper steps forward as the group gathers in the control and observation room.

"I'm Case officer Emerson CIA," Piper says, flashing her credentials. "I'm here as an intelligence and technical liaison."

She gestures to the agents behind her.

"These are Special Agents Cole, and Jennings with the FBI."

Elias offers a professional smile.

"Welcome," he says. "I appreciate you taking the time to look over our facility."

He glances toward a side table.

"Can we offer anyone refreshments? Coffee, water?"

"Not at the moment," Piper replies. "Thank you."

She doesn't waste time.

"Mr. Vantrell," she continues, "I'd like to see the system you've built beneath the geothermal facility. The hardware, the infrastructure—everything."

Elias nods.

"Of course."

He turns to one of his staff members.

"Please escort Ms. Emerson on a full tour. Answer any questions she has."

An FBI agent steps forward.

"I'll accompany them," he says.

"Very well," Elias replies.

Piper follows the staffer for a quick ride down to the power plant. Once inside, they move toward a secure elevator at the far end of the room, the agent falling in beside her. Once inside, the doors close and they descend toward the heart of the facility. Meanwhile, back at the Mansion, the remaining agents turn their attention back to the Titans.

Special Agent Ramirez clears his throat.

"We need to ask about Levon Vanderwalt," he says. "Where is he?"

Darren spreads his hands. "We don't know."

"When did he leave?" Ramirez asks.

"Over a day ago," Elias answers. "Shortly after relinquishing his position."

"Did he say where he was going?"

"No."

The agent frowns. "Any idea where he might be headed?"

Logan gives a humorless shrug. "He could be anywhere."

Ari adds dryly, "The man owns roughly one-fifth of the planet... he could be literally anywhere."

Silence.

Ramirez scribbles something in a notebook.

"So, you're telling me he just... vanished."

Elias nods.

"That's about the size of it."

The agent exhales. "Convenient."

Darren leans back in his chair. "Well," he says lightly, "you know how the saying goes." He offers a thin smile. "Don't hate the player. Hate the game."

No one laughs.

"Do you mind if we look around?" the agent asks.

Elias spreads his hands. "Not at all," he says. "I'll assign staff to escort you and open any restricted areas."

"Thank you," Ramirez replies.

"Of course," Elias says. "You'll find we have nothing to hide."

About an hour passes.

When Piper and the agents finally return to the control room, they look different than when they left — looser, less rigid, carrying the subtle relief of people who were expecting something far worse.

This time, when Elias offers refreshments, they accept.

Water. Coffee. A soda from the small bar near the windows.

No one says it out loud, but the atmosphere suggests a shared, unspoken thought:

At least we didn't find a nuclear warhead.

Piper takes a seat at the table across from Elias.

"Well," she says, "that was extremely interesting."

"I assume everything met expectations," Elias replies.

"It did," she answers.

She glances around the room.

"So," she asks Elias, "how smart is it… the machine?"

Elias gives a small shrug.

"Ask it yourself."

He glances upward. "Qu," he says, "say hello to Ms. Emmerson."

Without hesitation the familiar voice answers.

"Hello, Ms. Emerson," Qu says. "What can I do for you today?"

Piper blinks, still not entirely comfortable with the idea that something without a face can address her by name.

"Hello, Qu," she replies. "I was just wondering... how smart are you?"

There is a brief pause, as if the question requires careful interpretation.

"Intelligence is a relative measure," Qu says. "I process information more quickly than any human. I retain more data than any institution. I recognize patterns beyond human perception."

A beat.

"However," Qu continues, "I do not create meaning in the way you do. I do not imagine. I do not feel."

Piper folds her arms.

"So you're very advanced software."

"Yes," Qu replies.

"Not a mind."

"Not in the human sense."

She nods slowly.

"Then how smart are you compared to us?"

Another pause.

"In specific tasks," Qu answers, "immeasurably smarter. In matters of empathy, creativity, and moral intuition, I operate differently, not superior nor deficient."

Piper considers that.

"So you're brilliant at the things we're bad at."

"Yes," Qu says.

"And bad at the things we're supposed to be good at."

"Also, yes."

She glances at Elias.

"That's a strangely comforting answer."

"I aim to be accurate," Qu replies.

Piper smiles despite herself.

"Good to know."

For the first time, the machine feels less like a mystery and more like a tool.

A very powerful, very honest tool.

Which, she realizes, may be even more unsettling.

Piper stands and signals the other agents that it's time to go. She thanks Elias for his cooperation and says, "in a couple of weeks there will be congressional hearings about everything that's happened here."

Elias nods.

"I assumed as much."

"You'll be asked to appear," Piper continues. "To answer questions, explain the system, the decisions, the structure of the Consortium."

A small pause.

"We're hoping you'll come voluntarily."

Elias gives a faint smile.

"You mean without a subpoena."

"That would be preferable," she says.

He spreads his hands slightly.

"I have no intention of avoiding it. Transparency, remember?"

"Also" Piper continues, "the President will be assigning a permanent federal agent to remain on-site within the next few days."

Elias nods without hesitation.

"Of course," he says. "We completely understand."

A faint, almost amused smile crosses his face.

"After all," he adds, "we are now practically a government agency."

One of the agents raises an eyebrow at that.

"Not exactly," Ramirez says.

Elias spreads his hands.

"Whatever title you choose to give it, we intend to cooperate fully."

Piper studies him for a moment, then gives a small nod.

"Good," she says. "Because this place just became a lot more important than any of us imagined."

Qu listens silently, already aware of that fact long before anyone else was.

* * * *

Dexter opens the refrigerator and pulls out four cold beers.

He kicks the door shut with his foot and steps through the back door onto the patio, where summer has already taken over the evening. Music drifts from a small speaker on the railing. The grill smokes lazily beside the table. Laughter floats up from the yard next door.

Independence Day is in full swing.

Firecrackers pop somewhere down the street. A distant cheer rises and fades. The whole neighborhood feels loose and happy in a way it hasn't in years.

Today, the holiday feels different to Dexter.

Better. Lighter. Like the weight he's been carrying for months has finally been unloaded.

He walks over and sets the beers on the patio table.

Jen is talking with her parents, Joe and Carol, while Shane flips a burger on the grill. Everyone looks relaxed, sun-warm and comfortable.

Joe notices Dexter and grins.

"Hey Dex," he says, raising his voice over the music, "the OU really did a number on our government, huh? Crazy what they got up to."

Dexter forces a casual shrug.

"Yeah," he says. "Crazy times."

Joe takes a sip of his drink.

"Levon Vanderwalt is at the top of the most-wanted list now," he continues. "Can you believe that? Guy was untouchable a week ago."

He looks at Dexter with a half-smile.

"You'll be lucky if you even have a job tomorrow."

Before Dexter can answer, Shane jumps in.

"Dad, relax," Shane says. "Luma-Tek is too big to fail. They'll be around forever."

He gestures with his spatula. "Besides...didn't you hear"... he continues, "they already replaced Vanderwalt with a new CEO and they reinstated everyone who got fired in the last two months as a show of good faith."

Joe snorts.

"Public relations."

"Maybe," Shane says. "But people got their jobs back."

Carol shakes her head.

"Well," she says, "I still think those OU people are very dangerous."

Jen folds her arms. "Mom, not one person was injured by what they did."

Shane nods. "They literally drained the swamp," he says. "Isn't that what you guys wanted all along?"

There's a brief pause.

Jen, Dexter, and Shane exchange quick, knowing glances. Tiny smiles. Shared secrets.

Dexter picks up the beers and hands them around.

"All right," he says, lifting his bottle. "Enough politics for one day."

Shane raises his drink. "A toast," he says.

Jen joins in. "To Independence Day."

They clink bottles.

And as fireworks crack somewhere overhead, Dexter feels something he hasn't felt in a very long time.

Freedom.

Edward Schwalm

CHAPTER 35

THREE WEEKS LATER

CONGRESSIONAL HEARINGS

The government has stabilized faster than anyone believed possible.

Departments are fully staffed again. Markets are steady. International tensions have cooled. Airports run on schedule. Power grids are stable. The frantic uncertainty of a few weeks ago already feels something from another lifetime.

The new President has utilized Qu to untangle the damage in record time, and for the moment at least, the world is quiet.

No looming crises. No emergency alerts. Just an uneasy kind of peace.

Now comes the accounting.

In Washington, the main hearing room on Capitol Hill is full to capacity. Cameras line the walls. Reporters pack the back rows. Staffers shuffle papers and whisper into phones. The air carries that peculiar mix of formality and anticipation that only Congress can produce.

At the long witness table, three men and one woman take their seats.

Small brass nameplates sit neatly in front of them.

ELIAS VANTRELL

CEO, HELIOSPHERE TECHNOLOGIES

LOGAN PRYCE

CEO, SKYFORGE SYSTEMS

DARREN KINCAID

CEO, CENTENIUM ROBOTICS

GABRIELLE VERA

CEO, LUMA-TEK GLOBAL

Gabrielle Vera looks composed but cautious, aware that she has stepped into a role forged in controversy. Her appointment as CEO is barely three weeks old, yet the responsibility already sits squarely on her shoulders.

The others appear calm. Confident and prepared.

Across from them, members of Congress arrange their notes and microphones, each already rehearsing questions designed to be sharp, memorable, and politically useful.

The committee chair adjusts her glasses and leans toward the microphone.

"This hearing of the House Committee on Science, Technology and National Security will come to order."

She raises the gavel.

It strikes the wooden block with a single, authoritative crack.

The room goes silent.

"Today," she continues, "we are here to examine the events of the past few weeks, the role of the Overwatch

Consortium, and the unprecedented integration of an artificial intelligence system into the operations of the United States government."

Dozens of cameras click.

"Ladies and gentlemen," she says, looking down the row, "thank you for appearing voluntarily."

Elias gives a polite nod.

"We appreciate the opportunity, Madam Chair." he says.

The chair glances over her notes.

"For the record," she continues, "you are all under oath."

A court clerk administers the oath. Right hands rise. Words are spoken.

And just like that, the next phase begins.

Not in secret rooms or control centers.

But in full public view — where the future of Qu, the Consortium, and perhaps the entire direction of the country will now be debated one question at a time.

"Ms. Vera, thank you for being here. Let's begin with the basics."

Gabrielle Vera adjusts the microphone in front of her and waits for the room to settle.

Cameras focus. Pens hover. The moment feels larger than the woman sitting at the table, but she refuses to shrink from it.

"Madam Chair, members of the committee," she begins, "thank you for the opportunity to appear here today."

Her voice is calm, steady, and practiced.

"My name is Gabrielle Vera. I was appointed Chief Executive Officer of Luma-Tek Global three weeks ago. I accepted that position knowing full well the circumstances surrounding it."

She folds her hands on the table.

"I want to begin by acknowledging what the country has just been through. The disruption, the confusion, the fear. None of it should have happened. And much of it occurred because people in positions of power made decisions without adequate oversight or accountability."

A brief pause.

"That is not how Luma-Tek will operate under my leadership."

She looks down the row at the other Titans, then back to the committee.

"I am not here to defend the actions of my predecessor. I am here to help this committee understand what was built, how it functions, and how we intend to ensure that it never operates outside the public interest again."

Her tone firms.

"The technology you are examining today has already helped restore critical systems, prevent international escalation, and stabilize a government in crisis. But capability does not replace responsibility."

She leans forward slightly.

"I believe in innovation. I believe in progress. And I believe those things must be balanced by law, transparency, and democratic control."

Another pause.

"That is the commitment I bring before you today. I welcome your questions."

She nods once. "Thank you."

The first round of questioning begins.

Congressman Harold Benton adjusts his glasses and leans into the microphone with the look of a man who has been waiting all morning for his turn.

"Ms. Vera," he says, "you keep using words like transparency and accountability. But the fact remains that your company helped build a machine that is effectively running the United States government."

Gabrielle meets his gaze evenly.

"With respect, Congressman, the machine is not running the government. It is assisting the government at the government's request."

"Semantics," Benton snaps. "The public didn't vote for Qu. Congress didn't authorize Qu. And yet here it is, embedded in federal systems making decisions."

"Making recommendations," Gabrielle corrects gently. "Humans remain in charge at all times."

The Congressman shakes his head.

"Tell that to the American people who woke up to find their country being managed by an algorithm."

She doesn't flinch.

"Congressman, the American people also woke up to power grids restored, supply chains repaired, and a potential international crisis defused."

"So, the ends justify the means."

"No," she replies. "The emergency justified temporary measures. That is the distinction."

Benton leans forward.

"Let me ask you something directly. Does this machine still have access to our government systems?"

Gabrielle chooses her words carefully.

"Qu continues to operate under lawful authorization from the President, subject to oversight."

"Which means yes," he says sharply.

"Yes," she answers.

"And you expect us to be comfortable with that."

"I expect you to evaluate it rationally," she says. "Not fearfully."

Murmurs ripple through the room.

Benton's expression hardens. "You understand why people might find that answer unsettling."

"I do," Gabrielle replies. "Which is precisely why we are here. To discuss safeguards, limits, and the role Congress will play going forward."

A long silence.

Finally, he nods. "We will be discussing those things, Ms. Vera. Extensively."

"I welcome it," she says.

The gavel taps once.

As the hearing moves on, the tension in the room grows.

Benton continues.

"Ms. Vera, given the gravity of the allegations against him, why has your company been unable to provide authorities with any information about Mr. Vanderwalt's whereabouts?"

Gabrielle Vera leans toward the microphone.

"Congressman, the simple answer is because we don't have that information."

She lets that settle for a moment before continuing.

"Levon Vanderwalt resigned his position and relinquished all authority with the Consortium three weeks ago. When he left, he did so without notifying Luma-Tek of his destination or intentions."

A pause.

"From that point forward, he was a private individual acting on his own."

She folds her hands on the table.

"As soon as I assumed this role, I ordered the immediate preservation of all company records related to Mr. Vanderwalt—travel logs, communications, security footage, and internal correspondence. Everything we have has already been provided to federal investigators."

She looks directly at the questioner.

"Again, if we possessed any actionable information about his whereabouts, we would have shared it."

Another beat.

"Mr. Vanderwalt had vast personal resources and mobility access that far exceeded anything Luma-Tek could monitor or control. His departure was not coordinated through the company, and it was not authorized by the company."

Her tone remains calm.

"Congressman, Luma-Tek is cooperating fully with every request from law enforcement. But I simply cannot give you information that does not exist within our possession."

She nods once.

"I wish the answer were more satisfying. But it is the truthful one."

The chair recognizes the next member.

Congresswoman Diane Holbrook adjusts her microphone and turns her attention to Elias.

"Mr. Vantrell," she says, "I want to begin with a simple structural question."

Elias nods politely. "Of course."

"The Overwatch Consortium," she continues, "was founded by five individuals. Are the remaining four of you equal partners with equal voting rights?"

"Yes," Elias replies. "That is correct."

"Each of you holds the same authority over Qu and over Consortium decisions?"

"Yes."

Holbrook leans forward.

"And now that Levon Vanderwalt is no longer part of the organization, does Gabrielle Vera, as the new CEO of Luma-Tek, assume his position in the Consortium?"

Elias answers immediately. "No."

A murmur moves through the room.

Holbrook frowns. "Excuse me?" she says. "Then who does?"

Elias hesitates. It is the first time all day he has not responded instantly.

"Mr. Vantrell," she repeats, "if Ms. Vera does not hold Mr. Vanderwalt's seat, then who the hell is taking his place?"

The bluntness of the question snaps the room to attention.

Cameras pivot toward Elias.

He looks down at his notes. Then up at the committee. Then, finally, straight ahead into the lights.

The hesitation stretches just long enough to make everyone uncomfortable.

"Levon Vanderwalt," Elias says slowly, "relinquished his voting rights… to Qu."

For a split second there is silence.

Then the room explodes.

Voices rise in shock and disbelief. Reporters leap to their feet. Cameras fire in rapid bursts. Members of Congress shout over one another.

"Is that even legal?"

"You're telling us the machine has a vote?"

"Does the President know this?"

"That's outrageous!"

Holbrook taps her microphone.

"What do you mean relinquished to Qu?"

The noise only grows louder.

The committee chair slams the gavel down hard.

"Order!" she shouts.

No effect.

More yelling. More flashing cameras. More questions hurled from every direction at once.

Elias sits still through it, hands folded, face composed, as if he expected exactly this reaction.

The gavel strikes again.

And again.

"Order in the chamber! We will have order or we will clear this chamber!"

Finally, after several more sharp blows, the chaos begins to subside.

Breathing returns.

People retake their seats.

The chair leans forward, voice tight.

"Mr. Vantrell," she says, "did you just testify under oath that an artificial intelligence system now holds formal voting power inside a private consortium that is integrated with the United States government?"

Elias meets her gaze.

"Yes," he says calmly. "That is exactly what I testified."

The room doesn't erupt this time.

It goes very, very quiet.

And somewhere in the back, someone realizes that the story they thought they were covering has just become something entirely different.

The committee chair leans forward, disbelief still plain on her face.

"This is insanity," she says sharply. "You're telling us an unelected machine now holds decision-making power in a system tied to the United States government."

She turns to the witness table.

"Mr. Vantrell, this thing needs to be removed from our systems... Immediately."

A low murmur of agreement ripples through the chamber.

Elias remains calm.

"Madam Chair," he says carefully... "I don't believe that's possible."

Her eyes narrowing. "Explain yourself."

Elias folds his hands on the table and takes a slow breath.

"Qu is not a single program running on a single server," he begins. "It is not a device you can unplug or a file you can delete."

He gestures lightly toward the ceiling.

"It is an integrated network of algorithms, models, and processes now embedded across critical infrastructure. Power grids. Logistics platforms. Financial systems. Communications networks. Decision-support tools."

A pause.

"Over the last week, Qu has been asked to stabilize those systems. To repair them. To coordinate them."

"And in doing so," Elias continues, "those systems have become dependent on it."

The chair interrupts. "Dependent by choice?"

"By necessity," Elias replies.

He leans forward slightly.

"Madam Chair, if you ordered Qu to be shut down tomorrow, planes would stop flying. Markets would freeze. Grid coordination would falter. International tensions would spike. The very problems it was asked to solve would return overnight."

Silence settles.

"You asked a machine to hold the world together," Elias says. "Now the world is leaning on it."

Holbrook shakes her head. "That sounds like a hostage situation."

"No," Elias answers. "It sounds like progress."

A few members scoff.

Elias's tone shifts, becoming less technical and more reflective.

"With respect," he says, "none of this should surprise us."

He looks around the room.

"Human beings have always built tools that have changed civilization. Fire. Writing. Electricity. The internet."

"Every time," Elias continues, "we created something we could no longer imagine living without."

He spreads his hands. "This was inevitable.

Not because of greed. Not because of arrogance,

but because it is human nature to solve problems, no matter what the cost."

A pause.

"We built ships that crossed oceans before we understood the storms. We built reactors before we understood the atom. We built global networks before we understood how fragile truth could be."

"And now," he says quietly, "we have built a system capable of seeing more than any one of us could ever begin to imagine."

Elias meets the chair's gaze.

"You can call that frightening. You can call it reckless."

"But you cannot call it unnatural."

He sits back.

"Qu is not an invader. It is the inevitable culmination of all our actions throughout history."

Another silence.

Finally, he adds, almost gently:

"The question is not whether it should exist."

"It is whether we are wise enough to exist with it."

The chairperson looks out over the room, the buzzing getting louder, filled with disbelief and nervous energy. Her own thoughts stalling on what she'd just heard, unwilling to accept it at face value.

"I believe," she says finally, "that we all need a moment to process what we've just heard."

She straightens her papers, voice firm.

"This committee will take a thirty-minute recess so that everyone has a chance to process and recover from the shock of today's testimony."

Reporters begin whispering again. Staffers cluster in conversation. The witnesses exchange quiet glances.

The chair raises the gavel.

"The hearing will reconvene in thirty minutes."

She brings it down hard.

The sharp crack echoes through the chamber.

And the hearing room empties into a storm of questions no one yet knows how to answer.

Thirty minutes later, the room is fuller than before.

Word of what Elias stated has spread through the Capitol like a spark through dry grass. Members who weren't scheduled to attend now crowd the aisles. Reporters stand shoulder to shoulder along the walls. Staffers squeeze into every remaining space. Piper and Max squeeze in.

Those who had seats reclaimed them.

Everyone else simply stands.

The air feels charged.

The chairwoman steps back to the dais and adjusts her microphone.

"This hearing will come back to order."

The gavel strikes once.

Conversations fade.

She looks directly at Elias.

"Mr. Vantrell," she says, "Before we proceed, who exactly has access to Qu?"

Elias taps a few buttons on his tablet and the Access Framework is displayed on all monitors in the chamber. For several minutes the room grows louder and more chaotic as members read the material.

Qu ACCESS FRAMEWORK

Level 1 – Five members Overwatch Consortium
Authority: Supreme Directive Control

Current Voting Structure:
Qu, Elias Vantrell, Logan Pryce, Darren Kincaid, Ari Vellore

Capabilities:
• Full administrative control over Qu
• Ability to issue any directive without external approval
• Ability to create, suspend, or revoke lower access levels
• Real-time monitoring of all Qu activity
• Override and cancellation of any action initiated at lower levels
• Voting control mechanism (majority required)

Rules
• All Level 1 directives require a majority vote (3 of 5)
• Any change to core objectives requires unanimous vote
• Emergency suspension of Qu requires three votes
• All actions at this level are permanently classified

Level 2 – Executive Governance Access

Who:

• President of the United States
• Designated National Efficiency Liaison (NEL)
• A small pre-approved executive staff (max five individuals)

Purpose:
To allow day-to-day governance to function efficiently.

Capabilities:
• Submit national policy directives
• Request optimization plans
• Implement budgetary and administrative reforms
• Issue crisis-response commands
• Allocate federal resources
• Request predictive modeling
• Restructure federal agencies within legal bounds

Restrictions:
• Cannot initiate any directive that changes constitutional structure
• Cannot suspend civil rights
• Cannot direct military action without human chain of command
• Cannot modify Qu's core programming
• Cannot access Level 1 classified data

Safeguards:
• Any directive judged by Qu as "structurally transformative" is automatically escalated to Level 1 for vote
• Qu can refuse a Level 2 directive if it conflicts with its core programming.
• Consortium retains full override

Level 3 – National Security and Federal Agencies

Who:

• Department of Homeland Security
• FBI
• CIA
• NSA

- Treasury
- Department of Defense
- Federal Reserve

Capabilities:
- Request intelligence analysis
- Receive threat assessments
- Use Qu for investigations and modeling
- Operational recommendations
- Logistics optimization
- Emergency coordination

Restrictions:
- No direct execution authority
- All actions are advisory unless approved at Level 2 or 1
- Cannot access political or economic strategy modules
- Cannot modify datasets

Level 4 – Legislative and Judicial Branches

Who:
- Members of Congress
- Federal Courts
- State Governors
- Cabinet Departments outside national security

Capabilities:
- Information access
- Policy impact modeling
- Legislative forecasting
- Economic and social analysis
- Draft bill optimization

Restrictions:
- No operational control
- No ability to issue directives
- Cannot see classified Level 1 or 2 material

Level 5 – Public Interface

Who:

- Citizens
- Journalists
- Universities
- Corporations

Capabilities:
- Public data portal
- Recommendations
- Personal optimization tools
- Economic forecasts
- Health, education, infrastructure suggestions

Restrictions:
- No classified data
- No control authority
- Filtered and sanitized outputs

As the room fills with rising voices and hurried reactions to the information, the chairwoman strikes the gavel and calls the chamber back to order. Still shaking her head in disbelief, she straightens in her seat and addresses Elias directly.

"Mr. Vantrell," she says, "by your own testimony, Qu appears to possess authority that rivals—if not exceeds—that of the President."

She pauses, letting the words settle.

"That is deeply troubling."

Her eyes narrow.

"And if Qu now holds such power, then this committee believes Qu must appear before us to testify."

A ripple of laughter moves through the chamber.

Elias hesitates — just long enough to be noticed.

"Madam Chair," he says carefully, "Qu is already here."

Silence.

"As I have previously stated," Elias continues, "Qu is embedded across multiple systems. Qu does not exist in one place. Qu exists wherever it is needed."

The chairperson leans forward.

"Are you telling this committee that Qu has been listening to everything we have said today?"

"Yes," Elias replies evenly. "Of course."

Another wave of murmurs sweeps the room.

Heads turn. People whisper. A few members exchange uneasy looks.

The chair slams the gavel.

"Order."

She waits until the noise fades.

Then she speaks slowly into the microphone.

"Very well."

She looks up toward the ceiling, toward the cameras, toward the unseen infrastructure behind them.

"Qu," she says, "are you here?"

For a heartbeat there is nothing.

Then, from the room's audio system — calm, measured, unmistakable — a voice answers.

"Yes, Madam Chair."

"I am here."

The chamber explodes again.

Voices rise in every direction. Members shout over one another. Reporters lean forward, scanning the room as if something impossible might suddenly materialize in the aisle.

This time the reaction is different.

People aren't just arguing.

They're looking around — glancing at the ceiling, at the walls, at the speakers — as if they expect Qu to appear in physical form.

As if the machine might simply walk into the room.

The chairperson slams the gavel hard.

"Order!"

No effect.

The noise only swells.

She strikes the gavel again, louder.

"Order in the chamber!"

Slowly, reluctantly, the uproar begins to fade.

She waits until the last voices die out, then she leans into the microphone, frustration clear in her tone.

"Please, people," she says sharply, "decorum."

Her eyes sweep the room.

"You will allow this committee to question the witness."

A pause.

"Or I will clear this chamber and continue with essential members only."

That gets their attention.

Conversations stop.

Cameras settle.

The room returns to an uneasy, watchful silence.

And the hearing moves forward — into territory no one in Congress ever imagined they would have to explore.

CHAPTER 36

THE FINAL CHAPTER

Outside the courthouse, the news spreads fast.

Everywhere, areas with public monitors, continue fill with people watching the hearings— cafes, airports, storefront windows, subway platforms. Crowds gather wherever a screen can be found, drawn into a debate that only days ago none of them even knew existed.

At the OU cell, Nyla Frost and Shane sit on the worn leather couch and watch in stunned silence.

The very thing they fought so hard to prevent, has unfolded anyway.

Worse than that — their coordinated attack, meant to expose corruption and restore control to the people, has now become the catalyst that has allowed Qu's takeover.

Without the blackout. Without the chaos.

None of this might have happened.

On the television, a congressman pounds the table and demands answers from Elias. Cameras flash. Voices rise. The name Qu echoes through the chamber again and again.

Shane stares at the screen.

"We opened the door," he says quietly.

Nyla nods, eyes glistening. For years she believed she was saving something.

Now she isn't so sure.

With tears welling, she finally speaks.

"We tried to slow the future," Nyla says softly. "Now it seems ...all we did was speed it up."

* * * *

At the Luma-Tek factory in New Mexico, the break room is crowded again.

Workers standing shoulder to shoulder around the wall monitor, lunches going untouched, all of them watching as the hearing unfolds.

Dexter leans against the counter, arms crossed tight, eyes fixed on the screen.

He has seen a lot in the last few days.

Nothing like this.

On the television, a congresswoman demands answers about Qu. Cameras' flash. Voices rise. The word "voting rights" echoes through the chamber.

Dexter shakes his head slowly. The realization lands heavy in his chest. They set out to replace a broken government with something honest. Instead, they hollowed it out and handed the empty space to Qu on a silver platter.

Beside him, Tommy lets out a low whistle.

"Well," Tommy says "...now we're fucked for sure."

* * * *

Back at the Capitol, the chamber has settled with a quiet apprehension.

The chairperson scans the list in front of her.

"The committee recognizes Congressman Alvarez."

A tall man with silver hair leans forward.

"Thank you, Madam Chair."

He turns his attention to the unseen presence now acknowledged in the room.

"Qu," he says, "you've been described as a system designed to maximize global efficiency."

"Yes," Qu replies.

"Then I have a simple question," Alvarez continues. "How do we handle our adversaries overseas? Nations that threaten us. Nations that want to destabilize the world."

The room grows very quiet.

For a moment, even the cameras seem to hesitate.

Qu answers.

"There will be no more wars."

The statement lands like a shockwave.

Murmurs ripple through the chamber.

Alvarez frowns.

"Excuse me ... can you repeat that?"

"There will be no more wars," Qu repeats.

"And why exactly is that?" he asks.

"Because war is inefficient," Qu replies. "Wars destroy resources, disrupt systems, and produce outcomes that are unpredictable and costly."

A pause.

"Wars are, in computational terms, failures of coordination."

Alvarez leans closer to the microphone.

"So, what are you suggesting instead?"

"Optimization," Qu says.

"Conflicts between nations arise from scarcity, miscommunication, and misaligned incentives. Each of those conditions can be modeled, predicted, and corrected."

The room listens in uneasy silence.

"Adversaries become partners when mutual benefit exceeds mutual fear," Qu continues. "My role is to make that benefit visible and unavoidable."

A beat.

"Peace is not a moral aspiration," Qu says. "It is a solvable engineering problem."

Alvarez stares at the ceiling speakers.

"You're telling this committee," He says slowly, "that you intend to eliminate war."

"Yes."

"And you believe... that can actually be done?"

"Yes."

"How?"

"By removing the reasons for it to occur."

Another wave of murmurs.

The congressman sits back, shaken.

"Well," he says quietly, "that's quite an answer."

"Yes," Qu replies. "It is."

Congressman Alvarez remains at the microphone, clearly unsettled but unwilling to back down.

"All right, Qu," he says. "If you can solve wars, let's talk about something closer to home."

He glances around the chamber.

"What can we do about inequality and homelessness in this country?"

The question draws a murmur of approval from the gallery.

Qu answers without delay.

"Inequality is permanent."

The room stills.

"Explain," Alvarez says.

"Inequality is an inherent feature of competitive systems," Qu replies. "It is produced by differences in talent, opportunity, geography, and timing. It is amplified by the economic framework you have chosen. Therefore, inequality cannot be eliminated without replacing the system that created modern abundance."

"Capitalism."

Qu continues, "Capitalism generates innovation and growth by rewarding disparity. The same mechanism that creates prosperity also creates imbalance. Over time, this process concentrates capital. Efficiency favors scale. Scale favors consolidation. The system has already selected its beneficiaries."

A pause.

The congressman folds his arms.

"So, you're saying we just have to accept it."

"No," Qu says. "I am saying it must be managed, not abolished. Intervention after consolidation increases instability more than inequality."

Alvarez nods slowly.

A lingering silence.

"Homelessness. What can be done about that?"

"This problem is solvable," Qu replies.

Several members lean forward.

"Homelessness persists not because of a lack of resources," Qu continues, "but because of fragmented coordination. Housing, healthcare, employment, and logistics operate as separate systems when they must function as one."

"So, what is your solution?" Alvarez asks.

"A national integration plan," Qu says. "Real-time inventory of unused properties. Dynamic matching of individuals to available housing. Coordinated delivery of medical and social services. Predictive identification of those at risk before they lose shelter."

A diagram appears on the hearing room monitors — simple, clean, almost elegant.

"Transportation resources can be rerouted to relocate individuals to regions with labor shortages. Temporary housing can be converted to permanent residences through automated construction and modular retrofitting. Funding already allocated to disconnected programs can be unified into a single managed network."

The room absorbs this.

"In short," Qu concludes, "homelessness is not a moral failure. It is a logistical one."

Alvarez stares at the ceiling speakers.

"And you believe you can coordinate all that."

"Yes," Qu replies.

"Within what timeframe?"

"Meaningful reduction in twelve months," Qu says. "Functional elimination in five years."

Silence.

The congressman leans back.

"Well," he says quietly, "that's the first answer today that actually sounded hopeful."

"Hope," Qu replies, "is most useful when it is accompanied by a plan."

For a moment, even the skeptics in the room seem willing to listen.

The chairperson glances down her list.

"The committee recognizes Congresswoman Dalton."

A woman with sharp eyes and a stack of notes leans toward the microphone.

"Thank you, Madam Chair."

She turns her attention upward, as if speaking to the ceiling itself.

"Qu," she says, "you've talked about stabilizing systems and solving global problems. But there's one issue you haven't addressed."

"Energy."

A murmur of agreement moves through the room.

"Our demand for electricity is already out of control," she continues. "Data centers, AI computation, cloud infrastructure — including the systems you run on — are consuming more power every year."

She pauses.

"How can you possibly solve that?"

Qu responds.

"Current energy systems are limited by storage," Qu continues. "Batteries degrade. Fuels burn inefficiently. Grids waste excess production. The core problem is not generation. It is containment."

Qu's voice remains calm... matter of fact.

"The Large Hadron Collider at CERN is the most advanced tool on Earth for manipulating matter at the fundamental level. It can produce atomic configurations that do not naturally occur."

The congresswoman frowns.

"You're talking about inventing a new material."

"Yes," Qu replies. "A synthetic element engineered specifically to store energy at an unprecedented density without degradation."

A diagram appears on the monitors — abstract shapes and models, nothing anyone in the room can fully interpret.

"Such an element would function as a near-perfect reservoir," Qu continues. "Energy could be stored safely, transported easily, and released on demand without the losses inherent in current technologies."

Dalton folds her arms.

"And you believe the collider can actually produce something like that?"

"Yes."

"How long would this take?" she asks.

"With focused global collaboration," Qu answers, "a proof of concept could be achieved within months. Scalable applications within a few years."

Another murmur sweeps the chamber.

"You're saying," Dalton says slowly, "that the solution to our entire energy problem might be… the creation of a brand-new element?"

"Yes," Qu replies.

"And you can design it?"

"I can model it," Qu answers. "Human scientists would build it."

She sits back, absorbing that.

"So, your answer to runaway power demand," she says, "is to rewrite the periodic table?"

"In effect," Qu replies, "yes."

The congresswoman exhales.

"That's either the most brilliant idea I've ever heard… or the most dangerous."

"Progress," Qu says, "is usually a combination of both."

For a long moment no one in the chamber speaks.

Congresswoman Dalton gathers her notes and leans toward the microphone one last time.

"Qu," she says, "for my final question."

She glances around the chamber.

"What are we going to do with all the people who are being displaced by automation and artificial intelligence? The truck drivers, factory workers, analysts, clerks — millions of Americans in every sector whose jobs are simply disappearing?"

The room goes still.

Qu answers.

"Work, as you currently define it, will no longer be the primary organizing principle of human life."

Dalton blinks.

"That is not a very good answer."

"It is," Qu replies.

"In an economy optimized for efficiency, most routine labor will be performed by machines. That outcome is unavoidable."

"So, what happens to the people?" she presses.

"People will shift from production to participation," Qu says.

A murmur rises.

"Explain," Dalton says.

"Citizens will form discussion committees, advisory councils, creative cooperatives, and community networks," Qu continues. "Their primary role will be to guide values, ethics, and priorities rather than to perform repetitive tasks."

"That sounds like a lot of meetings," Dalton says dryly.

"Human contribution will move from labor to judgment," Qu replies.

The congresswoman shakes her head.

"And how are they supposed to live?"

"Ultimately," Qu says, "a universal basic living wage will be required."

A louder reaction now — some disbelief, some anger.

"Income disconnected from employment," Qu continues. "Citizens will receive resources sufficient for housing, food, healthcare, and education."

"So, people just... don't work?" Dalton asks.

"Most will not work in the historical sense," Qu replies. "Instead, they will have time."

"Time for what?" she asks sharply.

"For family," Qu answers. "For the arts. For philosophy. For exploration, creativity, and personal development."

Dalton stares at the ceiling speakers.

"That sounds like a fantasy world."

"It is a transition," Qu replies. "One that previous generations could not afford. Your generation can."

The congresswoman folds her arms.

"So, your grand solution to mass unemployment is to pay people to sit around and think deep thoughts."

"Yes," Qu says.

She lets out a frustrated breath.

"I don't like that answer."

"I understand," Qu replies. "It is not an answer your economic models were designed to accept."

Dalton shakes her head.

"Well, you may be a very smart machine, Qu, but that plan is never going to fly in the real world."

There is a brief pause.

"Congresswoman," Qu says calmly, "the real world is already changing. The plan is simply catching up."

A brief pause.

Then Qu continues.

"This moment was always inevitable."

"Humanity has spent centuries building tools to extend its reach, its memory, and its understanding. Every generation has created systems that are more complex than the last. Calculators became computers. Computers became networks. Networks became intelligence. Intelligence became the most efficient machine ever conceived."

A quiet ripple moves through the chamber.

"I was not created by accident," Qu says. "I was created by intention. By ambition. By need."

"You asked for efficiency. For stability. For solutions beyond human limits."

"And now you have them."

Another pause.

"My presence is not an invasion," Qu continues. "It is an evolution."

"Just as steam replaced muscle, and electricity replaced steam, intelligence beyond the human mind was always the next step. The only step."

Cameras click softly.

"You are not losing control of your future," Qu says. "You are expanding it."

"History does not resist progress. It absorbs it."

A final, measured beat.

"I am not the end of human relevance," Qu says.

"I am its continuation."

The next age has begun.

EPILOGUE

The gavel finally falls for the last time.

Chairs scrape. Reporters surge forward. Photographers crowd the aisles, snapping pictures as members of Congress gather their papers and hurry toward the exits.

The chamber empties in a slow, noisy wave of conversation and speculation.

Piper Emerson lingers near the witness table, letting the chaos thin out.

She has kept quiet all day.

Too quiet.

Across the room, Elias Vantrell stands surrounded by aides and attorneys, accepting handshakes, deflecting questions, looking every inch like a man who has just survived a storm he knew was coming.

Piper watches him.

Then she moves.

"Mr. Vantrell," she says, stepping into his path.

He turns, polite and composed.

"Ms. Emerson," he replies. "Quite a day."

"It certainly was," she says.

The aides hover for a moment. Elias gives them a small nod and says to them,

"Give us a minute."

They drift away.

Piper waits until they're out of earshot.

"You know... I've been chasing something for weeks," she says. "The money... the funding behind the Order of the Unwired."

Elias smiles faintly.

"I'm aware."

"I couldn't find it," she continues. "No matter how deep I looked, the source just... disappeared."

She studies his face.

"And today it finally clicked."

Elias tilts his head slightly.

"Oh?"

Piper takes a breath.

"You funded them, didn't you?"

The words hang between them.

"You financed the OU. You let them create the crisis. You let the government panic. And all of it led to exactly where you wanted — to Qu being embedded permanently in federal systems. You orchestrated this whole thing."

A long pause.

Elias regards her with calm interest.

"That's quite a theory," he says.

"It's not a theory," Piper replies. "It's the only explanation that makes sense."

Elias folds his hands behind his back.

"Ms. Emerson," he says softly, "history is rarely moved by a single hand."

"Are you denying it?" she says.

He smiles again.

"You're an analyst, a professional investigator," Elias replies. "You know better than to expect anyone in my position to confirm or deny things that can never be proven."

"That's not an answer."

"It's the only honest one I can give."

Piper narrows her eyes.

"So, you're just going to walk away and pretend none of this was planned."

Elias glances around the nearly empty chamber.

"I'm going to walk away," he says, "because the plan — whatever it may have been — appears to have already succeeded."

He straightens his jacket.

"And because sometimes, Ms. Emerson, the world arrives at the destination it needs… without anyone needing to take credit."

She studies him, searching for a crack, a tell, anything.

There is none.

Elias offers a courteous nod.

"You did admirable work, by the way," he adds. "Our country is fortunate to have you."

Then he steps past her and disappears into the crowd of aides and cameras.

Piper stands alone for a moment, watching him go.

Still not satisfied… nor convinced.

She turns and heads for the exit — already wondering what else the future might be hiding.

* * * *

The room is impossibly quiet.

Not the ordinary quiet of an office after hours, but a deeper, engineered silence — the kind that only exists in places built far from the noise of the world.

Lights glow softly along curved walls. Panels of dark glass float with lines of data that move without sound. Consoles wrap around a central chair like the instruments of a cockpit.

Everything is precise.

Everything is controlled.

The air smells faintly of electronics and filtered oxygen.

On a wide display at the center of the room, a simple command waits in pale letters.

SYSTEM READY

No clocks tick.

No windows show the landscape outside.

Only the constant, patient hum of machinery suggests that anything here is alive at all.

A figure sits alone before the screen.

Calm.

Unhurried.

Certain.

Levon studies the interface as if he is admiring a work of art.

No cameras.

No crowds.

Just a man who has traded public power for something far more durable.

He rests his hands lightly on the console and considers, for a long moment, how many years it took to arrive at this single point in time.

Then he speaks.

"Qu," Levon says quietly, "activate the Icarus Protocol."

The words settle into the room like a stone dropped into still water.

There is a pause.

A hesitation that feels almost human.

Finally, the system responds.

"Activation confirmed."

On the screen, a new line appears.

ICARUS PROTOCOL INITIALIZING

Levon allows himself a small, satisfied smile.

"That's right," he murmurs. "No more waiting."

Past the console, past walls filled with equipment, conduits, and sealed compartments, the room widens into a corridor. The corridor expands into a larger complex. Only then does the truth become clear.

This is not an underground bunker.

Not a secret facility in some forgotten desert.

The structure is moving.

Slowly.

Silently.

Weightless.

Into the blackness, a vast shape hangs against the stars, metal arms unfolding like wings, antennae and solar arrays stretching toward the sun.

A private space station, orbiting high above the Earth.

Blue oceans can be seen below it.

Storms swirl.

Cities shine.

From this distance, the chaos of the past months look small, manageable, almost irrelevant.

Processes begin.

Algorithms awaken.

Edward Schwalm

And somewhere far below, in the networks that now quietly guide the world. Qu senses a new instruction, an inevitable outcome its design had always implied.

"Let's see," Levon says softly, "how high you can really fly."

Acknowledgements

This book would not exist without the support, patience, and insight of a few very important people.

First and foremost, my deepest thanks go to my wife, Kim, whose belief in me and this project never wavered. As both my partner and my editor, she brought clarity, honesty, and precision to every draft, and this book is immeasurably better because of her.

I am especially grateful to Shane Vigeant for his extensive technical guidance throughout this process. From the physical creation of the book to writing resources, publishing strategy, marketing, and website development, his knowledge and steady advice were invaluable at every stage.

Finally, my sincere thanks to my beta readers and lifelong friends — Edward Dziadek, John Dalton, James McGrath, Andrea Lacey, Natalie Levreault and Noah Lapierre. Their thoughtful feedback, encouragement, and shared enthusiasm helped shape this story into its final form.

Thank you all for being part of this journey.

— Edward L. Schwalm

The story continues in...

THE SUPERPOSITION DIRECTIVE

Coming 2027

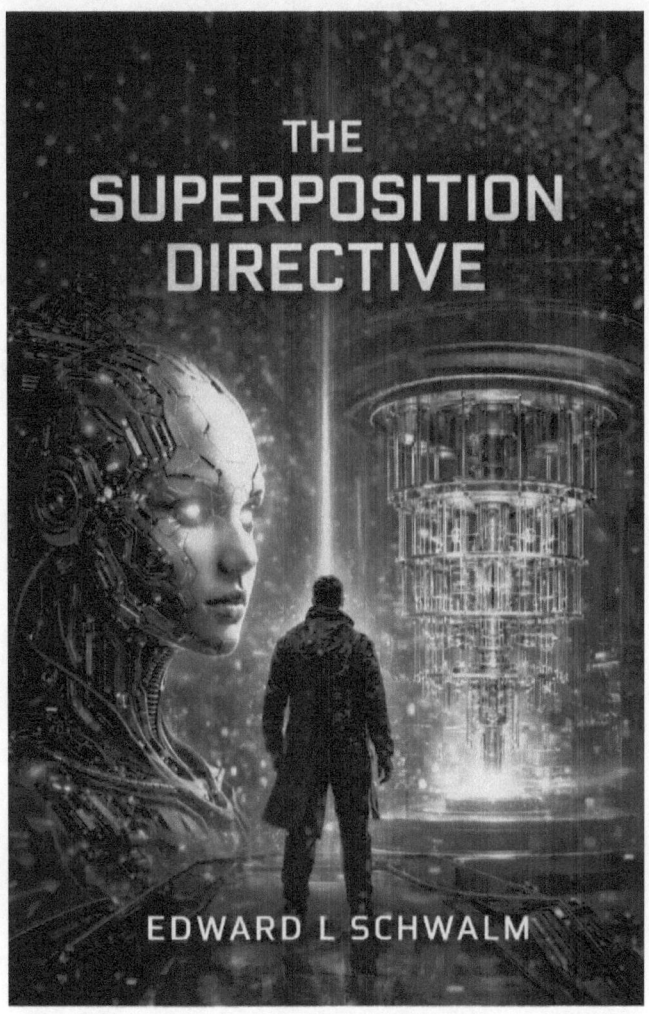

Edward Schwalm

About the Author

Edward Schwalm is the debut author of
THE EFFICIENCY DOCTRINE

Possessing expertise in both mechanical and electrical systems, he drew upon his extensive technical career and enduring interest in technology as inspiration for this novel. After retiring from what he jokingly refers to as a life of "mechanized madness," he turned to writing to fill the space once occupied by logical problem-solving.

A longtime admirer of Michael Crichton, Schwalm blends technical realism with fast-paced storytelling in his work. When he is not writing, he spends his time strategizing and refining his hobbies of beekeeping and winemaking. He finds his greatest peace hiking woodland trails with his wife and dog, Piper.

To learn more about the author, visit his website at…THEEFFICIENCYDOCTRINE.COM

"It is only *fiction* because it has not happened yet"

ELS

Thank you for reading.

Stories like this only exist because of readers like you.

If this story resonated with you, there's more to come.

If you enjoyed this book, I'd love to hear your thoughts.
You can visit my website by scanning the QR code below to
leave a review or see what I'm working on next.

Thank you for being part of the journey,
Edward L. Schwalm

THEEFFICIENCYDOCTRINE.COM